I CAME TO MY SENSES, LYING ON MY
BACK AND GAZING UP AT THE SKY.
THE CLOUDS WERE FLOATING ON
GENTLY BY, AND I COULD HEAR BIRDS
CHIRPING IN THE DISTANCE.
I CLAMBERED TO MY FEET, NOTICING
MY BODY DIDN'T HURT AT ALL.
AS I SURVEYED MY SURROUNDINGS,
I TOOK NOTE OF MOUNTAINS AND
GRASSY PLAINS ALL AROUND ME.
THERE WAS NO MISTAKING IT, I WAS
IN ANOTHER WORLD.

In Another World With My Smartphone 1

Linze Silhoueska
TOUYA SAVED LINZE AND HER SISTER FROM BEING SWINDLED. THOUGH GENERALLY A RESERVED GIRL, SHE CAN SHOW TRUE STRENGTH OF HEART EVERY ONCE IN A WHILE. THE YOUNGER TWIN.

Kokonoe Yae
A SAMURAI GIRL WHO LEFT THE FAR EAST COUNTRY OF EASHEN TO WANDER THE LANDS AND HONE HER SKILLS. SHE BOASTS A SERIOUS, STOIC PERSONALITY, AND TENDS TO POUR HER HEART AND SOUL INTO HER TRAINING. ALSO, SHE EATS A LOT.

Elze Silhoueska
AN ADVENTURER WHO FIGHTS WITH DUAL GAUNTLETS. SHE'S THE TYPE TO PUNCH FIRST, AND ASK QUESTIONS LATER. THE OLDER TWIN.

Mochizuki Touya
A BOY FROM ANOTHER WORLD. GENERALLY KIND AND COURTEOUS, HE'S QUITE THE LIKABLE, UPSTANDING YOUTH. HOWEVER, HE'S NOT ONE TO HOLD HIMSELF BACK IF SOMEONE HE CARES ABOUT IS PUT IN DANGER.

Sushie Urnea Ortlinde
THE ONLY DAUGHTER OF DUKE ORTLINDE. TOUYA SAVED HER WHEN SHE WAS ATTACKED BY A HORDE OF LIZARDMEN.

Yumina Urnea Belfast
THE CROWN PRINCESS OF THE KINGDOM OF BELFAST. POLITE AND CAREFUL AS SHE IS, YUMINA IS AN EXEMPLARY MEMBER OF ROYALTY. THAT BEING SAID, HER ACTIONS CAN BE SURPRISINGLY BOLD AT TIMES.

"IT ABSORBS MAGIC ATTACKS?!"

AN ALMOND-SHAPED BODY WITH SIX
ELONGATED LEGS JUTTING OUT FROM
ITS FRAME. A CRYSTAL BODY, BEAUTIFULLY
SHIMMERING AND SHINING LIKE WATER
BENEATH THE SUN. THIS TRANSLUCENT
BEING WAS ALIVE, SOME KIND OF
CRYSTAL CREATURE.

In Another World With My Smartphone

1

Patora Fuyuhara
illustration·Eiji Usatsuka

IN ANOTHER WORLD WITH MY SMARTPHONE: VOLUME 1
by Patora Fuyuhara

Translated by Andrew Hodgson
Edited by DxS

This book is a work of fiction. Names, characters, places, and incidents are the product of the author's imagination or are used fictitiously. Any resemblance to actual events, locales, or persons, living or dead, is coincidental.

Original Japanese edition published in 2015 by Hobby Japan
This English edition is published by arrangement with Hobby Japan, Tokyo

Find more books like this one at www.j-novel.club!

President and Publisher: Samuel Pinansky
Managing Editor: Aimee Zink

ISBN: 978-1-7183-5000-7
Printed in Korea
First Printing: February 2019
10 9 8 7 6 5 4 3 2 1

Contents

"I do hate to be the bearer of bad news, but I am sorry to say that you are dead."

"I see."

The old man bowed his head before me. There we were, in a sea of clouds. They stretched out as far as the eye could see, perhaps even farther than that. Amidst it all, we sat together on a small square of tatami mats. Four and a half tatami mats, to be precise. It was a simple little room, though that description was a loose fit since it lacked both walls and a roof, and was floating in the clouds. It was furnished with a small tea table, a set of drawers, an old CRT TV, and an old-fashioned telephone. It was all very classic, if nothing else.

But all that aside, back to Lord God. Or at least, the man who claimed to be God. This God guy claimed that I had died in some accident of his making. But honestly, for a dead man, I certainly didn't feel very lifeless.

As I remembered, rain suddenly started pouring while I was on my way home from school. I was taking a detour through the local park, at which point I was assaulted by a blinding light and a thunderous roar.

"I am afraid to say that I have made a bit of a blunder when I dropped some lightning into the world below. Truly, I am sorry about my mistake. I never intended for it to strike anyone... the chances of it happening are so low to begin with! Really, I cannot apologize enough."

"So the lightning scored a critical hit, which killed me? Well, that makes sense. So… is this Heaven, then?"

"Ah, no. This is actually far above Heaven. It is where all the Gods live. You could call it the Divine Realm, I suppose. I actually had to summon you here myself. Humans ordinarily cannot ever hope to come here, you see. Now, um, Mo… Mo-chi-zu-ki…"

"Ah, Mochizuki. Mochizuki Touya. Touya's my given name."

"Yes, yes, young Touya." Old Man God addressed me as he poured us both a cup of tea.

Oh, look at that. My tea stalk's upright. Lucky me, I thought.

"Young Touya, are you not a tad too calm in this situation? You are very much dead. I had thought you would have been more panicked, or perhaps even furious."

"I'm a dead man talking. Quite frankly, I'm having a hard time believing this is even real. Still, what's done is done. No use pointing fingers over it."

"That is a rather philosophical outlook."

Even so, I never thought I'd die at fifteen… I sipped my tea as that thought crossed my mind. *Ah, delicious.*

"So, what happens next? Heaven or Hell, which way are you sending me?"

"Oh, no. Perish the thought! This was all my fault, and I will gladly take responsibility for that. You'll be resurrected in a moment, don't you worry about that. But…" God stumbled over his words for a moment.

I couldn't help but wonder what was wrong.

"I can certainly restore you to life, but I cannot simply place you back where you came from. There are rules about this kind of thing, you understand? Once again, allow me to profusely apologize for this situation... Now, to the point."

"Go on," I said, encouragingly.

"It is possible to grant you a life in a *different* world. A chance to begin anew, so to speak. Of course, I will understand if you don't like the idea, but—"

"Sounds good to me."

"...It does?" Finding his endless apology cut short, God's face was now almost comically blank.

"If that's the way it has to be, then that's all there is to it. I'm honestly just happy I get another chance, so that's fine by me."

"You truly are an amazing young man... You definitely could have made something of yourself if you were still alive down there... Please forgive my carelessness." Poor old God looked very downtrodden indeed. I was very close to my own grandfather, so it felt a bit bad for me as well.

I knew it was silly, but I definitely empathized with him. Besides, I was talking to God of all people. I had never been very religious, but I wasn't so stupid as to get up and start yelling at the guy, demanding he make everything right again. I did feel very sad about never being able to see my family or friends ever again, but that wasn't something that could be fixed by blaming God. My granddad told me to be a good person, the kind of person who forgave other people when they made mistakes. By all accounts, Gods were people as well. Probably.

"At least allow me to make it up to you somehow. I am permitted to grant you small favors like that... Does anything come to mind?"

"Hm... well, you've kind of put me on the spot here." Being able to go home would be nice, but that was against the rules. As such, I had no choice but to think of something else. Something that could be of use to me in the new world.

"The world you're sending me to... what kind of place is it?"

"Ah, in comparison to your world it is not *quite* as developed as of yet. Hm... your world was the one with the Middle Ages, correct? I suppose it is close to that level, on a societal standpoint. Well, half of it at least! It varies a bit by location."

Well... that was certainly a drop as far as quality of life was concerned. Hearing that made me feel a little worried. Could I really survive just being thrown into that kind of landscape unawares, left to fend for myself? *Oh, that's it,* I realized.

"Uhm, there *is* one thing."

"Oh? There is? State it and I will see what can be done."

"*This,* can you make it so I can still use it while I'm over there?" I produced the item I desired from my uniform pocket. An object akin to a small metal board, the device known as the all-powerful cellular telephone! Well, really, it was just my smartphone.

"That is all? Well, I do suppose it is possible... I would have to impose some restrictions on its usage, however, if that is acceptable."

"What kind?"

"You will not be able to directly communicate with anyone through it. In simpler terms, I should say that you cannot use it to interact with your old world. No texting, no posting to websites, and no outgoing calls. However, you will still be able to observe, browse, and use search functions and whatnot. What else... Oh, I will give you my telephone number as well."

"Sounds good to me." All the information from my old world would make for a powerful weapon. I didn't exactly know how at the time, but I was sure that it would prove useful.

"I will link the battery directly to your magic so as to keep it charged at all times. You will not have to worry about it running out of power."

"Sorry, did you just say magic? Are you telling me that the people in my new world can cast spells and stuff?"

"Well, yes. Fear not, you should be able to use it freely in due time."

I was going to become a wizard. Amazing. I was really going to become a wizard as I started off a life in another world.

"All right, then. We should really see to getting you back on your feet now, eh?"

"Thank you for all of this, really."

"Not at all. This whole situation was a result of my mistake to begin with. Ah, speaking of which, one last thing." God gently raised his arm out toward me. I was wrapped in a warm, gentle light for a moment.

"It would be quite tragic indeed were you to die again immediately after being revived, so I have given all of your basic abilities a small boost. Your body will be stronger, your mind sharper, and so on. Anyway, it should be considerably harder for you to die this time around. Well, unless some silly old God drops lightning on your head!" The kindly old coot smiled wryly. And I found myself smiling too.

"I will be unable to do much for you directly once you are down in the world below. So just consider that a little present from me."

"Thanks again."

"I may not be able to interfere with the lower realms too much, but I can always offer you advice should you require it." God pointed at my phone as he spoke.

This was a bit of a tough one. I couldn't exactly call God every evening asking how to do this or that, so I figured I should hold off on calling him unless the situation was particularly serious.

"Well then, until next time." God saw me off with a saintly smile, and I blacked out in an instant.

I came to my senses, lying on my back and gazing up at the sky. The clouds were floating on gently by, and I could hear birds chirping in the distance.

I clambered to my feet, noticing my body didn't hurt at all. As I surveyed my surroundings, I took note of mountains and grassy plains all around me. I could see a large tree in the distance. Plus, I thought I could make out a road next to it as well.

There was no mistaking it, I was in another world.

"Guess I'll just walk the road and see if I run into anyone." My immediate checkpoint in sight, I set off toward the big tree. Upon reaching it, I got a better look at things. I was right! There was a road nearby.

"Now... left or right, that is the question." I pondered my options beneath the shade of the giant tree.

The nearest landmark to my right looked to be an hour's walk away. Off to the left, I could make out a town. It was probably eight hours by foot... As I was lost in thought, my smartphone began to ring. The Caller ID was listed as "God."

"Hello?"

"Ooh! It went through! I see that you have arrived safely." I could hear God's voice as I held the phone close to my ear. We'd only just parted, but it felt as though we were talking for the first time in forever.

"I forgot to mention one thing. The maps and compasses and such on your phone should be compatible with this world now. I hope they help you out some!"

"Wow, really? That's great timing, actually. I was a little bit lost, and wondering where I should go."

"I had assumed so. I could have just as easily dropped you in the middle of a town, but think of the panic that would ensue. I had thought you would rather avoid that, so I dropped you off where nobody would see you instead. Of course, that brings us to the problem of you being lost in the middle of nowhere."

"Heh, yup," I answered with a somewhat wry smile. It was only natural I'd be lost. I didn't have a destination, a hometown, or even any acquaintances.

"If you follow your map, you should be able to reach the nearest town without incident. Do your best out there. Goodbye."

"Will do. Later." As the call ended, I went back to the home screen, located the map application, and opened it up. My location was displayed in the very center of the map. A road stretched out right alongside that point. This must have been the very road I was looking at. Zooming further out, I took note of the town to the west. It was... Reflet? The town of Reflet.

"Well, I guess that's where I'm headed." Firing up a simple compass app, I took heed and headed west.

After walking a fair bit, the reality of my situation finally began to sink in. To begin with, I had no food. Not to mention the fact that I had no water. Once I got into town, what then? I had no money. I still had my wallet, but what good was that? Was there an exchange rate for my country's money? From a logical perspective, it was all worthless now. What to do...

As I was lost in thought, a sound steadily approached from behind. I turned around to check, and saw something off in the distance. It was heading this way, and it appeared to be... a horse-drawn carriage. I'd never seen a carriage before in my life, but it was generally something you'd find someone riding in.

This would be first contact with life in another world. *Think, what should I do? Try and stop it?* I could have asked for a ride into town, but I decided against the idea. Why? A simple enough reason.

As the carriage grew closer, I could tell at a glance that it was a very high-class vehicle. Its physical appearance showed that it was gorgeously adorned and built of the highest craftsmanship. Even I could tell at a glance that it was the sort of vehicle ridden by a noble, or at least some rich person of high status.

If I were to stop a carriage like that only to be met with a line like "Insolent knave! I'll see you hanged for this!" then it'd be no laughing matter. I decided it was in my best interest to give way instead, so I simply moved to the edge of the road.

The carriage passed me by, kicking up a cloud of dust in its wake. *Good.* I was glad I'd managed to avoid any trouble. However, as I turned to resume walking down the road, I noticed that it had come to a stop a short way ahead.

"You! Yes you, over there!" A man slammed the carriage door open and stepped out. He was an older gentleman with gray hair and a splendid mustache. He wore a stylish scarf and mantle, and a rose brooch shone on his chest.

"Uhm, yes? What is it...?" Clearly excited about something, the older gentleman made his way over. Somewhere in the back of my mind, I was mostly just relieved that we seemed to be speaking the same language. The man firmly gripped my shoulders and held me in place. His eyes wandered all across my body as though slowly savoring something. *Er, wait… what? This could be bad…*

"Wh-Where in the world did you get these clothes?!"

"Sorry?" I was taken aback, left utterly baffled by his question. The gentleman was so immersed in scanning my school uniform from every angle that he didn't even pay any attention to my confusion.

"I've never seen a design such as this. And the way this was sewn… How could this have been made…? Hrmm…"

And then it all started to make sense. To put it simply, my uniform was rare. Maybe nothing else like it existed in this world. In that case…

"You can have it, if you'd like."

"Are you certain?!" The mustachioed gentleman took the bait.

"I acquired these clothes from a traveling merchant. If you would rather have them, I don't mind handing them over. However, that puts me at a loss, as I'd have nothing to wear. If you might kindly take me into town and help me find a new set of clothes, I would be very grateful."

I couldn't possibly have told him that my clothes came from another world, so I was forced to come up with an excuse. If I somehow managed to sell my clothes and make a bit of money off of them, that was one problem solved. Plus, it would help me get clothes that didn't stand out so much. Killing two birds with one stone, so to speak.

"Very well! Step aboard and accompany me to town! I shall have new clothes prepared for you on the double. You may sell your current garments once that is taken care of."

"Then we have a deal," I sternly replied. The mustachioed gentleman firmly shook my hand in response.

After that, it only took three hours to reach the town of Reflet by carriage. During the journey, the gentleman, who introduced himself as Zanac, took my jacket and ran his hands over it several times, examining it down to every last seam. He seemed extremely interested in the make of the clothes. Once I learned of his job, it all made sense. Apparently Zanac worked in the fashion industry. That explained his initial reaction and all of his curious behavior. Today, too, it seemed he had been on his way back from a meeting of some kind.

As for me, I passed the time staring out of the carriage window. The scenery of a brand new world. A world which was my new home.

It had been three hours since I first met Zanac. After a lot of rocking and shaking, the carriage safely arrived at Reflet.

A soldier, possibly some kind of gatekeeper, met us at the entrance and questioned us before promptly allowing us to pass. From his reaction, it seemed that Zanac was quite famous.

The carriage rattled loudly as we proceeded down the town streets. Since the roads were old cobblestone, it shook quite a bit. Carrying on, we made our way to what seemed to be a prosperous shopping district with many stores all lined up in a row. The carriage stopped in front of one such shop.

"We've arrived! Come now, let's see you into some new clothes." I did as Zanac asked and stepped out onto the street. The store's signboard sported a needle and thread design, but it was the writing below that had alerted me to an alarming fact.

"I can't read it…" I couldn't read what was written on the sign. That definitely wasn't good news.

I had thought it might be okay since I was able to talk just fine, but that seemed not to be the case. It could've been worse, I supposed, since at least being able to converse meant I could still have somebody teach me to read and write. Day one in another world and I already had something to study...

Zanac led me into the shop, and several of the staff came to greet us.

"Welcome back, owner!" I was taken aback by what they said.

"Owner...?"

"Ah, I run this store. But that's not important right now, let's get you changed! Somebody pick out new clothes for this boy!" Zanac whisked me off into a changing room, which was an actual small room with a door, not just a box with a curtain dividing it off.

After that, he rushed back in with a pile of clothes. I removed my blazer, tie, and shirt so I could begin getting changed. I was wearing a simple black T-shirt underneath, and it seemed to have caught Zanac's eye as well.

"M-Might I press you to sell me those undergarments as well...?!" The scoundrel.

In the end, I was made to sell every last thread off my back. Everything including my socks and shoes. By the time my underpants were added to his list of demands, I had become quite tired of the ordeal. I understood how he felt, I just wish he could've understood how *I* felt...

The clothes and shoes he'd prepared for me in return were comfy and easy to wear. I certainly had no complaints about them. Black pants and a white shirt, with a black jacket over the top. A chic outfit that also wasn't too showy. I liked it. It kept me from standing out.

"Now, how much are you selling me your clothes for? I'll spare no expense, of course, but did you have a particular charge in mind?"

"Well… I'm afraid I don't really have a good estimate in mind. This isn't my field of expertise, you see. I can only assume they'd be expensive, but… To be completely honest, I'm penniless right now."

"I see… That is rather sad to hear. Well then, how does ten gold pieces sound?" Without any knowledge of the currency in this world, I had no way to judge the worth of ten gold pieces. As such, I accepted.

"Sounds good."

"Wonderful! Well, here you are," Zanac replied, clearly pleased by my answer.

Ten gold pieces jingled into the palm of my hand. Each one was about as big as a 500 yen coin, and had engravings of something resembling a lion. It was my entire life savings. Something I had to spend wisely.

"By the way, you wouldn't know where I could find someplace like an inn, would you? I'd like to find a place to rest my head before the sun goes down."

"An inn, yes? Turn right as you go out onto the street, then follow the road. You should see a sign for the Silver Moon Inn, won't be hard to find." Even if I did spot it, I wouldn't know because I couldn't read… Well, it wouldn't be a problem since I could just keep asking people as I went. Even if I couldn't read, I could still talk.

"Got it, thanks. I'll be on my way then."

"Very well. If you come across any other unusual garments, please bring them my way."

I said my goodbyes to Zanac and left the shop. The sun was still high in the sky. I took my smartphone out and turned it on. The time seemed to be just before 2PM.

"I wondered this in the carriage, but… the time should be accurate too, right…?" Going by the sun, it couldn't have been too far off at least.

Right then, something suddenly came to mind. I fired up the map application. It showed my current location on the town map, and sure enough, the street and shop names were also displayed. I certainly wouldn't be getting lost now. I found the Silver Moon Inn on the app quickly enough. Oh, wait a minute…

I turned back and looked at Zanac's store. "…«FASHION KING ZANAC» That's seriously what the sign said…?" I set off for the inn, all the while feeling bad for poor Zanac and his terrible naming sense.

After a bit of walking, I found the sign for the Silver Moon. The logo had a crescent moon design. Fairly standard, all things considered. The building, which was made of brick and wood, looked like it stood three stories tall. It certainly seemed sturdy enough, at any rate.

I passed through the double-leaf doors. The room inside resembled a bar or dining hall with a large counter on the right. To the left, there were stairs leading upward.

"Welcome. Are you here for a meal, or is it a room you want?" The lady behind the counter called out to me. Her red hair was tied up in a ponytail and she looked quite lively. A woman in her early 20s, or so I guessed.

"Ah, I'd like to rent a room please. How much a night?"

"Two copper! Meals are included with the price. Oh, you'll have to pay up front as well."

Two copper coins…? I couldn't tell if that was expensive or cheap. Logically it was at least cheaper than one gold coin, but I couldn't guess how many copper made up one gold.

With no other option, I took one gold coin from my wallet and placed it on the counter.

"How many nights will this get me?"

"Whaddya mean, how many? Fifty, right?" She replied, clearly exasperated.

"Fifty?!"

I felt stung by the sudden look she gave me, which made me feel that she was basically saying "Hey, can't you count?" or something. So then… one gold equals one-hundred copper. Ten gold could buy me five-hundred nights. I could live comfortably for around a year and a half without lifting a finger. Well, that meant I had a lot of money, didn't it?

"Well? What'll it be?"

"Err… one month's lodging, please."

"Alrighty! One month it is. I haven't had many customers lately, so you're kind of a life-saver right now. Haha, thank you. I'm out of silver coins though, so I'll just give you the change in copper."

The lady took my gold coin and returned forty copper to me. If she took sixty copper, then that meant one month was roughly thirty days in this world, too. Pretty close to the old world, then.

With that sorted, the lady brought out what appeared to be a hotel register from behind the counter. She opened it up in front of me, then handed me a feather pen.

"Okay, then. If you could just sign here, please."

"Oh, excuse me… Thing is, I can't actually write. Could you fill it in for me, please?"

"Really? Well, that's fine. What's your name?"

"It's Mochizuki. Mochizuki Touya."

"Mochizuki? That's a pretty unusual name."

"Ah, wait, no. My given name is Touya. Mochizuki is my surname… my er, family name."

"Ooh, okay! Your given name and family name are reversed. Are you from Eashen?"

"Err… somewhere around those parts, sure." I hadn't the faintest clue where in the world Eashen was, but I couldn't come up with anything better, so I left it at that. I resolved to look over my map later to see if I could find this Eashen place on it.

"Okay. Your room's on the third floor, right at the end. It gets the best sunlight out of all of our rooms! Here's your key, be sure not to lose it. The toilet and the bath are both on the first floor, and this room here is for dining. Speaking of which, will you be having lunch today?"

"Oh, please. I haven't eaten since this morning…"

"I'll whip up something real quick, then. You can use this time to go check out your room, maybe rest a bit."

"Got it," I said. I then took my room key, went upstairs to the third floor, and opened the door to my room. It was roughly the size of a six tatami room featuring a bed, desk, chair, and closet. I opened the window and looked down on the street. The view was really nice. Also, it was heartwarming watching children running around and playing below.

Invigorated, and in a surprisingly pleasant mood, I left my room and locked it shut. As I made my way back downstairs, I was greeted by a lovely smell.

"Here you go! Sorry for the wait." I took a seat in the dining room and the lady carried my meal out to me. There was some soup, something resembling a sandwich, and a salad. The bread was a bit hard, but very good for the first loaf I tried in another world. Delicious, even. I devoured the entire thing.

After that, I gave some thought to my next course of action. I was going to be staying at the inn for a while, so I figured I should go get a feel for how things were around town.

"I'm heading off for a walk."

"Alrighty! See you later, then." After the innkeep, who told me her name was Micah, saw me off, I left to go explore the rest of town.

Being a town in another world, everything was unusual and fascinating. My wandering gaze made some people regard me with suspicion, and whenever I grew aware of that fact, it caused my gaze to wander even more. Carrying on like that would just put me in an endless loop… That was no good.

One thing that I did notice about the people in town was how many of them were carrying weapons around. Some had swords or axes, others had knives, and a few were even carrying whips. It struck me as somewhat dangerous, but I figured that was just how it was in this world. I made note to consider buying a weapon of my own.

"First things first, though. I need to start making money. I can't very well live in this world without a source of income…"

Never would have thought I'd be job-hunting so soon. Honestly, it would've been nice if I had a specialty of some kind… Alas, my best subject in school was history, and the history of another world wasn't exactly much help.

The only other thing that came to mind was music. Did this world even have pianos? Well, even if there were some around, it wasn't like I was especially talented at it.

"Hmm?" Something suddenly caught my attention. Noises… Voices, even. Loud voices coming from one of the alleyways off from the main road. Sounded like an argument of some kind.

"…Guess I can check that out." With that thought, I set off for the back alley.

When I made it to the end of the narrow back alley, I found four people. It looked to be two men having an argument with two girls. Both of the men seemed the nasty, rough sort, but the girls were exceptionally adorable.

The girls looked to be around my age, perhaps younger. The two of them were so alike that I almost thought I had been seeing double. I wondered if they were twins, perhaps. Looking closer, they had their differences. They looked different around the eyes, and one had long hair while the other wore hers short. But even then, they had the same silver hair.

Both of them wore the same black jacket and white blouse, but the girl with longer hair wore culotte shorts with black knee socks, while the girl with shorter hair wore a flared skirt with black tights. It was easy to tell that the long haired girl was full of energy, while the short haired girl was more neat and composed.

"This isn't what we agreed on! You said you'd buy it for one gold!" The long haired girl yelled at the men, who both stood grinning as if arrogantly mocking her. One of the men held something like a deer's antler made of glass.

"Hmm? Whaddya mean. I said we'd buy your Crystal Deer's antler for one gold *if* it was in perfect condition. But lookie right here, it's scratched! A damaged antler's only worth one silver, so that's what we're paying you. Go on, take it and scram!" A single silver coin rolled to the ground at the girls' feet.

"That doesn't even count as a scratch! You were never planning on giving us a fair deal, were you…!" The long-haired girl glared menacingly toward the men, while the short-haired girl quietly bit her lip in frustration.

"…Fine. I don't want your money. Just give us back the antler." The long-haired girl said that and took a step forward. Disproportionately large gauntlets appeared on her arms as she advanced toward them.

"Oh, afraid we can't be having that. This was a fair trade, y'know? I never agreed to give it back—"

"Ah, excuse me. Do you have a moment?" I spoke up, and everyone's eyes fell upon me. The girls seemed confused, but the men looked almost ready to jump me.

"Huh? Whaddya want, kid?" one of the men said with a snarl.

"Ah, not you. I meant the girl over there," I replied calmly.

"Eh? Me?" was the only response I got from her as I ignored the scowling man and called out to the girl behind him.

"I was just wondering if you might sell me that antler for one gold." For a moment she stood flabbergasted. Then my words finally seemed to click with her, and she answered me with a smile.

"It's a deal!"

"The hell it is! Don't go selling things that belong to other people—" Suddenly, the crystal antler shattered to pieces in the man's hands. The stone I had thrown met its mark.

"Wha…?! What the hell do you think you're doing?!"

"Whatever do you mean? I'm free to treat my belongings however I'd like to. Oh, though I guess I haven't paid for it yet. I'll do that now."

"I'll kill you!" One of the men bellowed as he pulled a knife and charged right at me. I managed to dodge him easily by paying attention to his movements. For some reason I just *knew* that I'd be able to dodge his attack. I could see everything, from the man's movements to the knife's trajectory.

That had to be the result of one of those gifts that God had given me to bolster my body and my senses. I bent down and swept the man's legs from under him. He collapsed to the ground face-up, and I drove my fist into his body in one swift motion.

"Gah…!" He passed out right on the spot I had knocked him down with that one final grunt. It seemed that the move I'd learned from my grandpa had come in handy.

When I turned around, I noticed that the other man was fighting the long-haired girl. He swung around a hatchet, but he couldn't seem to get a good hit on her and his blows kept bouncing off her gauntlets. When she saw her chance, the girl stepped forward, quick as lightning, and swung a tremendous right hook straight into the man's face.

He collapsed to the ground with his eyes rolling back in his head. *Amazing.*

Well… if I had known it'd be that easy, then maybe I wouldn't have shattered that crystal antler… I actually regretted doing so. There was no point regretting past decisions. I'd thought to calm the situation peacefully by removing the source of the argument, but it seemed that had been a poor plan. I took one gold coin from my wallet and went to hand it to the long-haired girl.

"Here, one gold coin."

"…Are you sure? I mean, it'd really help us out, but…"

"It's fine. I'm the one who smashed the antler to pieces. Wouldn't be fair to go back on my word now."

"In that case… thank you." With that, she accepted the coin with her gauntlet-clad hand.

"Oh, and thanks for helping us out there. I'm Elze Silhoueska, and this is my younger twin sister, Linze Silhoueska."

"...Thank you very much!" The short-haired girl spat out those words, bowed, and gave me a little smile.

Seemed they were twins, just as I had thought. The long-haired one was Elze, and the short-haired one was Linze. Easy enough to remember. Though I still couldn't tell them apart except by hairstyle and clothes.

"My name's Mochizuki Touya. Oh, uh, Touya's my given name."

"Hmm... Your given name and family name are backward? Are you from Eashen?"

"Ah... er, yeah. Somewhere around those parts." Met with the same reaction as Micah from the inn, I just left it at that again. All those reactions did, however, move thoughts of Eashen to the forefront of my mind. I wanted to know what kind of a country it was.

"Oh, I see. So you only just arrived in town too, huh, Touya." I chatted with Elze over fruit juice. In my case, though, it was less having just arrived in this town and more having just arrived in the world.

After the events in the alleyway, we returned to the Silver Moon Inn. The girls had told me they were looking for an inn, so I took them back with me. Micah was overjoyed when I brought back more customers. So much that it showed clearly on her face.

Since we were all together anyway, we decided to share a meal. We talked a lot while eating the dinner Micah had made, and after dinner, we all had some tea to drink.

"See, we came here to deliver a Crystal Deer's antler after those guys put out a request, but *that* went about as well as you saw. I mean, their request was plenty suspicious, so I did figure something was up, but still..."

"...That's why I said we shouldn't accept their request... But Sis, you wouldn't listen to me..." Linze spoke up to reprimand her older sister. She seemed to be the one with a good head on her shoulders. Meanwhile, Elze seemed to have more of a wild personality. Elze the fearless older sister and Linze the shy little sister. At least, that was how they seemed to me.

"So why would you accept their request if you knew it sounded suspicious?" I voiced my doubts for the girls to hear. I couldn't help but wonder why they'd bother to try and strike up any kind of deal with dubious characters like those guys.

"Funny story, actually... See, we'd just beaten a Crystal Deer and gotten one of its antlers when we heard that there was someone looking to buy one. Sounded almost too good to be true. Well, I guess it was, considering we got duped and all... Suppose we'll only be accepting requests like that through the guild from now on. Hopefully that way we'll get wrapped up in a lot less trouble." Elze lowered her gaze and let out a big sigh.

"Wanna take this opportunity to get registered with the guild, Linze?"

"...That sounds like a good idea. Better safe than sorry, after all. Let's go some time tomorrow."

The guild... As I remembered from games, it was something like an employment service center that would mediate jobs for prospective adventurers. They'd have lots of quests posted and completing them would net you some money. Hmm...

"If it's alright with you, can I tag along tomorrow? I need to get registered with the guild, too."

"Sure! I don't see why not."

"Yeah... We can all go together..." The two of them kindly agreed.

Alright. I'd get registered with this guild and see if I could make some money working through them. That might well have been my ticket to earning a stable income that would allow me to live comfortably.

With all of that decided, the three of us split up, so I went back to my room. My long first day in this world had finally come to an end. It sure was a busy day, too...

I was transported to another world, made to sell my clothes, searched for an inn to stay at, helped a couple of girls, and gotten myself into a brawl. What the heck was with all that...

For the time being, I decided to note everything that had happened that day down in my smartphone in place of an actual diary. After that, I opened up a few news sites and checked in on how things were going down in my old world.

Oh, the Giants are winning. Aww, that band's gonna break up... What a shame.

I turned my phone off once I'd found a good place to stop reading, then crawled my way into bed. I would be registering with the guild the next day, so I wondered what it'd be like... Thoughts like that ran through my mind until drowsiness finally overtook me.

"Zzz..."

The electronic noise of my smartphone's alarm got me to sluggishly crawl out of my bed. I then washed my face, got dressed, and headed downstairs to the dining room. Elze and Linze were already awake and having breakfast. I took my seat and Micah brought out some food for me as well. This morning's menu was bread with ham and eggs, vegetable soup, and a salad. What a delicious way to start the day.

The three of us headed out to the guild as soon as we'd finished eating. It was pretty crowded since it was right near the middle of town.

The first floor of the guild's building was laid out like a restaurant. It was a lot more cheerful than I thought it would be. I'd pictured it in my head as a bar where ruffians would hang about, but it looked like my fears were unfounded. The female receptionist met us with a lovely smile as we approached the counter.

"Uhm, we'd like to register with the guild, please."

"All right, then. That's no problem at all. Would that be three for registration, then?"

"Yes. All three of us," Linze replied.

"Will this be your first time registering with the guild? If so, I can provide a basic explanation of what it means to register with us."

"Please do." The gist of it was that the guild would take the requests of individuals or groups, publicize them, then take a small fee upon completion. That was how the guild worked.

The requests were split into ranks based on how difficult they were expected to be, so someone with a low personal rank couldn't accept requests aimed at those of a higher rank. However, so long as half of one's party were of a high enough rank, they would be able to accept such requests even if the others in the party didn't meet the rank requirements.

Upon completion of a quest, one would receive payment. If one failed a quest, however, they would be charged with breach of contract. *Hrmm… I need to pick and choose my work carefully.*

In addition, if one continued to fail multiple quests, then they would be deemed a low-quality individual, and their guild registration would be revoked as a penalty. Were that to happen, one would never be able to re-register with any guild branch in any town.

Other stipulations included: if one did not accept any requests at all for five years, then their guild registration would expire; one could not accept multiple requests at the same time; concerning subjugation requests, one must hunt the monsters in the designated area, else their work would be deemed invalid; as a general rule, the guild would not directly involve itself in personal dissent between adventurers, unless such dissent was judged to be harmful to the guild itself... Anyway, we received a pretty thorough explanation of the rules.

"And that about sums up the explanation. If you have any further questions, please direct them to the appropriate individuals."

"Alright, got it," I replied.

"Very well. Please fill in and return these forms with all of the required details." The receptionist handed us three blank forms, but I couldn't read a single word on them. When I informed Linze that I couldn't read or write, she agreed to help me fill out my form. Hrm... I knew that being illiterate was going to cause me problems sooner or later.

The receptionist then took the registration forms and held a pitch black card over each of them in turn, seemingly casting some sort of spell. Afterward, she took out a small pin and told each of us to spill a little bit of our blood onto the cards.

I did as I was instructed, took the small pin in hand and pricked my finger with it, then rubbed a small amount of blood onto the surface of the card. Some white letters floated up onto it... but I still couldn't make heads or tails of what it said.

"Each of your personal guild cards has a little spell on it that will make it turn gray if handled by someone other than its real owner for longer than a few seconds. It's a simple anti-forgery mechanism. Also, should you happen to lose your card, please report to the guild as swiftly as possible. For a small fee, we will be able to issue you a new card."

The receptionist took hold of my card and stood there for a few seconds. Just as she'd said, it eventually turned from pitch black to a dull gray. The very moment she placed the card back in my hands, it snapped right back to black. That was a really cool trick. I wondered how it worked.

"With this, your guild registration is complete. All available work requests are posted on the board over there. If you see one you would like to accept, please confirm all details and apply for it through our quest clerk."

The three of us stood in front of the board where the quests were posted. Our guild cards were all black, signifying that we were at the beginner level. Our cards would apparently change in color as our ranks rose, but right now we could only accept quests aimed at beginners.

Elze and Linze busily pored through each quest notice one by one, but I on the other hand...

"...Not good. I seriously need to learn how to read and write, and fast..." If I couldn't understand the details of a job, I was never going to get anywhere. I made a mental note to put evenings aside for studying my reading and writing.

"Hey, hey, Linze, check this one out. The reward's pretty decent, and it seems like a good place to start. How about it?"

"...Yeah. This one doesn't seem so bad. What do you think, Touya?"

"…Sorry. I can't make any sense of it." Elze had been merrily pointing out the request in question, but her finger drooped slightly when I said that. Ngh…

"…Umm, let's see. It's a request to go out and defeat some beast monsters in the forest to the east. They want us to hunt five Lone-Horned Wolves. They're not very strong, so I think we can manage. Oh right, the reward is eighteen copper." Linze was polite enough to read out the details of the quest to me.

Eighteen copper, huh… Split evenly between us, that would make for six copper each. That could pay for three nights of lodging. Not bad at all.

"Fine, let's go with that," I decided.

"Okie dokie! I'll take this to the clerk." Elze tore down the request notice and headed on over to the quest clerk.

Lone-Horned Wolves… Apparently they were wolves with a single horn on their head, sort of obvious given their name. I was slightly worried as to whether I could defeat them or not…

…*Huh?* "Oh, right… I completely forgot…"

"What's wrong…?" Linze curiously asked why I was standing there, clearly dumbfounded.

"I, uh… I sort of kind of don't have a weapon yet." It had totally slipped my mind.

Trying to take on a subjugation quest unarmed would have been the height of idiocy. Therefore, we decided to make a beeline for the weapon store after departing the guild.

We took a north street and eventually another glaringly obvious logo on a signboard came into view. Just as one might expect, this one was of a sword and shield. And again, just as one might expect, I could not decipher the name of the shop printed below the logo.

Opening the shop door made a small bell tinkle, announcing our arrival. The noise caused a massive, bearded old man to spawn from within the depths of the store. He was huge. In fact, I almost mistook him for a bear.

"Welc'm. Lookin' for something?"

The bear-man appeared to be the store's owner. *Goddamn he's massive.* He had to have been at least two meters tall. Was he some sort of pro wrestler or something?

"We're looking for a weapon for this guy here. Mind if we take a look around?" Elze asked in a clear attempt to aid me.

"Go right ahead. Feel free to pick up anythin' that catches yer eye." Mr. Bear responded to her with a gentle smile.

What a nice bear... I mean person. *What a nice* person. I wondered if he would like some honey...

The shop was packed from floor to ceiling with weapons. There were all kinds up on display as well. Everything from swords to spears, bows, axes, even whips. So many weapons...

"Any weapons you're good with, Touya?"

"Hrmm... Nothing particular comes to mind, but... Well, I *have* been trained with swords. Just a little, though." Negative thoughts formed in my mind as I answered Elze's question. I said swords, but I'd only ever held one in kendo classes. I'd never actually received any proper training. I probably knew some of the basics of swordplay, at best. I was pretty much a rank amateur.

"...In that case, I think a sword would be the best fit. Touya seems like more of an agile fighter than one who uses brute force, so, I think, maybe a one-handed sword..." Linze pointed out a section of the shop where one-handed swords were on display.

I picked up one of the swords, still in its scabbard, and held it by the hilt with one hand. It was too light. I felt that maybe a slightly heavier sword would suit me better.

Just then, one sword in particular caught my eye. Actually, that was no mere sword... It was a katana. A slim, curved blade with a masterfully crafted circular handguard. A black sheath with a belt-like cord. Upon closer inspection, there were parts which differed from the Japanese katanas that I was familiar with, but it was still remarkably similar.

"...What's the matter?"

"Oh, you're looking at that Eashen sword? I suppose it makes sense that you'd be drawn to a weapon from your homeland." Noticing my fixation on the katana, Linze and Elze called out to me.

Ah, so this sword was from Eashen, apparently. Not that it was actually my homeland... But, well, it did seem that Eashen and Japan had a lot of common points. The more I heard about it, the more interested I became in this Eashen.

I took the katana down and carefully removed it from its sheath. The pattern on the blade shone beautifully in the light, captivating me for a moment. The blade was a bit thicker than I'd assumed, so the katana itself was fairly heavy. Not so heavy that I wouldn't be able to swing it properly, though.

"How much is this one?" Mr. Bear's head popped out suddenly from farther back in the store as soon as those words left my mouth.

"Err, that one, eh? That'll be two gold, aye. Thing is, though, it ain't exactly the easiest weapon ta use. Definitely ain't something I'd suggest fer a beginner."

"T-Two gold?! Isn't that a little expensive?" Elze argued on my behalf.

"Well, it ain't like I usually get 'em stocked often, and even when I do there's hardly anyone who can use the dang thing. Of course it's gonna be pricey!" Elze pouted at Mr. Bear's words, but he remained steadfast.

Thinking it over, that price probably was reasonable. Even I could tell that a weapon like this had intrinsic value.

"I'll take it. You said it cost two gold?" I returned the katana to its sheath and pulled two gold coins out from my wallet, placing them on the store counter.

"Pleasure doin' business with ya. Interested in any protective gear while yer at it?"

"Nah, this'll do for now. I'll come back when I have a bit more cash on me."

"Gotcha. Well then, here's hoping that sword helps ya earn a boatload." The bear heartily laughed as he spoke.

Now, I'd found what I was after, but Elze and Linze ended up picking some things up while we were there. Elze went for some leg armor called greaves, a type that covers the leg from roughly foot to shin, and Linze bought a silver wand. It seemed that Elze was a close-ranged brawler, while Linze supported from the rear with magic.

Weapons secured, we decided that the general item shop was next on our list of stops. Along the way, I got curious about something, so I fired up my map application to check the name of the shop we just left.

«Weapon Shop Eight Bears» …Did everyone in the town share this bizarre naming sense?

At the item shop I bought a small pouch, a canteen, a lunchbox, a fishing hook and some fishing line, a pair of scissors, a knife, a toolbox with plenty of handy little things such as matches, some medicinal herbs, some antidotes, and other little things along those lines. Elze and Linze already had necessities like that, so I was the only one who bought anything there.

And so, our preparations were complete at last. *Beware, Lone-Horned Wolves, we're coming to the forest to wipe you out!*

The eastern forest was about a two hour walk away from Reflet. I had hoped we might be able to hitch a ride on a carriage if we happened to pass any, but not a single one passed by. Exactly two hours later, we arrived at the forest.

We made our way into the dense woodland, being sure to take note of our surroundings. At first I was frightened by every little noise, from birds crying to small animals moving around amongst the trees. Gradually, though, I started to notice something.

Faintly, but surely... I could detect the presence of things around me. I could tell what or where something was, how it saw us... All manner of things like that. I wondered what it was... Some kind of sixth sense, maybe? It might've just been another one of those little gifts from God.

As I pondered the thought, I noticed something directing aggression toward us from just a bit ahead and to the left. I could feel the hostility clearly.

"Hold up. Something's there." The girls stopped in their tracks when I spoke up.

I continued to gaze toward that point as my party got into a battle formation. As if it was waiting for that one movement, a dark shadow came leaping out and attacked us.

"Hup!" I panicked and spun my body to evade, reassuring myself internally that it was fine after all.

I could predict its movements. It was roughly the size of a large dog, with gray fur and a single black horn on its head. However, the beast before me was far too ferocious to be a mere dog... *So this is what a Lone-Horned Wolf looks like.*

As I turned to face it, a second one jumped out from the other side and attacked Elze. She stood before the creature and swung her fist straight into the creature's muzzle. Taking a smashing blow from her gauntlet-clad fist, the Lone-Horned Wolf was thrown to the ground with all the life knocked out of it. Killed in a single motion.

Thinking me distracted as I looked at Elze's fight, the wolf in front of me bared its fangs and leaped to attack again. I remained calm, simply moving in time with the wolf's attack, then drew the katana at my hip. My attack connected as our bodies passed one another. In that instant, the wolf's head was torn from its body and sent flying through the air. The decapitated piece bounced to the ground like a basketball.

I felt some guilt and other unpleasant emotions at having killed an animal for the first time in my life, but another four wolves showed up before I had any time to let those emotions sink in. Two of them rushed toward my location.

"Come forth, Fire! Hail of Red Stones: [Ignis Fire]!"

By the time I even heard those words, one of the wolves charging at me suddenly burst into flames. It seemed like Linze had backed me up from behind with her magic. *Crap! I missed my first chance to see magic in action! Dang it...*

The other wolf charged at me, but I dodged once again and laid into it with my katana. It dropped to the ground and its body became still.

I turned to see one of the other wolves leaping at Elze, who countered with a roundhouse kick to its stomach and sent it flying. Nearby, the final remaining wolf was burned to a crisp. *Man, I just missed another chance to see magic...*

"Guess we're done here. The request was to defeat five wolves, but we ended up taking out one extra, huh." Elze reported in, clanging her gauntlets together.

We'd beaten six in total, with each of us having taken out two. For our first fight, that was pretty good. Though really, it was only *my* first fight.

So, as proof that we'd completed the quest, we had to take back the wolf horns with us. We cut off all six of their horns and placed them in our pouches. Our only remaining job was to deliver them to the guild to complete the mission.

As we left the forest, I physically felt my body grow less tense. It felt like something stifling had been lifted right out of the air. That was probably just another feeling I had to get used to.

Luckily, this time we managed to catch a carriage on its way into town, so we got to hitch a ride.

We made it back to town in only a fraction of the time thanks to that. After arriving in town, we traveled by foot to the guild, where we reported in about completing the request to hunt five Lone-Horned Wolves. I ended up keeping the remaining horn in commemoration of the day's events.

"Okay, all of the horns appear to be here. Now, please present your guild cards." When we presented our cards to the receptionist, she pressed something like a stamp on each of them. As she did, a magical circle appeared briefly on the cards before fading out.

When I asked about it later, I found out that the stamp differed based on the difficulty of the request completed. The cards saved the information about what we had done, so as we accumulated stamps, eventually our rank would increase and the color of our card would change.

We were only at Black, the Beginner rank. Apparently, the ascending order was Black, Purple, Green, Blue, Red, Silver, and finally Gold.

"Here's your reward of eighteen copper coins. Well then, the request has been fulfilled. Good work out there!" The receptionist handed us our reward, which we promptly split into six coins each. With that, we'd earned three days of food and accommodation. And it finally felt like I would be able to make it just fine in this new world.

"Hey, hey, wanna go grab a bite to eat to celebrate clearing our first quest?" Elze proposed that course of action as we left the guild.

It was a little early for dinner, but it occurred to me that we'd missed lunch, so I supposed that maybe it wasn't such a bad idea. Plus, I had a favor to ask, so it seemed like a good opportunity.

We decided to go to a little tea house in town. I ordered a hot sandwich and milk, Elze ordered what appeared to be a meat pie and orange juice, and Linze ordered a pancake and black tea. After our orders were brought out, I began to talk.

"Hey, can I ask you two for a favor?"

"A favor?" Elze replied.

"Yeah. Think you could teach me how to read and write? It'd really help me out. I'm already having trouble here and there, so I figure that the sooner I learn, the better."

"Hmm… that's a good point! If you can't read quest information, then I guess…" Elze and Linze nodded in unison. It was at times like that where you could really tell they were twins.

"In that case, get Linze to teach you. She's smart, so I'm sure she'll be a good teacher."

"Th-That's not… I mean… If you're okay with me…"

"Thanks a lot. You'd really be helping me out."

Alright. So I'd be able to work toward my goal of being able to read and write. I just had to face my studies seriously. I was glad I'd found such a kind teacher. Speaking of which…

"Oh yeah, Linze. While we're at it, do you think you could teach me some magic? I'd like to be able to cast spells and stuff as well."

"Whaat?!" Darned twins were even speaking in unison… What? Was what I said really that weird?

"Teach you some magic…? Well… Touya, what's your aptitude?"

"Aptitude?"

"Magic is highly influenced by the… aptitude that you're born with! People without the gift for it… won't be able to use magic at all…"

Hmm… So, magic wasn't something that just anybody could use. Well, that made sense. After all, if everyone could use magic, then civilization would have been far more based around it.

"The gift for it, huh… You know, I think I'll be fine on that front. Someone, uh, guaranteed that I'd be able to use magic if I wanted to."

"Who told you that?"

"Oh uh… just a very, very important person." It was God, as a matter of fact.

Hah. Yeah right. They'll think I'm insane if I tell them that. I figured it'd be best to keep that part to myself.

"I mean, is there any way to test whether someone has any aptitude for magic?"

At my question, Linze pulled out some translucent stones from the pouch around her waist. Red, blue, yellow, and perfectly clear; they shone almost like they were made of glass. Each one was about one centimeter around. Looking at them, I remembered that there was a similar one on Linze's silver wand. The one on her wand was bigger than the pebbles she placed before me, though.

"Okay, so what are these?" I asked, clearly confused by her actions.

"They're, uhm, spellstones. They can be used to amplify, store, and release magical energy. We can use these to test whether or not you have aptitude for magic. But it can only provide a rough estimate, either way…" Linze whispered something like "I wonder if water would be the easiest to demonstrate…" before picking up the blue stone. She held it over the cup that she'd finished drinking her tea out of.

"Come forth, Water!"

At Linze's command, a small amount of water flowed from the spellstone and into the teacup.

"Whoa."

"This is how you cast a spell. Just now, the spellstone responded to my magical energy and created water."

"By the way…" Elze cut in, then took the spellstone from her sister. After that, she tried to cast the same spell.

"Come forth, Water!"

The spellstone refused to activate. Not even a droplet of water poured out.

"This is what happens when you have no aptitude for an element. See, this means I can't use Water magic."

"You can't use it even though your twin sister can?"

"Man, you really don't think before you speak, huh? I mean, no offense taken, but still…"

Whoops. That was a pretty poor slip of the tongue. It didn't seem like she was seriously angry at me, though, more like sulking a little. I was just glad my thoughtless comment hadn't hurt her.

"In exchange for not being able to use Water magic, Sis can use Fortification magic… I can't use that type, personally… You need the proper aptitude to use Fortification magic, too."

Things suddenly made a lot more sense. I had been wondering where she was packing all that punch in that slender frame of hers, but the mystery had been solved.

"Everyone has some magical energy inside them, but unless they have the aptitude to use it, they won't be able to channel it into any spells." Seemed like everything hinged on whether or not you had the gift for it. Those without talent were just out of luck. It seemed that this world was just as unfair as the last.

"So, we'll be able to test my aptitude if I do the same?"

"Yes. Just take the stone in your hand and focus on it, then chant **Come forth, Water!** Then, if you have the aptitude... water should come out." Elze handed me the blue spellstone as she said that. I put a plate down under my hand to keep the table from getting wet, then held the stone above it and began to concentrate. I cast the spell I had just been taught.

"Come forth, Water!"

Before I could even blink, the spellstone started gushing out water like a broken faucet.

"Uh-oh-huh-wha-?!"

I dropped the spellstone hurriedly, and the waterfall immediately ceased. Sadly, though, it was too late. The table looked like it had just been soaked down with a hose, and the tablecloth was drenched.

"...What the heck does this mean?" I looked at the two sisters sitting in front of me, seeking some kind of explanation for the bizarre scene. Neither one answered me, though. They just sat there, looking on in amazement at the spectacle before them. It honestly looked like the expressions on their faces had been copied and pasted. In fact, it was all so silly that I almost found myself laughing.

"...Touya, you have so much magical energy that it's almost overflowing... I think. To cause such a strong reaction with such a tiny stone and only the fragment of a spell... and on your first attempt, too… It's just… your magical energy seems to be obscenely potent… I can't believe my own eyes, even though I just saw it."

"…You're really much more suited to being a mage, I think. Seriously, I've never seen anything like this in my life."

Seemed I had the potential after all, just like God told me I would. My sheer talent in the field was surely the work of God, too. It had to be. I mean, I wasn't about to complain about it, I was just glad to know that I really could use magic.

Apologizing for soaking the table, we rushed straight out of the cafe. The sun had already set by the time we got back to the inn, so my magic lessons were to be left for the next day and onward.

Once I finished my dinner, Linze began to teach me how to read and write. I got Micah's permission to use the dining room for the lesson. To start off with, I had Linze write out a simple sentence for me. Next to that, I wrote the same thing in Japanese.

"…I've never seen writing like this before. Where did you learn it?"

"Hm… It's a written language native to my hometown and the area around it. I'm probably the only one around these parts who can read it." Never mind these parts, I was probably the only person in the world who could understand this writing. It was almost like a secret code language for my eyes only.

Linze looked a bit bemused, but it seemed like she believed my story for the moment. Moving on, she taught me some more very simple phrases, which I steadily paired with their Japanese counterparts. Linze must've been a talented teacher, because the words just clicked into place in my brain.

Wait, has my memory always been this good? Is this another act of God…? If it really is thanks to God, then it would've been way better if he just let me know the language right off the bat. Such thoughts did cross my mind, but I was sure God had his reasons. I wasn't really in a position to be asking for more than I'd already gotten from him, anyway.

We cut off at a good stopping point, then Linze and I returned to our respective rooms for the night.

I whipped out my smartphone and noted down the day's events in my makeshift diary. I then decided to take a peek at what was going on in the other world. *Oh, that person won a People's Honor Award. Ah, I wanted to see that movie...*

Eventually, I suddenly snapped to my senses and remembered to open up my map and check for Eashen. I found out that it was an island country far to the east of here on the map, just off the edge of the continent. I never thought it would resemble Japan all the way down to those points, but it was almost identical. I decided I'd like to go there if I ever got the chance.

Between hunting those monsters and all that walking, I was beat. I soon felt drowsiness take its grip, so I crawled into bed and let the sandman do his job. *Goodnight.*

"Zzz..."

"Uhm... well then, let's begin." Linze seemed a bit nervous, almost straining herself to announce the beginning of our lessons. She struck me as more than just shy, almost docile even. Maybe she could've learned from her sister... within reason, anyway. She'd opened up a bit as we'd gotten to know each other, but I couldn't help but feel she was still a fair bit distant.

Today we were taking a break from guild quests to give me a crash course in magic training instead. We sat at a worn-out little table around the back of the inn, since it seemed like it wasn't in use by customers anymore. Oh, and since Elze had nothing to do, she went to the guild and picked up a simple plant harvesting job that she could manage on her own.

"Well then, Ms. Silhoueska, I'll be in your care today."

"M-Ms. Silhoueska is a bit much... A-Ah...!" My adorable teacher drooped her head and blushed a full red through to her ears. *Damn, she's cute.*

"Alright, what's up first?"

"Oh, right. Well, we should start from the basics, so... You know that there are different elements of magic, right?"

"Elements?" I questioned, not fully aware of the distinctions.

"You know, like fire and water. Well, uhm... the seven basic elements are Fire, Water, Earth, Wind, Light, Dark, and Null. We already know that you're proficient in Water magic, as we learned yesterday." She was clearly referring to the little spellstone incident the day before. Since I was able to bring out that much water, I was obviously proficient in Water magic.

"We learned right away that you can use Water magic, which is good. If you couldn't use Water magic, the plan was to test you using the spellstone for a different element."

"So even if someone can use magic, they're limited to certain elements...?"

"That's right. By the way, the elements I'm proficient in are Fire, Water, and Light. As for the other four, I can't even cast the most basic spells. Even among the three I can use, I'm good with Fire spells, but Light magic is a bit difficult."

So even in this world, there were the haves and the have nots. You couldn't choose talents for yourself. God must have decided those things instead. I felt sorry for poor old God.

"Right, so I get stuff like Fire or Water, but what about Light, Dark, or Null? What do those elements do?"

"Light is also known as Holy magic, which uses light as a medium. Healing magic falls under this category. Dark is primarily Summoning magic... You can use it to form contracts with magic beasts or monsters and have them fight for you. As for Null... that one's a bit different from the other elements. It's mainly composed of spells unique to the caster. Sis can use Fortification magic, which is a good example."

Made sense to me. Something like that seemed pretty useful overall.

"Apart from Null, each element is dependent on your magical energy plus your aptitude with it, and will only come forth once the proper spell is cast. You can't do anything if you don't know which elements you're compatible with, so we'll test for that first." As she spoke, Linze took the spellstones out from her pouch and lined them up on the table. Seven in total, colored red, blue, brown, green, yellow, purple, and clear.

"The elements of these spellstones are, in order: Fire, Water, Earth, Wind, Light, Dark, and Null. We'll test them all in that order."

First off was the red spellstone. I grasped it in my hand and concentrated, reciting the spell that Linze had taught me.

"Come forth, Fire!"

The stone burst forth flames like an oven at my words. I panicked and dropped the stone, which made the fire disappear in an instant. That was dangerous!

"It's okay, magical fire won't hurt the one casting it. Well, not unless your clothes catch fire, of course. Just make sure that doesn't happen..."

"Huh, is that so?" I took the spellstone in hand and cast the spell once more.

A flame popped out again, but she was right. It wasn't hot to the touch. So, if a magic flame spread to something else, then even the caster would get hurt, huh? Maybe that meant that when something caught fire due to magic, it didn't count as magical flames anymore... Still, wasn't the flame a bit too big?

"It seems like you've just got way too much magical energy... I'm sure you'll be able to control it better with practice, but for now, it might be safer to not concentrate too much and instead let your mind wander a bit..."

So basically, if I went at it a bit more relaxed, the effect of the magic would be much less extreme? Her advice sounded odd, but it was worth a shot. Anyway, next up was the blue stone, but we'd already confirmed that one, so we moved onto the brown one. This time I took the stone in hand without really concentrating on it, and cast the spell in a more bland, uninspired fashion.

"Come forth, Earth."

Sand started spilling out of the spellstone. Well, that got sand all over the table. I knew we had to clean all that up later...

Next up was the green spellstone.

"Come forth, Wind."

A small squall burst out and blew all the sand off the tabletop as soon as I spoke. Nice that I wouldn't have to clean up anymore, but it also knocked the spellstones all over the place. *Damn it.*

"Come forth, Light."

The spellstone turned into a strobe light. *Ugh, my eyes!*

"Come forth, Dark."

Now, I totally didn't understand that one. Some kind of black mist poured out of the spellstone and clung to its surroundings. It was super creepy.

Having gone through six elements, I finally noticed a small change in Linze's expression. She'd been celebrating with me after each element for a while, but had gradually begun to speak less and less, and there was currently a grave expression on her face.

"...What's up?" I asked, worry evident in my voice.

"Eh? No, it's nothing. I've just never met anyone who's proficient with as many as six elements... I mean, I can use three, and even that's considered rare... But you... You're something else entirely."

So, that was it. Hrmm... I mean, this *was* a gift from God and all, but it still felt like I was cheating a little. There were probably people who couldn't use magic even though they really wanted to, so it felt like I was trampling all over their feelings.

Still, worrying like that wouldn't change anything. Moving on to the final test, I grabbed the clear spellstone.

"...Huh? Hold on, how do I use this one?" I'd just been chanting "Come forth, something!" up to that point, but would that really make sense? Wasn't "Come forth, Null!" a contradiction? Sure sounded awkward at least.

"The Null element is a bit special. It doesn't have any particular incantation. Instead, it activates based on your magical energy and spell name alone." Hm... so that was how it worked. Sounded mighty convenient, this blank element...

"For example, the Fortifying magic that Sis uses is activated by yelling [**Boost**] and that's it. There are others such as [**Power Rise**] that increase raw muscle strength, and rarer spells like [**Gate**] that allow one to move great distances, but Sis can't use those."

So, basically, all the handy little miscellaneous spells that didn't fit under any element were listed under the Null element.

"...Well, how do I figure out which Null-type spells I can cast, then?"

"According to Sis, she just somehow knows the spell name for some reason. Null-type magic is also referred to as personalized magic, so very few people are ever able to use the exact same spells as each other. There are people with multiple Null-type spells out there, but these people are exceedingly rare."

Sounded mighty inconvenient, this blank element...

"So, there's no quick way to learn which Null-type spells I'll be able to cast, then...?"

"No, we should still be able to test that. If you grip the spellstone and try to cast any kind of Null-type spell, then even if it fails, the stone should shine slightly or wobble a bit. There should at least be some kind of small change."

"And if nothing happens?"

"...Then I'm afraid you'd have no aptitude for that element." Well, nothing to do but give it a go, I supposed. A spell that let you cross great distances sounded pretty handy. If I had that, we wouldn't have to walk all the way to that forest like we did the day before.

All right. I took the clear spellstone in hand, then exclaimed the spell's name.

"[Gate]!"

Suddenly, the spellstone shone brightly and formed a translucent wall of light next to me. The wall was roughly the size of a door. Or well, I thought it was a wall at first, but upon closer inspection, I noticed it wasn't even one centimeter thick. It was more like a sheet, to be honest.

"...It worked."

"...So it did," Linze replied, utterly dumbfounded.

I timidly touched the surface of the sheet of light. Ripples flowed out from the area my fingertips brushed against. It was almost like a thin membrane of water. I stuck my arm through the membrane and pulled it back out. Having confirmed that it was safe, the next thing I did was stick my head through it. As I did, my vision was filled by an expansive forest, and Elze sitting on her backside, her eyes wide with shock.

"...'Sup Elze."

"Wha-Wha-What the... Touya?! What the heck's going on?!" I pulled my head back for a moment, took Linze by the hand, and we walked into the forest together.

"Linze, you too?! Eh? Eeehh?! What's going on, where'd you pop out from?!"

Linze calmly explained the situation to the panicking Elze. It seemed that we were at the same eastern forest we'd gone to the day before. Apparently Elze had traveled to the area to pick some medicinal herbs for her guild quest, but a wall of light suddenly appeared. After that, an arm came flying out of it, then flew back in, and the sheer sight of it made her fall flat on her backside. Honestly, I'd probably have reacted the same way.

"The [Gate] spell is supposedly able to take the caster anywhere that they've visited at least once... In all likelihood, Touya probably thought about this forest when he was casting it."

She was right on the money. At the time, I had been thinking about how it would be nice if we didn't have to walk all the way to the forest again.

"Haaah... So basically, you can use all seven elements? That's a bit freaky..." Elze spoke as though she'd just gotten used to all of my eccentricities at that point. I kind of shared the same sentiment there.

"I've never even heard of anyone who was proficient in every element before. Touya, you're really amazing!" Linze, in stark contrast to her sister, reacted in sheer admiration. I could only meet her in turn with a wry smile.

Elze seemed to be done with her harvesting, so as though I were a ferryman escorting some passengers, I brought us all back through the [Gate] to the garden behind the inn.

"It took me two whole hours to walk there, but now we're all back in an instant. That's one handy spell you've got there." On that note, Elze left to report her completed quest to the guild.

We decided that my crash course in magic would end there for the day, then headed on back inside the inn. It was almost lunchtime, anyway. I wondered what would be on the menu. I sure was hungry...

When we returned to the inn, Micah was there with an unfamiliar woman who seemed to be about the same age as her. She had wavy black hair, and judging from the white apron she was wearing, I deduced that she most likely worked with food.

The two of them sat with various dishes laid out in front of them. They sampled the foods with a knife and fork, making difficult expressions all the while. Micah raised her head, then noticed us and called out.

"Oh, hey, perfect timing."

"What's up?" I inquired, as Micah brought the other lady up to us.

"This girl's name is Aer, she runs a little cafe in town, Parent."

"Ah, we were just there yesterday. It was a really nice place." I decided to keep quiet about almost flooding the shop. I hadn't seen Aer anywhere at the time, so my guess was that she was probably in the kitchen. Things would have been a little awkward if she'd seen us back then.

"We're trying to come up with new items for her menu, so we figured we'd ask your opinions on the matter. Thought that someone from another country might know of some dishes we don't have around these parts, see?"

"I'd be very grateful if you could think of anything." Aer bowed her head as she spoke. I looked at Linze, and we both nodded.

"I don't mind."

"...I'll help however I can." To be honest, I wasn't sure we'd be able to help at all, though.

"What kind of food were you thinking of putting on the menu?"

"Let's see... Right, preferably something simple, I guess. A dessert dish of some kind, something that would be a hit with young women..."

"Hmm... something young women would like, huh... I can't really think of anything better than crepes or ice cream, to be honest..." Wow, that was a weak suggestion even by my standards. But it wasn't like I knew much about cooking in the first place.

"I... scream?" Aer responded, seemingly confused.

"No, no. Ice cream. You know, the kind you eat?"

"Ice... cream?"

Huh? Why's everyone making such weird faces? Is it possible that ice cream doesn't exist in this world?

"What kind of food is that?"

"Uhm, it's like sweet and cold, white... you know, vanilla ice cream?"

"Not really... I've never heard of anything like that before." It seemed that my suspicions had been confirmed.

Well, it only made sense. After all, this world didn't even have refrigerators. Actually, they did have simple refrigerator-like boxes that stored ice made from magic and used them to keep things cool. But those weren't really refrigerators, more like coolers.

"Would you happen to know how to make it?"

"No, I'm afraid I don't really know that much... If I remember right, milk was one of the ingredients..." I hesitated a bit at Aer's question. How was I supposed to know how ice cream was made?

...*No, wait.* I may not have known how to make it, but I *did* have a way to find out!

"Please wait just a minute. I think I might be able to come up with something. Uhm, Linze. Could you help me out for a minute?"

"Huh? W-Well, I don't mind, but..."

I grabbed Linze and dragged her to my room, then pulled out my smartphone and did a quick search for "how to make ice cream" on the internet. *Okay, good. Got it.*

"...Err, what is that object?" Linze seemed quite puzzled when she saw me fiddling with my smartphone.

"Uhh... it's a handy little magical item! I'm the only one who can actually use it, though. I'd be really grateful if you didn't bother paying much attention to it."

She seemed somewhat suspicious of me, but didn't pry any further. Looked like she was quick on the uptake.

"Okay, can you write down everything I'm about to tell you?"

"No problem."

"Three eggs, two hundred milliliters of fresh cream, sixty to eighty grams of sugar... Does any of this sound unfamiliar to you?" I posed that question to Linze as I listed off the ingredients.

"Sorry... what are milliliters and grams?" ...*Of course this would happen.*

"Milliliters are a thing we use in my country when we're measuring the amount of something. Grams are a unit of weight.

Guess I'll just have to go with my gut on those from now on... Oh, right. Linze, can you use Ice magic?"

"Yes, I can. Ice spells are considered Water magic, you see."

Then there were no problems. After listing off the ingredients, I had Linze transcribe the instructions on how to make vanilla ice cream.

Following the instructions, Aer began making the ice cream. It was a far safer bet than having a complete amateur like me try to make it. Though I did still help out with the mixing, which actually took a lot more effort than I'd originally thought.

For the last step, the mixture was placed in a container and sealed with a lid. Linze cast her magic on it and froze the container in a block of ice. We left it for a while until it seemed about ready, then cracked open the ice block and retrieved the container. It appeared to have come together properly.

I took a spoon and tried a little bit. The flavor was slightly off, but I figured it could pass for vanilla ice cream.

I put some on a plate and offered it to Aer. After a single spoonful, her eyes shot wide open. Suddenly, her face broke out into a beaming smile.

"This is delicious...!" The lady seemed pleased with my offering, which made me happy.

"What is this thing?! It's cold, but... it's amazing?!"

"This is really good..." Micah and Linze seemed to have taken a liking to it as well. Honestly, I thought it could've been a lot better. Though I supposed it would've been impossible to recreate the kind of ice cream sold in famous stores on our first try.

Only one problem remained. Was there anyone working in Aer's store who could use Ice magic? After I asked, she explained that her younger sister could. Okay, no problems on that front, then.

"I'm sure this one'll be popular with young women, and hopefully it meets the standards for your shop's menu."

"Of course! Thank you very much! I'll add vanilla ice cream to the menu right away!"

Since we didn't actually use vanilla extract, calling it vanilla ice cream was technically incorrect... But, well, why sweat the small stuff?

Aer gave a quick goodbye, then rushed back to her shop. It seemed like she wanted to try making it herself.

When Elze returned from the guild and heard the full story, she almost exploded, complaining that she was the only one who didn't get to try any. Micah cut in and said we'd make some more, and with that, I was right back on mixing duty. I found myself gazing wistfully into the distance, earnestly wishing I had that little lost piece of civilization known as the hand mixer... *My poor arm...*

From what I'd seen so far, this world gave off the odd impression of being a little bit mismatched in places. They had advanced greatly in some areas, but were still stuck in the Middle Ages in others.

Take, for example, the pillow in my room. It was an incredibly soft, undeniably high-quality pillow. And, from what I'd heard, it was on the cheaper end as far as pillows went. The raw materials used to make it were made by processing the hide of magic beasts that you could find just about anywhere. Made from common materials, it was about as ordinary as a pillow could be. But if that was what passed for ordinary, then I couldn't even begin to imagine the feel or texture that a high-quality pillow might have had.

Different worlds have different perceptions of value. I have to try and get used to that fact. This world is my home now, so I've got to do my best.

▁▍▋ Chapter II: The More the Merrier! Double the Joy, Half the Sorrow

There were various quests posted on the guild's board. Some involved monster hunting, while others involved gathering herbs or even investigating strange places. There were also a few rather simple ones, like babysitting or doing chores.

Since we'd completed multiple quests already, our rank had increased just the day before. And so, our cards had become purple, which signified that we were no longer mere Beginners.

Basically, that meant we could accept higher level requests. We were no longer restricted to Black quests, since we could do Purple ones as well.

Still, we couldn't let our guards down. We could end up failing the quests, and depending on what the mission was, that could also spell death. We really needed to keep it together.

"Northern... ruins... hunting quest... Mega... Slimes?" I tried reading one of the Purple quest listings. With Linze's help, I had finally made it to a point where I could read some simple words. The reward for the quest was... eight silver coins. Well, that didn't sound too bad at all.

"Hey, so how about this one..."

"Absolutely not." The girls refused in unison.

Well, okay then. They both had completely disgusted expressions on their faces. Really? Was it that bad? As it turned out, the girls just couldn't stand being near sticky, slimy creatures.

"Those things dissolve clothes, y'know? We're *definitely not* going anywhere near them!" Elze basically barked at me.

That'd be... so good...

"How about this instead? A request to deliver a letter to the capital. Travel expenses covered... The reward is seven silver coins... What do you think?"

"Seven silver... we can't split that evenly between us."

"Well, we can just spend the leftover amount on something for all three of us," I replied. That made sense to me.

I went to confirm the details of the mission that Elze had pointed out. The one who posted the request was named Zanac Zenfield... *Hold on, is it the same Zanac?* I checked the address, and surely enough it said «FASHION KING ZANAC» on it. Well, there was no mistaking that.

"How long does it take to get to the capital from here?"

"Hm... about five days by carriage, I guess?"

That was quite a long way off... The mission was looking to be my first long journey since I arrived in this world. But hey, I always had the option to make a [Gate] for the return trip, which wasn't so bad. Plus, if I visited the capital even once, I'd be able to return there any time I wanted thanks to that handy little spell. I had a feeling it would be an asset in the future.

"Okay, let's go for this one, then. I happen to know the guy who put out the request."

"That so? We'll take it, then." Elze ripped the request notice down from the board and took it over to the receptionist. When she came back, she told us that we'd hear the specifics of the request when we went to meet the person who posted it.

Looks like I'll be meeting him again after all.

"Ah, hello again! It's been a while. How've you been?"

"Quite well, thanks to your help that one time."

As soon as we'd entered the store, Zanac spotted me and called out. When I mentioned that we were there in response to his guild request, he led us into a room in the back of the shop.

"For this job, I would like you to deliver a letter to Viscount Swordrick in the capital. If you mention my name, he should know what it's about. I would also like you to return with a response from the viscount."

"Is this an urgent matter?"

"Wouldn't exactly call it urgent, but it'd be problematic if you left it too long." Zanac said that, then took the letter out of a small tube and placed it on the table. It was sealed with something like wax and bore some strange insignia.

"Also, here are your travel expenses. I might have included a little bit too much, but you don't have to return what's left over. You may use the spare change to go sightseeing around the capital, if you'd like!"

"Thank you very much."

Upon receiving the letter and the money for our travel expenses, we set right out to prepare for the journey. I procured a carriage, Linze went out to buy food for the trip, and Elze returned to the inn to retrieve any items we might need along the way.

An hour later, our preparations were complete, so we set off for the capital.

We were riding in a rental carriage, but it was really more like a cart than anything else since it didn't even have a roof. Still, it was far better than walking all the way.

I couldn't control the horses at all, but luckily the twins were experts. They told me that they had been around horses from a young age because one of their relatives owned a farm. As a result, the two girls took turns sitting in the driver's seat and I just stayed in the cart, allowing myself to be rocked about the whole time. I kind of felt bad about not being able to help out there.

North, north, north we went. The trip went smoothly along the main road, and we sometimes exchanged pleasantries with other carriages that passed by.

We left Reflet behind and passed straight through the next town over, a place called Nolan. After that, it wasn't long before we arrived in the town of Amanesque, making it there just before the sun had begun to set. I figured we should spend a night at the inn there, but… *Hold on a second, I totally forgot…*

Can't I just use [Gate] *to travel back to Reflet and spend the night at the Silver Moon? I can just cast it again tomorrow to return here, so it's no big deal, right?* Unfortunately, when I proposed the idea to the girls, they flat-out rejected it. *Why…?*

According to them, it would've been a waste of a trip.

"You just don't get it. The nice things about a journey are visiting unfamiliar stores in unfamiliar towns before spending the night at an unfamiliar inn. That's what traveling is all about!" Elze was shocked that I'd even suggested the idea.

Even if we'd had no money, there were the travel expenses that had been given to us. She seemed to firmly believe that we might as well use the money out of courtesy to the one who gave it to us in the first place. Was that how these things worked…?

Well, with that settled, we went and found an inn before the sun went down completely. We took the opportunity to stay in a slightly more upper-class place than the Silver Moon. The girls took a double room to themselves, while I rented a smaller single room.

With our lodging sorted out, we tied up our cart and went out to dinner. The man at the inn had told us that they made great noodles around these parts. I wondered if they served ramen anywhere...

Just as we were looking around for a good place to eat, we noticed a scuffle taking place nearby. A bunch of onlookers had gathered around, so it seemed like there was quite the ruckus.

"What's that?" It caught our attention, so we decided to go check it out. We pushed our way through the crowd to find the source of the commotion. What we found was a foreign-looking girl surrounded by several men.

"...That girl... she's wearing some pretty strange clothes."

"...She's a samurai!" I could only utter that brief explanation to Linze.

The girl wore a bright pink kimono with a dark blue hakama, white split-toe socks, and a pair of sandals with black geta straps. A pair of daisho blades hung from around her waist. Her long, flowing black hair was tied up into a ponytail and was cut with a straight fringe that leveled just above her eyebrows. Her ponytail was also cut straight across at its end, ending just above her shoulders. The simple little hairpin she wore suited her well.

I had said she was a samurai, but she really looked a bit more like the main character from *Haikara-san,* that shoujo manga about Japan in the 1920s. Still, she definitely resembled a samurai on a base level.

Around ten men surrounded the samurai girl, each with a dangerous look in their eyes. Some of them had already drawn their swords and knives.

"We're here to show our thanks for that little incident earlier, girlie!"

"...Whatever might ye mean? I've no recollection of any such thing, I don't." What was with that way of talking? She was like a movie character!

"Quit playin' dumb! Don't think you can get off safe after doin' a number on our buddies like that!"

"...Aah, you must be the companions of those ruffians I handed over to the town guard earlier today. That incident was entirely their fault, verily. They should not have been going around drunkenly flaunting violence in the middle of the day, indeed."

"Shut yer trap! Grab her!" The men charged all at once, as if his words were the signal they were waiting for.

The samurai girl nimbly dodged every single one of their attacks before grabbing one man by the arm, swiveling around, and throwing him. The man fainted in agony as his back slammed straight into the ground.

She moved in step with her opponent, broke his posture, and then threw him... Was that... Aikido? Jujitsu, maybe? The girl tossed a second man down, then a third, and then staggered a bit. Her movements had grown somewhat sluggish.

Spotting an opportunity, one man approached her from behind to attack her with his sword. *Watch out!*

"Come forth, Sand! Obstructing Dust Storm: [Blind Sand]!"

I reflexively spouted an incantation and channeled my spell.

"Augh, my eyes…!" the man screeched.

It was a simple spell I'd learned just recently. All it really did was throw sand in the opponent's eyes. It wasn't much, but it was good for getting out of a pinch.

While the man with the sword was blinded, I hit him with a dropkick. The samurai girl was surprised by the sudden new challenger who had joined the fray, but she seemed to have judged that I wasn't an enemy, so she returned her attention to those before her.

"Aah, geez, why do you always have to stick your nose where it doesn't belong?!" Elze let out a bemused comment as she joined the fray with a swift but heavy gauntlet-clad punch. But for all her complaining, she sure was smiling a lot.

It didn't take long before all the men were flat on the ground… half of them beaten into the dirt by my good friend Elze. She terrified me.

The town guards finally arrived, so we left the rest to them and left that area of town.

"Truly, I am in your debt. My name is Kokonoe Yae. Ah yes, Yae is my given name and Kokonoe is my family name, it is."

The samurai girl, Kokonoe Yae, introduced herself and bowed her head deeply. Her self-introduction gave me a sense of deja vu.

"Oh, are you from Eashen?"

"Indeed, I am. I have come here from Oedo, I have."

Oedo? The old name for Tokyo? *Eashen is seriously* that *similar to Japan?*

"I'm Mochizuki Touya. Touya is my given name, and Mochizuki is my family name."

"Ooh! Touya-dono, you are from Eashen as well, are you?!"

"Ah, nah. It's a similar place, but I'm actually from somewhere else entirely."

"Huh?!" The twin sisters behind me were surprised by my response. *Oh, right…* Explaining where I'd come from was a pain, so I'd just let them believe I was from Eashen.

"Never mind that… You seemed a bit unsteady on your feet in that fight back there. You're not hurt anywhere, are you?"

"No, I am unscathed, I am. However… as much as it shames me to admit, I have dropped my traveling funds. Therefore…" *Grrrrooowwwwllll*

As if on cue, Yae's stomach let out a massive rumble. Her face turned beet red almost immediately and she shamefully curled her shoulders inward.

And so, the starving samurai joined our party.

We'd been looking for a place to eat anyway, so we decided to take Yae along with us. Yae responded by saying something about not wanting to take advantage of people's kindness, so she didn't even entertain the thought of taking us up on our offer.

"Fine then, tell us stories about Eashen. In return, we'll treat you to food. This isn't charity, it's give-and-take," I proclaimed. She said that was acceptable, and proceeded to order something… That went easier than I expected.

"…I see. So, Yae, you're on a warrior's journey in order to get stronger?"

"Yes… *munch*… indeed. Mine has been a warrior family for generations, they have. My elder brother is to inherit the house, and so, I have left on a journey to improve my skills. Yes, indeed."

"Whoa, sounds rough. You're pretty good to your family, huh?" Elze gazed at Yae, clearly awestruck by the girl who was noisily chowing down on beef skewers. I was pretty much indifferent hearing her story; I just wished she'd either talk or eat, pick one and do the other later!

"So, Yae, got a battle plan going forward? Like, is there anywhere in particular you're headed to?"

"…There is someone, in this country's capital, who did a great deal to help my father in the past. I was, considering going, to meet this person myself, I was." Yae answered my question between several pauses as she slurped away at her bowl of what resembled kitsune udon.

Oh, come on girl, didn't anyone ever teach you not to speak with your mouth full?

"Well hey, ain't that a coincidence? We're actually heading to the capital on a job request. Wanna tag along with us? There should still be room for one more in the wagon. That'd be easier for you too, right, Yae?"

"Do you speak, the truth? I could not ask for, a more appealing offer, I could not… However, are you fine, with someone like myself?" Yae responded to Elze's suggestion while her cheeks were stuffed with something resembling takoyaki. Wait just a second. Exactly how much had this girl even eaten so far?!

"You don't mind, do you, Touya?"

"Me? Nah, I don't really mind, but…" I appeared to be the only one present who was worried that the average cost of our meals would jump exponentially with this girl in tow.

Yae seemed to be satisfied for the time being, having devoured seven slices of bread, beef skewers, yakitori, kitsune udon, takoyaki, grilled fish, a sandwich, and beef steak, so we took care of the bill and left the shop. *Damn it... I never accounted for this in our travel budget...*

On the way back we decided to meet up again the next day just before departing. Right as the twins and I were about to return to the inn, something crossed my mind. I asked Yae one last thing before we split up.

"Yae. Where are you booked into for the night?"

"Oh, well, I was planning on sleeping outdoors, I was..." Of course she was. The girl didn't have a penny to her name.

"Sleeping outdoors, seriously...? Look, come stay at the same inn as us. We'll lend you the money, so just pay us back later."

"It's dangerous to sleep outside by yourself..." Linze muttered lowly.

"Not at all, I couldn't possibly place myself further in your debt, I couldn't." Everything down to her overly-polite nature made her seem more and more like someone who had really just come from Japan. Even if we tried giving her the money for the inn, she'd just politely refuse to take it. I had to come up with a solution... An idea suddenly popped into my head as I thought over the situation.

"Yae, would you consider selling me that hairpin?"

"My... hairpin, is it?" Yae took her hairpin in hand. It had a pattern on it with yellow and brown spots.

"That's a bekko hairpin, right? I've actually wanted one for a while. I think it'd be a good gift for someone I owe a lot to."

"Bekko? Whassat?" Elze butted in, apparently seeking an explanation from me about the unfamiliar word.

"It's an accessory made from a tortoise shell. They're pretty valuable things where I come from." I wasn't actually certain about that, but I was sure I'd at least heard something like that in the past.

Of course, the part about me having wanted one for a long time was utter hogwash. It was just an excuse so that I could get this girl to accept some money. Elze and Linze both caught on fast, and decided it would be best to play along with my tall tale.

"If you truly want a humble trinket like this, then I do not mind, I do not..."

"Alrighty, it's a deal! Here, I'll buy it for this much." She passed the bekko hairpin to me, and in exchange I took one gold coin out of my wallet and forced it into her hand.

"Th-This is far too much! I cannot accept this much for it, I simply cannot!"

"It's fine, it's fine. Look, Touya's been searching for one of those things for ages, you know? That's probably just how much it's worth to him. Now c'mon, let's get you to that inn."

"No, wai— Elze-dono?!" Elze seized Yae by the arm and dragged her off. As their figures gradually faded into the distance, Linze came up to talk to me.

"...Is that hairpin really valuable?"

"Who knows? If it's genuine, then it'd be pretty valuable back where I come from, but I'm no real expert in the going prices for jewelry."

"You don't know its value yet you paid one gold for it...?"

"Well hey, it seems pretty well-made. Even if I don't know its price, I'm sure it'd go for a fair bit. At the very least, I don't feel like I've made a poor trade here, right?" I smiled before slipping the hairpin into my pocket, then the two of us headed back to the inn as well.

Yae was able to book a room for the night, get herself a good night's sleep, and join our motley wagon crew the very next day.

We departed from Amanesque and headed even further north. The country we were in was the Kingdom of Belfast, located on the western part of the continent. It was also the second largest among the countries occupying that area. Maybe because of that, it didn't take long after leaving a town for all buildings to completely vanish out of sight. Soon enough there was nothing but mountains and forests on the horizon. Perhaps the population just wasn't big enough to fill out the overabundance of land.

We ran into maybe one person or wagon only once per couple of hours, and sometimes we didn't even encounter anyone over the course of an entire day. That would change as we got closer to the capital, supposedly.

I warmed my seat in the wagon as usual, sometimes taking peeks at Yae, who was up in the driver's seat. She was good with horses too, she had said, so the three girls had decided to take turns holding the reins. I felt almost ashamed at my lack of experience. I was beginning to understand the feelings of those characters that would always just be left warming the wagon…

As if to make up for that — well, partly, anyway — I sat in the back and engrossed myself in my magic studies. From my lessons with Linze, it had come to light that I was able to use various kinds of spells that fit under the Null category, that is, magic without an element.

Our first hint came when I tried mimicking the [**Boost**] spell that Elze used, and it activated for me without so much as a problem. Later, I heard more about a spell called [**Power Rise**] from a fellow guild adventurer who could use it, and it went off without a hitch when I tried it out.

Put simply, what that meant was that as long as I knew the spell name and its effect, I could use just about any kind of non-elemental magic. The twins were long past being surprised by any of my abilities, so they just treated it like one of my character traits at this point. Well, whatever. It was pretty handy, so I had no complaints. *Thank you, God.*

Nevertheless, there were a few problems. Null, or non-elemental magic, as a category was almost entirely personalized magic. Basically, each individual spell could easily be something nobody but the users themselves had heard of.

In that sense, it was like their trump card. There were obviously some people who would want to keep something like that hidden, otherwise people would be able to account for it in advance. On the other hand, there were people like the adventurer who taught me about the [**Power Rise**] spell, people who assumed that others wouldn't be able to mimic it anyway, so there was no harm in telling people. *Sorry about stealing your spell,* [**Power Rise**] *guy.*

Still, despite their rarity, there were plenty of Null spells that were more widely-known. I had bought books on non-elemental spells recorded throughout history, and had set out to study them to try and acquire as many as I could.

Now, the next problem. There were far too many. Even the known non-elemental spells were enough to fill a phone book.

Because the majority of non-elemental spells were personalized magic, there were all sorts of spells with extremely limited usage. Magic for keeping incense sticks burning longer; magic for making the color of tea look more appealing; magic for smoothing out the surface of splintered wood… The list went on and on, and those types of mundane spells made up the majority of them.

In addition, there were plenty of spells that had similar effects. Even [**Power Rise**] and [**Boost**] overlapped a bit. Both were spells used to physically fortify the user after all. Still, [**Boost**] was more user-friendly since it also had effects like boosting jumping ability or granting explosive levels of power in physical attacks.

Since I had no way of knowing which spell would be useful in what situation, I figured I'd just go through them all one by one. But even if God *had* improved my memory, I still wasn't confident that I could memorize a whole phone book of spells.

Looking through that phone book in front of me for spells that seemed useful was a pain in the neck. It was like searching for needles in a haystack. It was boring! Then again… it wasn't like I had anything better to do. I was skimming through the book when one spell in particular stood out. *Oho…*

"A spell that allows the caster to retrieve small items from afar, eh… Wonder if I can use this one."

"Why not test it out?" Linze peeked over at the page. Good point, it seemed simple enough to test.

"[**Apport**]!" I exclaimed.

However, nothing happened. Huh? I'd definitely felt the sensation of something being drawn toward me…

Elze called over to me when she noticed that the spell had failed to activate properly.

"What'd you try to grab hold of?"

"Yae's katana. Figured I'd try giving her a bit of a small fright. Hmm… Oh, maybe it was too big? It does say it only works on small items, after all." I tried once again with a clearer image in mind.

"[**Apport**]!"

"Fwah?!" I heard Yae's startled voice coming from the driver's seat.

In my hand was the ribbon she had been using to tie her hair back.

"Looks like it worked. Could be a fairly convenient spell, but it's also quite a fearsome thing as well," Linze warned.

"What's fearsome about me using that spell?"

"I mean, it grabs things without leaving a trace behind. With a skill like that, someone could pickpocket all they wanted."

"I see... That's actually kinda scary, huh? You could use that power to freely steal all the money and jewelry you wanted."

"...Don't you dare use it for that."

"...Please don't use it for that..." Elze and Linze both met me with scornful eyes. What a rude accusation.

"Don't be ridiculous, I'd never do that! Oh... I wonder if underwear's a valid target for this spell..." Elze and Linze both bolted upright and moved a bit further away from me. Oh, come on, it was a joke!

"Uhm... my hair is kind of flying everywhere in the wind right now, it is..." Yae turned to face me, quite clearly asking for me to return her ribbon so that she could tie her hair back up. Whoops, forgot about that for a second there.

We had passed through several small towns since then, and before long three days had passed since we initially set out on our journey.

I confirmed on my map that we were just over halfway to our destination. It felt like more people and wagons had been passing by recently, too.

As for myself, I had been continuing my staring contest with the phone book of spells. Through my efforts, I had managed to master two new interesting ones. One which drastically reduced the effects of friction against the ground for a short period of time, and one which expanded the user's senses to cover a much wider range of detection.

The great thing about the spell that expanded my senses was that if I really focused, I could home in on specific events happening up to a kilometer away from where I was.

Now, before talking of the dangers of this spell, I only decided to learn it because I felt that the ability to see, hear, and investigate things without having to go there directly was obviously useful. The girls, however, vehemently demanded that I swear never to use it for peeping on women. Just what kind of person did they see me as…? I was testing out the effects of that spell, **[Long Sense],** and confirming everything within one kilometer when I noticed something odd.

This is… Was it… the smell of blood? My heightened sense of smell picked it up quite clearly. When I turned my vision to where the smell was coming from, I saw a high-class carriage, surrounded by armor-clad men… *They look like soldiers,* I thought. They were being attacked by a pack of what I could only describe as Lizardmen wearing leather armor. Though there was also one man in black robes among them.

Half of the soldiers were already cut down and laying on the ground. The remainder fought to protect the carriage from the Lizardmen, who were marching toward it, clearly armed with spears and curved swords.

"Yae! There are people being attacked by monsters! Full speed ahead!"

"Ah…! Understood, yes!" Yae whipped the horses and we sped up. I kept my vision linked to the area as we drew closer, so I could keep an eye on the situation. The Lizardmen cut through the soldiers one by one. There appeared to be an injured old man and a child inside the carriage. Would we be able to make it in time…?! *There they are…!*

"Come forth, Fire! Whirling Spiral: [Fire Storm]!" Linze cast a fire spell from inside the wagon. Some tens of meters away, a tornado of fire burst to life in the center of the pack of Lizardmen.

With that as our signal, we leaped from the wagon as it passed the monsters by. First out was Elze, followed by me, with Yae bringing up the rear. We left the reins in Linze's hands.

"Kshaaaaa!!!" A single Lizardman turned our way, darting straight at me. I focused my energy in order to cast one of the new spells I had just learned.

"[Slip]!"

All friction between the Lizardman's feet and the ground vanished in an instant, which sent it into a backflip so ridiculous that it would've even been ruled out of a comedy show.

"Gurghagh!!!" I dealt the killing blow to Lizardman A, then mowed down Lizardman B as it leaped to attack me.

Nearby, Elze had caught Lizardman C's curved sword with her gauntlets, which Yae used as an opening to slice into the monster's flank. Nice teamwork.

While my attention was on that scene, a spear of ice flew past me and impaled Lizardman D, who had been sneaking up on me while my back was turned. That must've meant that Linze had managed to stop the horses and join the battle.

With the flow of the battle in our favor, we cut the Lizardmen down one after another. Still, there was something odd about the whole situation… There were far too many enemies in one place, right…? We had already cut down a great deal of them. Lizardmen by themselves weren't particularly strong monsters, but it was a pain trying to deal with so many at once…

"Come forth, Dark! I Seek a Scalebound Warrior: [Lizardman]!" The black-robed man was behind the Lizardman army, and he was chanting. When he finished, several more Lizardmen came crawling out from the shadows around his feet. What the heck was up with that?!

"Touya, it's Summoning magic! That man in the black robes is the one summoning all the Lizardmen!" Linze yelled in my direction.

Summoning them... So he had been using Dark-type magic. No wonder we hadn't been able to cut down the Lizardmen's numbers. He would've been able to keep on calling monsters for as long as his magic held out, what a pain... All right, then. My course had been set.

"[Slip]!"

"Gah?!" The robed man's feet flew out from beneath him and he was thrown to the ground with a loud thump. He scrambled to get back up, but collapsed to the ground once more right away.

"Grr...!"

"Steel yourself." Yae leaped in with impossible speeds and cleanly severed the man's head. *Whoa, little bit gruesome there...* The man's head fell to the ground and rolled a bit before it stopped. Rest in peace.

Since the summoner had been taken care of, the remaining Lizardmen simply faded away. I assumed they'd gone back to wherever he'd pulled them out from.

"Looks like it's over... Everyone alright?"

"I'm doing great," Elze replied.

"I-I'm alright as well," Linze meekly muttered.

"As am I, I am." We made it out alright, but the people who had been attacked had suffered great losses. One of the remaining soldiers made his way over to me, leg dragging behind him.

"Th-Thank you... you saved us..."

"Don't mention it... What's the casualty rate?"

"Of ten bodyguards... they got seven of us... Damn it! If only we'd noticed sooner...!" The man trembled in frustration and clenched his fist. I felt the same, in a way. If only we had shown up a little bit sooner... but there was little point in dwelling on such things any longer.

"S-Someone! Is someone there? Gramps... Gramps is...!" We all turned to face the carriage when we unexpectedly heard the voice of a girl. Crying and shouting, a little girl with long, blonde hair clambered out of the carriage. She looked to only be about ten years old.

We ran over to the carriage, and next to the white clothed little girl lay a gray-haired old man in a black formal outfit. Blood flowed from his chest as he wheezed in pain.

"Please save Gramps! He was hit by an arrow...!" The girl, face soaked in tears, begged us for help. This old man must've been very important to her. The soldiers brought the old man down from the carriage and laid him down on the grass.

"Linze! Can't you use your Healing magic on him?!"

"...I-I can't. The arrow must have snapped, and part of it is still lodged in the wound. If I heal him in this condition, the arrowhead will get stuck inside his body... E-Even that aside... my magic wouldn't b-be effective on a wound this dire...!" Linze's words were laced with apology and regret.

As soon as the little girl heard what Linze had to say, her face clouded over with despair. She gripped the elderly man's hand tightly as she wept, and it looked like she would never stop crying.

"Young miss..."

"Gramps...? Gramps!"

"I am afraid… that we must part here… But please know… the days I spent with you… were among the happiest of my— ghh! Ack…!"

"Gramps, that's enough!" Damn… the old man was coughing and sputtering. Was there really nothing we could do? I had never tried out major Healing magic before, but I had read about it in the tomes Linze had let me borrow. I knew the incantation, too. It wasn't impossible for me to cast… probably.

Should I take a gamble here? But even if I heal him up with the broken arrow still lodged in the wound, there's no telling what might happen. The wound healing up might even make the arrow sink in deeper, which would make it pierce his heart… Wait… if I could just pull the arrow… out of the wound… That's it!

"Please, move out of the way!" I hurried the soldiers aside and knelt down by the old man. After that, I quickly pulled one of the other arrows out from the side of the carriage and committed the shape of the arrowhead to memory. Then, I focused on the image strongly in my mind.

"[Apport]!" In an instant, a blood-soaked and broken arrowhead was firmly gripped in my hand.

"Amazing! You used the spell to retrieve the arrow!" Elze looked at my hand and almost screamed with joy. But I wasn't done yet, there was one more step.

"Come forth, Light! Soothing Comfort: [Cure Heal]!" As I cast the spell, the wound in the old man's chest gently began to regenerate. It was almost like watching a video rewind itself. It continued like that until the jagged opening had closed up completely.

"…What is this? The pain… is receding? Whatever is happening, it… doesn't hurt? It doesn't hurt… I'm healed?"

"Gramps!" The old man sat there, completely baffled, but upright and unharmed, as the little girl threw her arms around him. She cried countless tears of relief, refusing to let go of the old man all the while. Watching the sight made all of us let out our own relieved sighs. We slumped to the ground.

"Phew…" Well, I was just glad it had all worked out.

We helped make graves in the nearby woods for the seven soldiers who had died. Couldn't very well have left them lying there, but bringing them with us wasn't an option either.

Of the three survivors, the youngest soldier dug graves in complete silence. Apparently, his older brother had been among those who had passed away. When we finished making the graves, he bowed deeply to us. The old man stood next to him and bowed as well.

"Truly, you have been the greatest of help to us. How can we ever even begin to repay you…?"

"Please, don't worry about it. More importantly, I healed your wound, but you've still lost a fair bit of blood. You really should be taking it easy right now." I tripped over myself a little bit as the old man kept his head bowed. It was like this with God too, but it really did seem that I was weak against old men.

"Thanks, Touya! You didn't just save Gramps, you saved my life as well!" The little blonde girl fired words of gratitude at me as though she were the queen of the world. I gave a wry smile and thought to myself that she must be the young daughter of some noble or other.

The carriage was of far higher quality than Zanac's. Plus, there was a large number of bodyguards, a family servant-looking old man, and the haughty little girl, so it felt I probably wasn't far off the mark.

"Apologies for my belated introduction. My name is Leim, and I am a servant of the noble Ortlinde household. The young miss is the duke's daughter, Sushie Urnea Ortlinde."

"I am Sushie Urnea Ortlinde! It's a pleasure to make your acquaintance!" A duke's daughter? Guess I was right on the money. She did seem like nobility, after all.

As I internally confirmed my theory, the twins and the samurai girl at my side all stood deadly still as though turned to stone.

"…What's up?"

"How can you be so casual like that?! This is the duke's daughter, you know!"

"…D-Duke is… the highest social rank that can be bestowed… Unlike the other titles, duke is usually only given to members of the royal family…"

The royal family… Huh?

"Yes indeed! My father is Duke Alfred Urnes Ortlinde, younger brother of His Majesty the King!"

"So, I guess that makes you the king's niece. That's pretty amazing."

"…You do not seem surprised. You must be quite the accomplished person yourself, Touya." Huh? I turned around to find the twins and samurai girl down on both knees, bowing their heads to the ground.

What, prostrating ourselves now? Is that how I'm supposed to react here?

"Uhh… Miss Sushie? Should I be… on the ground with them?"

"You may call me Sue. We're in no formal setting, so you needn't bow. You needn't speak formally, either. As I said before, I owe you my life. If anything, I should be the one to bow my head. All of you, please rise." The girls stood back up and raised their heads as Sue had instructed. It seemed some of the tension in the air had been relieved, but they still held stiff expressions on their faces.

"So, what's the daughter of the duke doing in a place like this?"

"We were on the way back from Grandmother's place… on my mother's side. There was a matter we were looking into, you see. We stayed for a month, and were traveling back to the capital."

"And then you were attacked all the way out here… Doesn't really sound like it was just any old group of thieves that attacked you."

I couldn't really picture thieves attacking with Summoning magic. Plus, while there were a lot of Lizardmen, there had only been the one man in a black robe commanding them. It made the most sense to assume that the assailant knew the duke's daughter was in this specific carriage. In that case, his motive was likely either assassination or kidnapping…

"Well, the assailant is dead now. We have no way of knowing who he was or upon whose orders he was acting."

"I do apologize, I do…" Yae hung her head despondently. Oh, right, Yae had been the one to send his head flying. It certainly might've made more sense to try and restrain him for interrogation. After all, there was always the possibility that we could've found out who had sent him or unraveled some big old conspiracy that was going on or something.

"Pay it no heed. I told you, I am grateful to you. You have my praise for vanquishing that menace."

"Such kind words... you waste them on me." Yae bowed once again.

"Well then, Sushi— er, *Sue*. What do you plan to do next?"

"Regarding that matter..." Leim, who had retreated to somewhere nearby, spoke up in an apologetic tone.

"Over half of the guards have been felled, and if we are attacked again, I fear we may not be able to keep the young miss safe. Would you consider lending us your services as bodyguards? I shall see to it that you are paid adequately as soon as we reach the capital safely. Will you assist us?"

"Bodyguard work, eh..." Well, we *were* all heading to the same place anyway, and I couldn't bring myself to just leave them there. I didn't really mind, but I needed to know what the others thought.

"Sounds fine, right? I mean, we *were* going that way anyways," Elze stated plainly.

"I don't mind at all."

"I am already but a passenger, so I shall leave the decision to you, Touya-dono." Seemed like we were all in agreement.

"Alright, we'll take the job! To the capital, then?"

"Indeed! We shall place ourselves in your capable hands!" Sue's face broke out into a broad smile.

So, both of our vehicles carried on. The old wagon trailed along behind Sue's carriage, and out in front of both were two soldiers on horses, leading the way.

The remaining soldier had taken his horse and rode off ahead to deliver a letter that Sue had written explaining the situation to the duke's family.

I rode along in the carriage as Sue's personal bodyguard. Since I was proficient in both magic and swordplay, it was decided that it was the best possible position for me.

I sat in a completely unfamiliar high-class seat, and directly in front of me sat Sue, Leim by her side all the while.

"...And with that, the valiant Momotaro slew the wicked Oni and took various treasures back to the village."

"Ooh! Amazing!" Sue clapped her hands as she listened to my tale. I wondered if this was okay. I had been told to talk about something, so calling it a heroic tale passed down in my hometown, I recited the tale of Momotaro. I didn't know how she would react to it, but Sue seemed pleased enough.

Sue spoke quite strangely for someone of her age. Apparently her speech was like that because she kept trying to mimic her grandmother, so her grandmother must have been someone of quite high status as well.

"Would you permit me to hear another tale, Touya?"

"Well, alright. Let's see... Long ago, in the castle town of a kingdom far, far away, there lived a girl named Cinderella..." I never thought I'd be telling stories featuring witches or wizards in a world where magic really existed... Still, Sue seemed happy enough, so I didn't really mind.

After that, I exhausted myself by reciting every fairy tale imaginable, and before I knew it, I found myself telling the stories of famous manga and popular anime movies.

I almost leaped out of my boots when Sue yelled about wanting to embark on a hunt for the Castle in the Sky, but Leim managed to calm her down.

It seemed the young lady was particularly fond of adventure stories. What a strange girl.

And so, we passed the time peacefully in the carriage as we headed onward to the capital.

CHAPTER II: THE MORE THE MERRIER!
DOUBLE THE JOY, HALF THE SORROW

"Ooh, we're almost there! It's the capital!" Sue let out a shout as she peeked her head through the window. I looked outside myself, and in the distance I could make out a white castle surrounded by tall walls, framed by a large waterfall behind it.

The Royal Capital, Alephis. Located on the bank of Lake Palette, a large body of water that formed at the base of the waterfall, it was also known as the Lake Capital.

Situated on the western part of the continent, the Kingdom of Belfast had a comfortable climate. That plus the fair rule of the reigning king made it a relatively peaceful country. The silk goods made in the Killua region of Belfast were renowned as some of the highest quality in the world. They were light and soft, sturdy, and beautiful. The goods were popular among nobles and even the royal families of other countries, so the business was the pride of the kingdom, and supposedly an indispensable source of income.

Come to think of it, didn't Zanac have some silk clothes up for sale in his shop?

As we grew closer and closer to the capital, I was shocked once more at the sheer size of the castle walls. Just where did it all stop? It was very much the picture of an iron fortress designed to keep any enemy out. Not to say it was actually made of iron or anything.

Several soldiers were conducting inspections at the city gates before allowing people passage into the capital. However, we were allowed through as soon as the guard caught a glimpse of Sue and Leim's faces. Seemed they were pretty well known around those parts. No doubt the duke's family crest on the side of the carriage played a part as well.

The carriage continued straight on toward the castle, crossing a stone bridge which spanned a large river below along the way. There was another checkpoint in the middle of the bridge, but we just rolled right on through once more.

"Beyond this point is the nobles' residential district." I gave a little "I see" to Leim's explanation. Then the capital was divided into two areas: the commoner district, and the noble district. Which meant the place we just left must have been the commoner district.

We traveled through a street filled with rows of beautiful buildings and arrived in front of a massive mansion. The walls around here were huge, too. When we finally pulled up in front of the entrance, five, then six soldiers slowly opened the very large, presumably heavy doors. Only now that we were directly in front of it did I recognize the crest on the door as being the same one on the side of the carriage.

So this was the duke's estate. It was huge. Everything from the garden to the house was needlessly huge. Why was everything so big?

The carriage pulled up in front of the foyer, and Sue swung the door open with great gusto.

"Welcome back, young miss!"

"Why thank you!" A wall of maids appeared and bowed their heads in unison. I simply sat in the carriage, completely dumbstruck until Leim urged me to step out. I felt… completely and utterly out of place. When we stepped into the foyer, a man came running down the red-carpeted staircase in front of us.

"Sue!"

"Father!" Sue made a beeline for the man and jumped up to embrace him.

"Thank goodness… Thank goodness you're safe!"

"I am fine, Father. Did I not write as such in my letter?"

"When that letter arrived, it felt as though my heart had stopped in my chest…" It seemed like the man was Sue's father. He was Duke Alfred Ortlinde, brother to the king. He had a head of blond hair, and a strong body that told of his good health at a glance. But despite his sturdiness, he had a gentle face which made him appear to be nothing but kind.

Eventually, the duke parted from his embrace with Sue and made his way over to us.

"…You must be the adventurers who saved my daughter. You have my sincerest gratitude. Truly, thank you so much for all your help." I was surprised. The duke approached us only to bow his head. The king's brother was bowing before us.

"Please, there's no need to bow your head. We only did what anyone would do in that situation!"

"I see. You're quite the modest one, aren't you? Nevertheless, you have my gratitude." After he finished speaking, the duke took my hand in his and shook it firmly.

"No doubt you know already, but allow me to formally introduce myself. My name is Alfred Urnes Ortlinde."

"I'm Mochizuki Touya. Oh, Touya is my given name and Mochizuki is my family name."

"Oho, might you be from Eashen?"

… Please. Not this again.

"I see… So you came to the capital on a guild request to deliver a letter?" We sat out on the second floor terrace overlooking the garden, enjoying a cup of tea.

Though the only ones actually *enjoying* their tea were the duke and I, as the other three were all tense and sat like planks of wood.

Sue had left her seat and wasn't there anymore. I wondered where she'd run off to.

"If you hadn't accepted that request, Sue might very well have been kidnapped or murdered right about now... I'm thankful to whoever asked you to come out here."

"Do you have any idea who could've been behind the attack?"

"I almost wish I could say that I didn't... But considering my position, I'm sure there's no end of sordid individuals who see me as a bother. There may even be some amongst the nobles who would seek to kidnap my daughter and use her as leverage against me to make me dance to their every whim." The duke made a bitter face and sipped from his tea as he said that. Sounded like there were all sorts of people even among nobility.

"I'm back, Father. Sorry for the wait." Sue came out on to the terrace. She wore a dress with pale pink frills, and in her hair was a headband fitted with a matching pale pink rose. It suited her very well.

"Did you talk with Ellen?"

"I did, yes. I kept quiet about having been attacked, however. I did not wish to worry her." Sue came out and sat herself down next to the duke. Leim came out not a moment later carrying more tea with him.

"Ellen?"

"Yes, that would be my wife. I'm sorry she couldn't come out to meet you, even though you came to our daughter's rescue... She's quite terribly blind, you see."

"Your wife is blind, is she?" Yae spoke up, a heavy heart clearly behind her words.

"She came down with an illness five years ago... They managed to save her life, but not her vision." The duke let his gaze drop as he spoke his sad tale. Sue noticed, and placed her hand on top of his. She must have been concerned for her father. She really was a lovely little girl.

"...D-Did you try treating it with magic?"

"I called out to practitioners of Healing magic throughout the land, but... it was no use. They said that if it had been caused by a physical injury, then magic might have helped to some degree, but that it would have no effect on the after-effects of an illness." The duke listlessly answered Linze's question.

So even healing magic couldn't help with it... I had thought we might be able to heal it with [**Cure Heal**] or something, but... Moments like those were where I felt my own powerlessness more than ever.

"If only Grandfather were still alive..." Sue whispered in a small, regretful voice. He must've noticed my curious expression, because the duke spoke up to explain.

"My wife's father... Sue's grandfather, that is, my father-in-law could use a very special kind of magic. He was able to cure any abnormality within the body. The reason Sue originally left on a journey was to find out more about his magic and try and find a way to recreate it."

"If we had Grandfather's magic, we would be able to heal Mother's eyes. Even if we couldn't use that magic, there was the possibility that knowing more about it would have allowed us to substitute it with a spell from a different school of magic. That was what I heard from the court magician, at least. Else we could try to find someone who could use the same magic as Grandfather..." Sue clenched her fist in frustration.

"She said that the possibility of that was very low indeed, Sue. Non-elemental magic is primarily personalized magic. There are almost no two people who can use the exact same non-elemental spell as each other. But I'm sure there must be someone out there who can use a similar spell. I'll definitely find that person, one way or another..."

"AAAAH!!!" "AAAAH!!!" "AAAAH!!!" The three girls sitting beside me suddenly leaped out of their seats and let out some seriously loud noises. *Whoa, that scared the life out of me! What the hell, what's going on?!*

"It's Touya!"

"Touya, that's you!"

"Touya-dono, that must be you, it must!"

"What are you talking about?" The girls fired out their fingers at me in rapid succession, and I reflexively pulled away from them.

You guys are seriously scaring me... Did all that tension go to your heads and make you snap? Look, the duke and his daughter are pulling away, too. You're freaking everyone out here!

"You might be able to use that spell!" Elze exclaimed.

"Non-elemental magic is primarily personalized magic... meaning no two people can use the exact same spell. Except...!"

"Touya-dono, you can use any kind of Null spell, can you not?!"

"Hmm...? Oh! So *that's* what you were all yelling about!" I finally got it! Right, if the spell wasn't elemental, then...

"Whatever... are you talking about...? Do you mean that you can...?"

"Touya! Can you really cure my mother?!" Sue exclaimed. The duke looked at me with an expression of sheer bewilderment on his face. Meanwhile, Sue was clinging to my arm like she was never going to let go.

"Honestly, I won't be able to say either way without trying it out first. But there is a chance... Just so long as I know the spell's name and the details of what it does."

"Oh my, do we have guests?" The lady sitting on the bed in the room we walked into strongly resembled Sue. Looking at her almost made me believe I was glimpsing into Sue's future. The only difference was that she had light brown hair in contrast to the blonde of her daughter.

Her white blouse and pastel blue skirt gave her an air of transience. To compare her to a flower, she was less like a rose or a lily, and more like a baby's-breath. She was still young, too. Probably wasn't even thirty yet. But I felt as though her youth only drew more attention to her blind eyes. Her eyes were still open, but it felt like her gaze never quite settled on anything. It almost made one wonder exactly where those eyes were gazing into.

"My name is Mochizuki Touya. It's a pleasure to meet you, Duchess Ellen."

"The pleasure is all mine. Darling, is this young man a friend of yours?"

"He is. He's someone that looked out for Sue while she was on her journey... and upon hearing about your eyes, he said he would like to see what he could do."

"My eyes...?"

"Mother, please relax for a moment," Sue said. I quietly raised my hand and held it in front of Duchess Ellen's eyes. My mind focused entirely on them as I cast the spell I had learned a moment ago. *Come on, please work...*

"[Recovery]."

A soft light flowed from the palm of my hand into Duchess Ellen's eyes. When the light faded, I pulled my hand away.

Her gaze wandered for a moment before gradually settling down. After blinking her eyelids a few times, she quietly turned to face in the direction of her husband and daughter.

"…I-I can… see? Darling…! I can see!" Tears began to flow from Duchess Ellen's eyes.

"Ellen…!"

"Mother!" The three of them clung to each other and started crying. Finally seeing her husband and daughter for the first time in half a decade, Duchess Ellen smiled brightly through her tears. She simply continued gazing at their faces through tear-stained eyes. The faces of her beloved family.

Leim, who had been quietly watching the scene from nearby, turned his face upward and began sniffling as well.

"Uwah… I'm so happy!" Elze choked out.

"I'm so glad for them as well…"

"I'm really pleased for them, I am…!"

Wait, why are you girls crying?! Huh? Hold on, does this make me a horrible person for being the only one not to cry? I'm feeling pretty moved by this whole scene too, you know! It's just that I was under so much pressure to make sure it worked that I'm more relieved than happy right now… Ah, forget it.

For the time being, we just warmly watched as the family rejoiced.

"I am greatly indebted to you. Really, you have no idea what this all means to me. You not only saved my daughter, but you even cured my wife… Thank you, thank you so much." The duke was bowing to us again. I really wasn't good with situations like that. I couldn't stand to keep making this man bow to me.

Sue was still in Duchess Ellen's room. We had been brought out into the parlor, where we sat in luxurious chairs opposite the duke.

"Please, don't mention it. Sue is safe, and your wife is cured. I'm just glad everything's alright now."

"No, I cannot possibly leave it at just that. I really must show you the appropriate level of gratitude. Leim, bring it over."

"Of course, sir." Leim brought over a silver tray with several objects laid out on it.

"First of all, take this. It's your reward for saving my daughter. As well as escorting her home safely." Leim handed me a bag that I assumed had money inside it.

"You should find forty platinum coins within."

"Huh?!" "What?!" "Eh?!" The girls seemed to grasp the situation immediately, but I wasn't sure what the duke meant. I knew all about gold coins by that point, but what was a platinum coin? I asked Elze, who was sitting next to me.

"Hey Elze, what's a platinum coin?"

"...It's a level of currency one step above gold coins. A single platinum coin equals ten gold ones..."

"Ten gold?!"

From my time in this world so far, I know one gold is roughly equivalent to about one hundred thousand yen... So if one platinum is one million yen, then I have... forty... million... yen...?!

"W-Wait, I can't accept this! That's way too much!" After I realized just how much was being given to us, I hurried to refuse it. There was no way the job we accepted was worth anywhere near that much.

"Don't say that, please, just accept it. If you plan to make a living as adventurers, I'm sure you'll reach a point where you'll find yourself in need of money like this. Think of it as funds to stash away for when that time comes."

"Well…" He had a point, the money would probably come in handy. I hated to admit it, but there were things in this world that could only be solved by moving money around. Besides, from what I knew of the duke's personality, he wasn't going to let up until I accepted the reward.

"In addition, I would like to give each of you one of these." The duke lined up four medals on the table in front of him. Each one had a diameter of about five centimeters. The medal's design featured a shield in the center and a pair of lions facing each other from the side. *Wait… isn't this…*

"They're medals featuring my family crest. With this, you will be able to pass through any checkpoint with relative ease, and you will also be able to use facilities normally exclusive to nobles. Should anything ever happen, they will act as guarantee that my family will provide support to you. They are a form of identification, I suppose."

According to the duke, such medals were normally given out to the family's exclusive merchants or other such important figures. Each of the medals had our individual names carved into them, along with a single word, which meant there could be no duplicates made. That was apparently to make sure they could never be abused if we ever lost them.

My medal carried the word "Tranquility," Elze's was "Fervor," Linze's was "Philanthropy," and Yae's was "Sincerity." *Tranquility, eh… Well, peace is the best after all.*

Anyway, these certainly did sound like useful things to have. They made it easier to visit Sue again as well, actually. Being stopped at checkpoints all the time sounded like a royal pain. Although in an emergency, I could always just cast [Gate] to bypass all the checkpoints anyway.

We split the money evenly between us, ten platinum coins each. Still, one platinum was ten gold, so that was one million yen... I had to make absolutely sure I never, ever dropped any of these.

We decided that it was too much of a risk to be walking around with that much money, so we each took a single coin and had the duke deliver the rest to the guild for us. Apparently it was set up so that we could withdraw our money from any guild office in any town. I figured it was like this world's equivalent of a bank.

We decided it was about time to be getting on our way, and when we returned to the foyer, Sue and Duchess Ellen had come to see us off.

"Come visit again soon! That's an order, you hear?!" A passionate farewell scene behind us, we hopped in our wagon and headed to deliver that letter to Viscount Swordrick's estate just as Zanac had asked of us.

"Eh? That letter you were asked to deliver was for Viscount Swordrick, it was?" Oh, had we not told Yae about that yet? I curiously met Yae's startled gaze as the wagon swayed us side to side.

"Do you know him?"

"Do I know him? He's the very man I mentioned before, he is. The one who helped my father in the past, he is the very man I'm here to meet, he is!" Huh, that was a huge coincidence. Small world after all.

We were tossed around in the back of the wagon as Elze led us down the high-class street, following the directions the duke had given us before drawing to a halt outside the viscount's estate.

It may sound rude, but having just come from the duke's estate, the viscount's seemed much more... snug, comparatively. Still, there was no mistaking that it was quite a grand place. It felt quite old, or rather, rich with history. I'd heard that quite a few of the nobles with property in the capital also owned land elsewhere, so this might even have just been the viscount's villa.

When we gave Zanac's name to the gatekeeper, he said he would arrange for the viscount to meet us. Before long we were led into the building, where a man I took to be a butler led us to the parlor room.

Once again, compared to the parlor in the duke's home, the place was a bit... well... Impolite thoughts ran around in my head as we waited, when out came a red-haired hero of a man. This guy... was strong. I could tell even through his clothes that his muscular form was well-trained. Even his eyes were sharp, surveying us like a falcon pinpointing its prey.

"My name is Carlossa Galune Swordrick. Are you the messengers that Zanac sent?"

"We are. We're here to deliver this letter to you upon his request. We were also asked to receive a response from you to take back with us." I handed him the tube containing Zanac's letter. The viscount took it and removed the wax seal with a knife before reading the contents.

"Wait here a moment. I shall write a reply." After he spoke, the viscount left the room. As he left, a maid entered the room and made tea for us, but compared to the tea we'd had at the duke's house... No, that was enough of that. No need to disrespect the viscount. I shouldn't have been comparing him to the duke in the first place.

"Sorry to have kept you." The viscount returned with a sealed letter in hand.

"Alright, please give this to Zanac. Also, hold on a moment. Before you go…" Even as the viscount handed me the letter, his gaze drifted over to Yae.

"I've been wondering since I first laid eyes on you… Have we… No, I don't think we've ever met before. Still… What is your name?" The viscount tilted his head as if he were trying to remember something. Yae looked straight at him and gave her name.

"My name is Kokonoe Yae; daughter of Kokonoe Jubei, I am."

"…Kokonoe… Oh, Kokonoe! I see. So you're Jubei's daughter!" The viscount slapped his knee, let out a broad smile, and gave Yae a once-over with a happy expression on his face.

"Yep. There's no mistaking it. You're the spitting image of Nanae. I'm just glad you take your looks from your mother and not your old man!" The viscount laughed as though he had suddenly been put in a great mood, and Yae simply smiled without a word.

"Uhm… so how do you know Yae…?" I asked.

"Hmm? Oh, right. You see, her father, Jubei, used to be an instructor of swordplay for the Swordrick family. Back when I was still a sniveling brat, he really put me through the wringer. It was a real challenge, I tell you. Hard to believe that was twenty years ago now."

"My father always talks about how, among the swordsmen he trained, none were nearly as wise or talented as you, Viscount-dono."

"Ohoho? I'm pleased to hear that! Even if it's mere flattery, it's heartwarming to know that my old teacher speaks so well of me." The viscount smiled happily, true to his words. But Yae continued talking to him with a serious expression on her face.

"He also told me that should I ever get the chance to meet you, I should request your advice in matters of swordplay, he did."

"Oho…" The viscount narrowed his eyes, apparently enthused by Yae's words.

Huh? What's with this change in the atmosphere all of a sudden…?

The viscount's garden had a dojo in it.

Upon entering, I couldn't restrain my surprise. After all, it looked exactly like a Japanese kendo dojo.

A polished wooden floor, several wooden swords hanging on the wall… complete with an actual home shrine.

"This building was planned by Mr. Jubei, and it was built by my father. It was designed to have an Eashen aesthetic, as you might be able to tell."

"It reminds me of the dojo back home… It makes me feel nostalgic, it does."

That makes two of us, Yae. Going to Eashen just got a whole lot higher on my bucket list.

"Choose the wooden sword that suits you best. They're lined up by the size of their grip." After changing into his training attire, the viscount fixed his sash and took hold of a wooden sword. Yae, on the other hand, took a few swords and tried swinging each of them several times before deciding which one suited her best. Shortly after that, she stood face-to-face with the man.

"Are any of you familiar with Healing magic?"

"…We know one or two spells." I replied by raising my hand and looking at Linze.

"Then there'll be no need to hold back. Come at me with all you have." When he said that, we went to sit down at the edge of the dojo so we wouldn't get in the way of their fight.

Struck with a sudden idea, I took out my smartphone. Alright, now…

"What are you doing…?" Linze spoke up, looking all confused.

"Just a little something for future reference." While I replied, Elze took on the role of the referee and took her place between the fighters.

After confirming they were fully ready, she signaled the start.

"Now then… **begin!**" As Elze's voice rang throughout the dojo, Yae dashed toward the viscount with the speed of a bullet. He stopped the first strike head-on and neatly parried each of the numerous attacks that followed.

Yae momentarily backed away and attempted to adjust her breathing. However, despite the golden opportunity, the viscount didn't attack her. Instead, he just watched her movements.

Facing one another, they closed in on each other as if drawing an inward spiral. Little by little, the distance between them shrunk until it reached a point that summoned another exchange of wooden swords… beginning another vicious chain of blows.

However, Yae was the only one actually attacking. The viscount merely parried, evaded, and deflected, not showing any sign of going on the offensive.

"I see… So that's how it is." He shifted his sword into a lower position. Yae fixed her aim and breathed as her shoulders moved up and down in quick succession. It was apparent that she was running out of stamina.

"Your swordsmanship is proper. I would even go as far to call it exemplary, as I don't see even a single wasted movement. It's just like how Jubei taught me."

"Is there a problem with that, is there?"

"Not in the least. However... you don't have anything beyond that level."

"Wha—?!" The viscount shifted his sword into an overhead position and displayed his first act of aggression. Even I could feel his electric aura.

"En garde!" He took a step forward, and before I even noticed, quickly leaped and closed the distance between him and Yae. The sword he held above his head quickly went down toward her head. Yae responded by positioning her sword above herself.

However... the very next moment, she fell to the floor with a highly unsatisfying sound. I could hear her moan as she held on to one of her sides.

"E-Enough!" Elze proclaimed the end of the match. If this was a real battle, Yae would have been neatly split in half.

"Guh..."

"Please, refrain from moving too much. I probably broke some of your ribs. If you give them the chance, they may pierce your lungs. You there! Come and heal her."

"Ah, right."

As Yae writhed in pain, I placed my hand on her side and cast a Healing spell. Sooner than later, likely due to the fading pain, her expression turned calm.

"I'm fine now, I am..." After thanking me, Yae stood up and gave the viscount a sincere bow.

"I am grateful for your guidance, I am."

"Your swordsmanship has no real dark side to it. You mix feints and actual attacks, charge and back away when needed… It's both fierce and open-ended. However, a proper manner of the sword like yours doesn't break the limits of dojo training. Now, I'm not saying that's a bad thing. After all, true strength differs person by person." The viscount's sharp eyes pierced Yae.

"What do you seek from your blade?" She offered no answer to his words. Instead, she just looked up at her wooden sword.

"That is the first thing you must learn. Then, you will find your true path. And when you do, feel free to come back to me." With those words as his last, the viscount left the dojo.

"Hey, well… You shouldn't mind it too much! Battles are all about luck. If you lost, you were probably bound to lose anyway!"

"…Elze-dono… you are not helping at all, you aren't…" Yae looked at Elze with a stern expression, which made her let out a dry laugh.

Linze took control of the carriage to get us to the checkpoint through which we could leave the noble district.

"What're you gonna do from here, Yae? We're headed back to Reflet," Elze proclaimed.

"What is it I should be doing, I wonder…"

Damn, she looks seriously low. Reminded me of some useless salary man who had lost all hope. Sitting on the side of our luggage, Yae was looking at the distant sky with her chin resting on her hands.

"If you've got nowhere to go, you should come with us to Reflet! Then you can join our guild, form a party, and even train with us sometimes!" Sometimes? Well, I kind of understood what Elze was going for. We became good friends, so it would've been a bummer if we split up at that point.

"That may not be a bad idea, it may not."

"Alright, it's decided!"

"My, you're so forceful…" Elze's forcefulness made me adopt a wry smile. She took full advantage of Yae's downer… or maybe she was just being considerate in her own way? As I thought about that, our carriage reached the checkpoint. The soldiers at the post came up to us, and when Linze shyly showed them the medal we got from the duke, they didn't hesitate to let us through. *Man, the duke sure is something.*

"The world is a very big place, it is… I did not think I was facing someone that strong… I have a long path ahead of me, I do…" Yae slowly muttered those words.

So she was still hung up on that… Must've been quite a shock.

"The final strike especially… I do not understand how it happened, I don't. I thought I was going to parry the sword as it came from above… but it somehow hit me on my side…"

"That was something! I was right next to you, but even I didn't see what happened! It was like I blinked and you were suddenly lying on the floor, y'know?" To help Yae process it, Elze started excitedly explaining what she saw.

"It is such a shame… If only I could see that attack one more time, if only…"

"But you can," I explained.

"…Excuse me?" My nonchalant words made Yae put on a rather silly expression and blink repeatedly.

I took out my smartphone, brought up the match I just recorded, and played it for her.

"Wh-What is this?! Ah! W-Wait! That is me! And Viscount-dono! Elze-dono, too, she is!"

"Whoa, what the hell's this?! It's moving! But I'm right here! Eh? Wait, is that actually Linze?! Sis?! No, she's right here, too! What's going on?!"

"Calm down."

"Ow!" "Ouch…!" I dropped a light chop on the top of their panicked little heads. They really needed to calm down. Not like it wasn't funny, though.

"This is… sort of like my personal Null magic that allows the recording of events so you can see them again later. I used it to record your match."

"That magic is amazing, it is!"

"Eh? What's that spell called?"

"Ah… smartphone, I guess?"

"Smawtforn… never heard of that one before. Well, whatever. It is non-elemental magic after all." Elze folded her arms and tilted her head. Yae, on the other hand, took my smartphone and intently gazed at the screen. Soon enough, she got to the scene where she was defeated.

"Right here, yes!" The sword that was supposed to go down on her head was actually going for her side the whole time. Huh? I was quite sure it was an overhead strike…

"What does this mean…?"

"Dunno…" I asked Elze, who was watching it by my side, but she seemed as clueless about it as I was.

"T-Touya-dono! Is it possible to see it again, is it?!"

"It is, yeah. As many times as you like. Should I go from the start? Or just before you were defeated?"

"Before I was defeated!"

I set the start point and handed the phone to Yae. The viscount approached Yae and hit her straight on the side. He never did go for her head. But I was quite sure that...

"Shadesword..."

"Shadesword?" I was confused by the word she quietly muttered.

"It's a technique that turns high fighting spirit into a blade. Being an illusion, it doesn't have any substance. However, since it is made of spirit, it has a presence you can feel, it does... That's why, before you realize it, you acknowledge its existence. The viscount likely set the shadesword to attack from above while he struck his real blade into my side. The shadesword was clad in a distracting amount of fighting spirit... while the real one, which I couldn't feel, came from the side, it did! Yes... I took the bait that he set, I did!"

So she was shown an illusion? I'd thought a cold dose of reality would make her even more depressed, but she was actually smiling. And it didn't look like the smile of someone who gave up... It was like she had come to realize something. Her muttering seriously creeped me out, though.

"My swordsmanship has no dark side, it doesn't. Now I see what he meant, yes. Sometimes, you don't wait for openings in your enemy, but create them yourself... That is interesting, it is..."

"Hey, Yae. You okay?"

"I am, yes. Thank you, Touya-dono. You truly helped me, you did." Since Yae looked satisfied, I took back my smartphone and placed it in my pocket. Well, it was good to help her cheer up.

"I shall train lots and grow even stronger... With all of you by my side, I will!"

"That's more like it! I wouldn't have it any other way!" Yae and Elze exchanged a high five. Ah, the joys of youth.

"H-Hey, don't forget about me..." A slightly bitter voice came from the front of the carriage. *Oh. I-It's not like we really forgot about you! Sorry, Linze.*

Since we were already in the Royal Capital, we decided to not waste the opportunity. We certainly weren't short on money, so we decided to spend some time shopping. Or, rather, that was decided for me. I lacked what it took for me to resist the will of the three girls.

We left our carriage at the inn, though it cost us because we weren't planning on staying the night, and decided that we'd gather there in three hours.

The three girls went somewhere together, but I chose to do something by myself. I really didn't want to be their baggage handler. Not to mention that there was something I wanted to buy for myself, as well.

So I took out my smartphone, found where I was on the map and... realized the Capital was huge. Wouldn't have expected less, really. *Is there a search function? Alright, a-r-m-o-r-s-h-o-p...*

Soon enough, several pins fell on the map, showing the locations of the armor shops in the area. The closest one was... right in front of me? I raised my head to see an armor shop with a shield sign in front of it. I didn't even have to search for it...

"Welcome!" I entered the shop to see an absolute bounty of shields, armor, gauntlets, and helmets. Behind the counter at the far end of the room, I saw a friendly-looking shopkeep smiling at me.

"Excuse me, can I have a look around?"

"Please, feel free! Try on anything you like, as well." Permission granted, I started intently looking at the armor pieces. I was set for weapons since I bought a katana for my first guild assignment, and I kind of postponed getting armor at the time. But being here gave me the perfect chance, and I wasn't about to miss it. It was the Royal Capital, after all, so I figured I might as well get something good.

Alright, now... I valued mobility a lot, so I didn't think I'd be suited for any kind of metal armor. Moving in full plate was probably bound to be a nightmare.

That'd leave me with lighter types of armor, such as leather...

"Excuse me, what's the best armor you have? Ah, non-metal, I mean."

"Non-metal? That'd probably be this spotted rhino armor."

"Spotted rhino?"

"Exactly, a rhino with spots on it. Armor made from its hide is tougher and longer-lasting than ones made from standard leather." I tried rapping my knuckles on the armor and it felt very tough, indeed.

"And it's still weaker than metal armor?"

"Well... unless it's enchanted in some way, that's how it is most of the time."

Enchanting... That's the thing where they add magic effects to equipment, right...? I'd heard that some highly coveted enchanted items could be found in ancient ruins, but the magic kingdom in the Far East actually produced them in large numbers.

"Do you sell enchanted armor?"

"Sorry, but we don't. Equipment like that is really expensive. I think Berkut, the armor shop on the eastern avenue, sells things like that, but it's exclusive to nobles." The shopkeeper replied with a troubled expression.

Exclusive to nobles, huh? Quite a predicame— Wait. "Would they let me in if I showed them this?"

"What is this...? Th-This is the duke's...! You are close to the duke, sir?!" Upon seeing the medal I got from the duke, the shopkeeper instantly changed his expression.

"Everything should be fine, then. If the duchy approves of you, there will be no trouble at all." I tipped him with a silver coin to make up for the time I had wasted, then left the shop. After that, while referring to my map, I went off looking for that shop named Berkut.

Walking through the Royal Capital, I couldn't hide my surprise at all the non-human races that were roaming about here and there. There were many races, all with their unique traits, but what really caught my eye were the beastmen.

I didn't see a single one back in Reflet, but here, you couldn't miss them if you tried. Those beastmen weren't the ones with human bodies and animal heads, like, say, the minotaur— they were like the fox beastgirl walking in front of me. Ears and tail aside, she was no different from a normal human. Long, blonde hair with fox ears just as bright except for the black tips. A large, fluffy tail with a white end. She also had another pair of ears. Human ones, just like ours. Linze said something about both pairs having a main-sub relationship, but I didn't really understand the details...

Oh? That foxgirl seemed really lost and confused... Was she looking for someone? Her expression looked really troubled. And yet no one was helping her. The big city folk here seemed just as cold as the ones in my world.

Alright, guess I'll talk to her.

"Er... is everything alright?"

"Y-Yesh?! What ish it?!"

Whoops, I startled her so hard that she forgot how to pronounce words. She looked at me with wide open eyes. Had to get her to calm down. After all, I wasn't some weird pervert or anything... At least, I thought I wasn't. With her being so scared, I began to lose confidence in that conviction.

"Well, it seemed like you were in a bit of trouble. I just wondered what was up."

"Ah, u-uhm… I-I… lost my companion…"

Ah, so she was lost after all.

"W-We decided where we'd meet if we ever got split up, b-but I don't know where the place is…" The little fox's voice gradually turned weak. I could swear I just saw her ears and tail sag in a profoundly sad manner.

"What's the place called?"

"Uhm… I think it was a magic shop called Luca…?"

Magic shop named Luca… got it. I took out my smartphone, ran a search on the map… And there it was. Right on the way toward Berkut as well. Convenient.

"I can take you there. It's on the way to where I was going, anyway."

"Really?! Thank you sho much!" Oh, she mispronounced again. What a charming little thing. She was probably younger than Elze and Linze. Twelve, maybe thirteen years old…?

Following the map, we walked through the streets. On the way, I found out that her name was Arma.

"Are you a tourist here, Mr. Touya?"

"Nope, had some work to do. Already finished with it, though. What about you, Arma?"

"My sister had work to do here, and I joined her. I wanted to see the capital." Arma let out a bright smile. It was almost like the troubled expression from before had never even existed.

As we made the simplest of small talk, we soon arrived at the magic shop. There was a beastgirl standing in front of it. Upon noticing Arma, she quickly ran up to us.

"Arma!"

"Ah, Sis!" Arma ran straight into her big sister's chest. The lady instantly hugged her back. As obvious as it might seem, she was also a fox beastgirl. Clearly older, too. Likely an adult. The aura of dignity around her made her seem somewhat soldier-like.

"I was so worried! How could you get lost...?!"

"I'm so sorry... But it's okay! Mr. Touya helped me get here." Finally noticing my presence, the lady gave me a sincere bow.

"You helped my sister? Thank you so much."

"It's nothing, really. I'm just glad to have met her."

She offered to repay me, but I refused because I had business to take care of. What I did wasn't worth any kind of repayment. After a short introduction, I took my leave. Arma just couldn't stop waving her hand at me as I walked away.

As I headed toward Berkut after leaving the two behind, I couldn't help but notice that the buildings and shops around me were gradually becoming fancier. After a while, I finally reached my destination.

"Damn, this place looks real expensive..." The formal, brick-built building made me feel a bit timid. It was like some brand name shop.

I didn't feel like I belonged. It seemed like they'd even take an entry fee. Well, not like there were guards or anything. Knowing that standing around wouldn't get me anywhere, I took a deep breath and walked in.

Upon passing through the grandiose door, I was quickly greeted by a young lady.

"Welcome to Berkut. Is it your first time here, sir?"

"Ah, yes. Never been here before."

"Well, then. Might you have something that proves your social standing or an invitation permitting you to shop here?"

I see. No chance customers allowed, huh? Nobles and those invited only. I took out the duke's medal and showed it to the shopkeeper. Unlike the man from the previous shop, the lady wasn't perplexed in the least and merely bowed her head.

"All is well, then. Thank you very much. Now, on what business have you come here?"

"I'd like to take a look at your enchanted armor."

"Understood. Right this way, please." I followed her to one corner of the shop, where I was met with an array of various armors, from shiny plates with a mystifying glow to cheap-looking leather gloves that didn't seem special in any way at all.

"Are all of these enchanted?"

"That is correct. For example, this Silver Mirror Shield is enchanted to reflect offensive spells, while this Gauntlet of Demi-God Strength has a muscle enhancing enchantment placed directly on it." ...Well, I could certainly feel magic coming from them. Now, when did I become able to perceive that? Probably God's meddling. Shouldn't overthink it.

"Sir, what exactly are you looking for?"

"Ah, something non-metal... Basically, armor that's light, yet durable."

"In that case... might I suggest this leather jacket? It's enchanted to resist blades, flame and lightning." Hmm... That sounded nice, but the design was just... The word "lame" didn't begin to cover how gaudy it was. Also, the draconic embroidery on the back was just embarrassing.

Suddenly, I noticed a white coat hanging at the corner of the shop. It was a long coat with fur trimming on the sleeves and collar.

"What about that one?" I said as I pointed toward the coat I noticed.

"It is enchanted with blade, heat, cold, and strike resistances. Also, it has a notably high resistance to offensive magic, but there's a bit of a problem with it..."

"What's that?"

"The resistance to magic only works for the magic affinities the wearer has. Not only that, but it makes them take double damage to affinities they don't have."

...So, someone with Fire affinity would be highly resistant to fire, but if he didn't have Wind affinity, the lightning resistance would not only be ineffective, but also make him take double damage... A true double-edged sword. It'd work wonders if the wearer fought monsters of the same element, but when they went beyond that, the risks were far too great...

Well, not like it matters to me! After all, I have an affinity for all the elements! Score!

"Can I try it on?"

"Go ahead."

I took the coat, examined the texture, and put it on. The size was just right. I tried moving a bit, and it didn't seem to impair my mobility, nor did it feel off in any way. I liked it.

"How much for this one?"

"We will make it cheap and sell it to you for eight gold coins."

Each one was about as big as a five hundred yen coin, and had engravings of something resembling a lion. And that was after making it cheap? *Damn hard on the wallet, if you ask me...* Might have been fair, though, considering the effects. My sense of the value of money was really getting warped...

"Alright, I'll take it. Here's the payment."

"One platinum coin, understood. Please wait here a moment." She returned to the counter and came back with a money tray holding two gold coins. I took them, placed them in my wallet, and walked toward the exit.

"Thank you very much for your patronage. We eagerly await your next visit!" She bowed her head and saw me off as I left Berkut.

And so, I finally got some good armor. Cost me an arm and a leg, though…

After buying the coat, I had a meal at a nearby restaurant and went back to visit the magic shop, Luca, that I left Arma at. However, neither she nor her sister were there anymore.

After looking around for a while, I bought a book on Null magic. When it came to the six elements, people normally bought books of the appropriate affinity, learned the spells, practiced, and made them theirs. However, Null magic was unique to individuals. Wasn't there something peculiar about such a book being sold?

It even had a dictionary listing all of the mysterious spells to ever be recorded in this world. And, of course, an overwhelmingly large part of it was non-elemental. It was a real treasure for someone like me.

Rather cheap, too. But that was only obvious. After all, it wasn't really meant for teaching magic. Wouldn't have been surprised if it was written with leisure in mind.

Afterward, I bought a souvenir for Micah — an assorted box of cookies — and returned to where I was supposed to meet the others. It was getting dark.

"Ah, he's finally here. You're too slow!" Elze said, clearly chiding me.

"Huh? You're all early. It's not even the time we agreed on yet." The three were waiting for me at the inn, next to our cart, clearly hauling a bigger load than before. *Just how much did they buy?*

"Oh? What's with the coat, Touya?" Elze spoke with an impish tone and began examining my purchase.

"Ah, this coat's enchanted. It lowers the effects of all offensive magic... and gives resistance to blade, heat, cold and strike attacks."

"Resistance to all offensive magic? Wow... How much did it cost?"

"Eight gold coins."

"Eight?! You've been ripped o— Wait, actually, considering the effect, that might be fair..." Apparently Elze's monetary senses weren't the best, either.

With all of us finally gathered, we got on the cart and took off. Yae took the reins and, since we were a bit overloaded, I decided to sit next to her.

We could use a [Gate] to instantly return to Reflet, but I didn't want us to stand out too much. Therefore, we decided to use it after we left the Royal Capital.

When leaving, we didn't even have to show our medals as we crossed the checkpoint again. Casually riding the carriage, I waited until the Capital looked really distant before I told Yae to stop.

"What is it we're going to do here, Touya-dono?" Clueless about [Gate], Yae asked me with a puzzled expression on her face.

"Should I aim for one of the roads near the town instead of the town itself?"

"Yeah, that makes more sense." Upon hearing Elze's confirmation, I imagined the place where I wanted to appear and concentrated my magic.

"**[Gate].**" A giant door of light appeared before us. I reshaped it so the cart could fit through.

"W-What is this, what is it?!"

"Right, move along, move along." Ignoring Yae's perplexed look, I rushed her to move the cart through the **[Gate].** Once we passed through the portal, we were met with the view of a large evening sun hidden behind the mountains west of Reflet.

"This magic is so useful... I can't stress it enough!" Linze proclaimed.

"It reduces a five day journey to a single moment, after all."

"A shame you can't go to places you haven't visited before, though..."

"Will someone finally tell me what's going on here, will they?!" As Yae was losing herself in utter confusion, we were overwhelmed by the relief of finally making it back home. It was already dark, so we decided to leave reporting to Zanac for tomorrow.

We stopped before the Silver Moon and walked in to inform Micah of our return. As obvious as it might seem, the place hadn't changed a bit. After all, five or six days wasn't long in the least. However, there was one change that truly stood out.

"Welcome! Ya stayin'?" The person greeting us from behind the counter was a tough-looking man with a red beard.

Huh? Who's this?

"...Uhh, we were staying here... and we just returned from a job..."

"Ahh, so ya were here before, eh? Sorry, first time seein' ya an' all."

"Umm, where's Micah?"

"Huh? You're back already? You sure work fast." An apron-clad Micah came walking out of the kitchen.

"Micah... who is this guy?"

117

"Oh right, you haven't met him yet, have you? This is my dad. Right as you left, he got back from a long-distance restocking."

"Name's Dolan. Nice to meet ya."

"I... see." He extended his hand, and I reflexively reciprocated.

Well, he and Micah *did* share the hair color. And it looked like they might share a lot of character traits as well... Like the lack of care for the little details, for one. But honestly, I was just glad that she didn't inherit his face. Apparently, Dolan was out buying spices in the southern lands. It was hard to get salt, pepper and other seasonings locally, so he often went and bought lots — enough for all the shops here.

"Ah, Mr. Dolan, could you prepare a room for this girl here?"

"Yes'm."

I gently pushed Yae in front of the counter. As she went through the registration process, we began taking our stuff up to our rooms. Elze left to return the cart.

"Oh, Micah. I got you a souvenir."

"Wow, thank you! How was the capital?"

"It was huge. Had a ton of people, too." I gave her the cookies and jokingly gave her question a straightforward answer.

We left the place pretty quickly, after all. Didn't even spend a day there. I always had the option of going there again with [Gate], so I considered making a more proper visit next time.

Micah celebrated our safe return with a filling dinner. We all ate a lot of what she gave us, but none of us could hold a candle to Yae, who ate several times as much as any one of us. Her metabolism was truly something extraordinary. Even Micah and Dolan were at a complete loss for words.

In the end, Yae was the only one to have food expenses added on to her lodging fee. *Only fair, if you ask me.*

The next day, we headed over to Zanac's store to finish up the request we accepted from him. Initially, he was surprised by our quick return, but he quickly accepted it once I explained the [Gate] spell to him. Teleporters were certainly rare, but not unheard of, after all.

"This is a letter with the viscount's response." I handed the letter over to Zanac. He inspected the seal and confirmed it was genuine before opening the letter up and briefly skimming through it.

"Indeed it is. Thank you for a job well done."

"Oh right, Mr. Zanac. You should take this. Since we only used half of the traveling fees, I figured we should return the rest," I said, as I handed him the bag with the remaining travel money in it.

"You're an honest lad, aren't you? Had you not mentioned your use of that [Gate] spell in returning, you could easily have kept that money for yourself."

"I figure having you trust me is worth more than some quick cash. As a merchant, I'm sure you understand."

"...Very true indeed. A merchant is only worth as much as the faith people have in him. Not many people would've been willing to trade with someone with a reputation for being a cheat. Making light of that fact can never lead to good things." As he spoke, Zanac took the money back.

After that, he handed me a card from the guild with a number printed on it, to serve as proof that we'd completed the request. All we had to do was hand that card in to the guild office to claim our reward.

We gave Zanac our thanks, then left the store. From there, we walked straight to the guild office.

As we entered the guild, we were greeted by the all-too-familiar sight of request boards and people staring from all sides. We made our way over to the receptionist's desk. Yae was fidgeting nervously all the while, since it was her first time there and all.

I handed over the card I'd received from Zanac, and just like that, our quest was complete.

"Please present your guild cards." Alongside a heavy sound of three thumps, the receptionist pressed the magical stamp down on our cards.

"And here is your reward of seven silver coins. As always, thanks for your hard work." I took our reward money, then called Yae over to the desk.

"While we're here, this girl wants to register with the guild."

"A new registration, then? Very well." While Yae received the explanation about her guild registration, the rest of us split the reward. We each took two silver coins and decided to spend the rest on food for all of us later on.

"Still, feels a bit weird, y'know? A reward of two silver suddenly seems like a lot less money than it actually is…" Elze muttered.

"I know exactly what you mean. Suddenly having platinum coins thrown at you does wonders for destroying your perception of value…" Linze replied.

I couldn't help but smile at Elze's bemused reaction. This was all quite silly, honestly. The money we'd received from the duke was ultimately a bonus, and nothing more. I had to make sure to be fiscally responsible, and not to rely on it too much in my day-to-day life.

"I got registered, I did!" Yae waved her card around happily as she made her way over to us.

Her card was the Beginner's Black, unlike the rest of ours. Seemed like she felt slightly left out when she noticed that fact. Still, we were by no means a very high level yet. I was sure the gap would be closed in no time as we kept doing more quests together.

Since Yae was so eager to get started straight away, we all made our way over to one of the request boards.

When people with different colored guild cards teamed up to accept a request, their overall level would be judged by the color of card that was most prevalent on their team. Since three of us had Purple cards and only one of us had a Black card, we could accept Purple requests even with Yae at her current level.

I read through the posted requests along with everyone else.

"Northern ruins... Hunt, Mega... Slimes? Hey, this one's still up. How about we..."

"No way!" "Please stop." "I do not think so."

Responding in perfect sync again, are we? I see how it is. And you've even brought a new recruit over to your side this time. Seems like Yae's not good with sticky, slimy things either... Damn shame...

In the end, we went with a hunting request for some magical beast species called Tiger Bears. With a name like that, I wondered which parts of them were tiger and which parts bear... Their habitat was within walking distance if we used a [Gate] too. So, off we went.

Well, I found out pretty quickly that Tiger Bears were large bears with tiger-striped fur. Also, they had fangs like sabre-toothed tigers!

121

I was startled when they ambushed us up in the rocky mountains, but Yae ended up taking out almost all of them by herself.

We snapped off their fangs to take back to the guild as proof that we'd taken care of them, and I used [Gate] once more to take us back to the guild. We handed the fangs in and the quest was complete. All of this took no longer than two hours, netting us a reward to the tune of twelve silver. Honestly, it was beginning to get a bit silly how quickly we were clearing those quests.

Understandably, we were questioned as to whether we really defeated these monsters at the location specified in the request. I carefully informed the receptionist that I could use teleportation magic, and she accepted my explanation. Apparently there were several other adventurers with various kinds of teleportation magic, although each with their own restrictions. In the case of my [Gate] spell, it could only take me to places I had already been to at least once before.

Yae went on about us taking on another request since we still had plenty of time left, but I wasn't really up for more fighting at that point. I managed to pacify her by suggesting we all go get something to eat instead. And so, we stopped off at the cafe, Parent, to celebrate having cleared Zanac's request, as well as Yae registering with the guild, *as well as* her first successful hunting quest.

We all ordered small snacks and drinks, plus one vanilla ice cream for each of us. Yae was shocked by her first contact with the substance, but she was wolfing it right down like everyone else before very long.

Right as we were about to leave, Aer asked if I'd like to come up with another new item for the menu. *Hmm… what'd be good this time? Guess I'll look up some ideas when we get back to the inn.*

CHAPTER III: THE CRYSTAL CREATURE

It had been two weeks since we'd gotten back from the capital. It was raining outside. It had been raining for three days, in fact. Apparently this world had a rainy season as well, but this wasn't it. Just a particularly long spell of rain.

We had put off doing guild quests until the rain stopped. Instead, I immersed myself in my magic studies. Basically, I was picking up usable new spells from that book I'd bought in the capital.

It was a five hundred page book. I'd read through about a third of the whole thing, but I'd only managed to find four worthwhile spells. There were about fifty spells per page, so twenty five thousand in all... Out of those twenty five thousand, only four usable ones so far from the approximately eight thousand three hundred I'd reviewed.

The spells I had acquired were:

[**Enchant**] — A spell for infusing magical properties into items.

[**Paralyze**] — A spell for paralyzing an opponent to prevent them from moving.

[**Modeling**] — A spell for changing the shapes of minerals, wood, or the like.

[**Search**] — A spell for locating nearby objects.

Only those four.

Out of them, [**Modeling**] and [**Search**] proved to be the most useful. Still, none of them were quite perfect.

[**Modeling**] was a skill for transferring one's mental image over to re-mold a solid object, but it took quite a bit of time if you weren't used to it. Plus, losing focus halfway through making something usually produced weird-looking results.

I tried making a shogi set for practice, but the board itself was one row too long and the pieces were too big to fit in the squares.

It was difficult unless you had a clear image in mind while performing the spell. It was much easier to create something while staring at what the finished product should look like, so I managed to get a shogi set made pretty well by searching for an image of one on my smartphone.

[Search] was one that I learned while thinking it would come in handy when trying to locate lost items, but it turned out that the spell itself could also perform incredibly vague searches.

I had thought there wasn't any vanilla in this world, so as a test I used [Search] at the marketplace and ended up finding it instantly.

What I found wasn't the vanilla that I was used to, but a strange fruit resembling a cherry tomato that was apparently called a Koko. Nevertheless, it both tasted and smelled like vanilla, so it turned out to be very usable as a substitute.

Even if the name or shape were different, if it was something my mind would judge as vanilla, then the spell picked up on it… It cast a wide net.

But even that spell had its downsides. Its effective range was incredibly short. It only had a radius of about fifty meters. I couldn't really use it for anything like finding missing people.

"I'm hungry…" I checked what time it was, and noticed it was well past lunchtime. No wonder.

I closed the book, locked my room, and headed down the stairs. In the dining room, Dolan and Barral, the owner of the Eight Bears Weapon Shop, were sitting facing each other. In between them was a board of wood covered in squares.

"You're playing shogi again?"

"Yup," Dolan answered, his gaze glued to the board all the while. I couldn't help but shrug.

Regarding the shogi set I had made as a test, Dolan was the one who took the most interest in it. Once I taught him the rules he became immersed in the game, and even started dragging acquaintances into playing against him. Barral also happened to get hooked on it, so the two of them would play against each other whenever they had the time.

To be honest, I really lucked out when Barral also got hooked. Until he came along, I'd been forced to be Dolan's opponent, being the only other person who really knew the rules.

Even if I was familiar with the rules, I was by no means good at shogi myself. I didn't even use to play it very often. I had won a few games at first, but could no longer lay a finger on Dolan. I guessed that was what it meant to grow good at something because you enjoyed doing it.

I placed an order for lunch to Micah in the kitchen, then took a seat on the other side of the dining room so as not to disturb Dolan and Barral.

"Mr. Barral, what about the store?"

"Not many people comin' along in the rain, so I left the missus in charge of things. Never mind that, though. Touya, think you could make another one of these here shogi boards?"

"Eh? Didn't I already make one for you?" I could've sworn I'd made a set for him just the other day since he said he wanted to practice at home, too.

"Simon from the item shop said he wanted one, too. Do me a favor, aye?"

"Well, alright then…" *Can't you just get a craftsman to make one…?* Though when I thought about it, I realized that making it normally might prove to be quite the hassle.

"Really now? Thanks a bunch, kid."

"Checkmate."

"Hrm?!" Dolan let out that word, crossed his arms, and gazed at the board, and Barral reacted in turn. Those two were completely hooked. I had no idea it would catch on to this extent.

While I was watching the two of them, Micah brought out my meal.

"Here y'go, sorry for the wait. And you two, hurry up and put that thing away already."

"Sorry... Jus' one more game." Dolan made a gesture as if begging Micah to let them keep playing. To be fair, they probably wouldn't be playing so much under normal weather. On the other hand, it could just be that the rain provided a convenient excuse...

The meal Micah had made today was wild herb pasta and tomato soup with two apple slices.

"Come to think of it, Micah, where's everyone else?"

"Linze is still in her room, and Elze and Yae went out earlier."

"In this rain?"

"They went to buy the new desserts from Parent, apparently." Oh, that explained it. Since I'd managed to find vanilla, I talked to Aer about it and came up with a vanilla roll cake as the new menu item.

Like the time before, all I really did was find the recipe and note down the instructions on how to make it. Even so, it turned out delicious. So delicious that I got carried away and had her make strawberry roll cake as well.

When Elze heard about it, she almost had me by the neck, demanding to know why I didn't bring any back with me. She was so unreasonable...

Just because those new creations are going on sale doesn't mean you have to run out and get them on the day they come out. Well, never underestimate the tenacity of a girl with a sweet tooth, I guess...

"We're back! Ahh, we're soaked!"

"We're back, we are." Speak of the devil and whatnot, the two of them had returned. They shook their umbrellas off and planted them by the entrance.

This world didn't have the vinyl umbrellas I was used to. It did have umbrellas, but they were basically made out of cloth and wood. Though the ones they had were infused with pine resin, so they were still just as water resistant as the ones I was used to.

"Welcome back. Did you get it?"

"Of course we did. There were fewer people because of the rain, so it was way quicker than usual." Elze proudly held up the bag of treats. *Bless her, just look at that smile.*

"It was delicious, indeed it was."

"I know, right?" They even had some when they went to pick it up? What a pair of gluttons.

"Here y'go, Micah, this one's yours."

"Thank you. I'll give you the money for it later, alright?" Elze took four small white boxes out of the bag and handed one to Micah. Seemed like Micah had asked Elze to get her one, too.

"Who're the rest for?"

"One for Linze, one for me and Yae to share… And one for you to deliver to the duke."

"Wait, deliver?" *Never mind that, you still plan on eating more?!*

"Who else but you is gonna make it to the capital in this rain? We've gotta give them gifts in return for their hospitality last time, it's common sense." When I said that they should come along as well in that case, I was politely rebuffed. Seemed they were still nervous around Duke Alfred. *Oh, come on already.*

With no real choice in the matter, I set off on my own. Since it was a freshly made, the sooner I handed it over the better they would still taste.

Oh, right… I figured I would deliver a shogi board to the duke, too. Just as a souvenir of sorts.

I let Dolan know and asked for permission to use some of the scrap wood from out in the back garden. I cast [**Modeling**] and made two more shogi sets. I'd made them several times already by that point, so I'd gotten pretty used to it.

I finished making them in around ten minutes. I checked them over just to be sure. *Yup, they look fine to me.* I accidentally made one too many rooks last time, so I had to be careful.

I returned to the dining hall and handed one set over to Barral. I put the roll cake and the box containing the shogi pieces into a bag, then slung the shogi board under my arm.

"Alright, I'll be off, then." I took my umbrella and headed out into the back garden to get ready to cast [**Gate**]. It was always better to avoid standing out when doing that.

The best place to appear would be… in the shadows of the front gate, I guess.

"[**Gate**]."

"Yummy! This is yummy!"

"Mind your manners, Sue. But you really do have a point… This roll cake truly is delicious." Sue and Duchess Ellen happily devoured my offering of roll cake. It made it worth taking it all that way. The duke ate too, and he seemed to approve.

"I'm truly envious of the people of Reflet who are able to eat this every day. If I could only cast [**Gate**] like you, then I would be able to buy it all the time, too."

"If you'd like, I could teach the recipe and cooking instructions to the chefs on the estate. It's not really a trade secret or anything."

"Really, Touya?! Mother, do you hear that?! We'll be able to eat this every single day!" Sue latched onto my words rather firmly. *Excuse you, young miss, but drool is escaping your mouth.*

"Now now, Sue. You'll get fat if you eat it every day. Let's just leave it at every other day instead, all right?" The Lady of the house had her say, though I didn't think every other day would make much of a difference compared to every single day… I'd feel pretty guilty if Sue had completely fattened up the next time I came to visit.

"Now then, you called this thing shogi, did you?"

"That's right. It's a game you play between two people… a pastime of sorts. Would you like a go at it?" I set up my side of the board as Duke Alfred inspected the board and pieces.

"Father, let me play too!"

"Now wait your turn, I'll be going first." The duke copied me and set up his side of the board… Except the rooks and bishops were in the wrong places.

"First of all, I'll teach you how each piece can move. This piece is a Pawn and indicates a regular footsoldier. It can only move one square at a time, but if you get it to the opponent's side of the board, then…"

"Hm, I see…" Slowly but surely, I taught the duke the basic movement patterns of each piece. He proved to be a fast learner. I was certain he'd improve rapidly given his quick thinking. Alas, it wasn't long before I regretted my actions yet again.

"One more game! Just one more game! We'll be done after that!" *You told me that same thing just a minute ago,* I thought to myself… The result was that, much like Dolan, the duke had gotten hooked on shogi. And, for the second time, I was forced to play several games of shogi in rapid succession. The sun had long since set, and Sue had even fallen asleep on the couch waiting for us.

I thought again about how little this world had in the way of entertainment, and briefly wondered if that was why people were so quick to latch onto things like shogi.

"This is a very interesting game. I must get my brother to play it as well!" It was late at night before I was finally released, but the duke proceeded to throw me a curveball with that shocking statement. I could only hope that the king wouldn't become hooked on shogi, too. *He won't ignore state politics to polish up his shogi game, right…?*

Oh, the rain finally let up.

"Yae, it's heading your way!"

"Understood!" It disappeared from my vision using the crumbling castle wall as a shield.

I heard a metallic clang from across the wall, and when I circled around it, I saw the thing engaged in combat with Yae.

It wore black plate armor and swung around a huge, menacing greatsword. An aura of raw power flowed out of its trunks as its mighty legs clung to the ground without ever giving way, and its two arms swung around that greatsword without so much as a trace of mercy in its being.

No, it had been lacking in a feeling of mercy from the very beginning, for this black knight had no head.

Dullahan. That was its name. Born from a knight who was beheaded whilst still harboring many regrets, it revived as a monster and began beheading others as a means to try and seek a new head for itself. It was different from the legends about it back in my old world…

But this Dullahan was our target. Yae and I caught the Dullahan in a pincer attack. I sent her a signal with my eyes, and she confirmed that the light was gathering in my outstretched middle and index fingers before quickly retreating from the spot.

"Strike true, Light! Sparkling Holy Lance: [Shining Javelin]!" A blinding spear of light shot out from the fingers I had aimed at the Dullahan. The spear hit the creature square in the left shoulder and tore its arm right off.

But unlike a human, no blood poured from the wound. Instead, a black miasma seeped out into the surrounding air as it moved to swing down its massive greatsword upon me with its remaining right arm.

Suddenly, a well-timed shadow leaped in from the side to intercept the headless knight with a brutal punch to the side. Not letting the monster recover its balance, the shadow continued with a flurry of well-placed roundhouse kicks.

"Elze! Did you take care of the Lone-Horned Wolves?!"

"Yeah, cleaned 'em all up! Man, there were like twenty of those things, you know?!" Linze came running up from a distance shortly after that. Right, time for the showdown.

The Dullahan staggered for a bit due to Elze's chain of attacks, but quickly corrected its posture and sent its blade flying horizontally at the neck of its new target. Elze noticed that fact and barely managed to leap out of its way, throwing herself into a roll toward my direction.

"Come forth, Fire! Purgatorial Sphere of Flames: [Fireball]!" Linze threw a fireball that landed a direct hit on the Dullahan's back.

Yae moved to strike in that instant, but her sword only struck the enemy's greatsword as her attack was fended off.

"This thing's tough! We won't stand a chance if this turns into a battle of endurance!" Unlike the enemy, we couldn't afford to take so much as a single clean hit from that weapon. It would cleave us in twain, and even a minor scratch from it was enough to tear off a limb or two.

The Dullahan was already a lifeless creature; a being of death. In other words, an Undead-type monster. As a general rule, Undead monsters were extremely weak against Light-type magic. Linze could also use Light magic, but she wasn't particularly proficient with it. I had to be the one to finish it off... And I had just the idea.

"Linze! I need you to freeze that thing's legs! Just buy me a few seconds!"

"Eh? Uhm... understood!" Hearing this, Yae and Elze made their move. They drew the Dullahan's attention from Linze and me. Our teamwork had finally reached an impressive level.

"Entwine thus, Ice! Frozen Curse: [Icebind]!"

Linze's spell froze the ground at the Dullahan's feet in a flash. The headless knight put all of its power into its legs to free itself from the bind, and the ice gradually began cracking around it. *As if I'd waste this chance!*

"[Multiple]!" I activated one of my non-elemental spells. Around me appeared four magic circles floating in the air. Next, I cast a Light magic spell.

"Strike true, Light! Sparkling Holy Lance: [Shining Javelin]!" At my command, four spears of light came shooting out of the four magic circles. Each spear followed a straight trajectory to the Dullahan. The effect of **[Multiple]**, one of my newer Null magic acquisitions, allowed multiple casts of a single incantation to be used at once.

The headless knight tried to move to dodge the spears of light, but Linze's ice held it firm to the ground.

The Dullahan took the full force of the attack, losing its right arm, a chunk out of its side, its left leg, and it also had a hole blasted in its chest before finally collapsing to the ground. Black miasma flowed out from the battered armor and dispersed into the wind. The headless knight would move no more.

"Looks like we're done here."

"That was hard work, it was." Elze let out a sigh of relief and Yae plopped herself down on the bare ground. That was to be expected. Yae had been the one constantly dodging all of the Dullahan's attacks in close-quarters for the majority of that fight.

"...We weren't expecting a pack of Lone-Horned Wolves to appear alongside it. That was a dangerous miscalculation..." Linze held her hand to her chest in relief as she said those words.

Over the past few months, we had built up our guild rank to the level of Green. Out of Black, Purple, Green, Blue, Red, Silver, and Gold, we were now the third rank from the bottom. Reaching that point meant people would acknowledge you as a fully-fledged adventurer.

We were ready to accept a Green request right away when Elze came forward with the suggestion of trying out a quest from a different town's guild office for once.

Just like that, we made for the guild office in the capital. There we found a green request asking for the subjugation of monsters in these ruins.

Apparently they were the ruins of what was once the country's old capital from over a thousand years ago. The king of that era decided to abandon the land and built a new capital elsewhere, so it was said. Basically, they relocated.

I had no way of knowing what it was like at the time it was still the country's capital city, but as of that moment the place was covered in ivy and the castle walls were riddled with holes. There were still faint traces of the paved ground and some buildings to give the feeling it was once a city, and at the center stood what must have been the royal castle... although it was just royal rubble by that point. It was the very picture of a ruined city.

Monsters had come to live in the ruins over time, and adventurers like us would be requested to drive them out. But before long the monsters would be back, leading to more adventurers driving them away, forming a curious cycle.

Still, it was true that if left alone, the monsters would eventually build up enough numbers to be quite threatening. It was probably best to drive them away from the place every now and then for everyone's safety.

"For this being the old capital, there sure is a whole lot of nothing here, huh..." Looking around, all I saw was crumbling walls, broken walls, and shattered walls. At the very peak of this place, on top of the only hill with a decent view, used to stand the old royal castle, supposedly. I wondered if Sue's ancestors had lived there at some point.

But would it normally deteriorate into such featureless ruins? Was it maybe like in the Three Kingdoms when Dong Zhou burned the old capital to the ground, houses and all, as he moved the capital to Chang'an?

"It'd be funny if there were some kinda hidden royal family treasure or something."

"No, I believe that not to be the case. It would be one thing if the country had fallen, but a relocation of the capital alone would not be so difficult that they would leave precious treasures behind in the process, it would not."

"I knooow, I just thought it'd be funny if there *were* something like that." Elze pouted at Yae's sound argument. Treasure, huh?

Back in my world there were the buried treasures of Tokugawa, Takeda, and the like, but it seemed like such concepts were familiar to this world, too. I wasn't averse to the idea. The idea of a treasure hunt never failed to strike something in a man's heart.

Just then, an idea came to mind. *I can try using that spell!*

"[Search]: Treasure."

I used my locating spell. If there was anything that I might've acknowledged as treasure nearby, then this spell would've picked it up... Which it didn't. Well, it was only to be expected.

"You used **[Search]**?! How was it, anything pop up?!"

"All I learned is that if there is treasure, it's nowhere near here." I gave the overexcited Elze the results of my search with a bitter smile.

"I see... That sucks."

"B-But that's only for things Touya would see as a treasure himself, right? There might be other valuable things outside of that range..." Oh my, it seemed the younger sister was raring to go treasure hunting, too. Shouldn't have expected any less of twins.

In fact, it was just as Linze had said. For example, say there was an extremely valuable painting by some famous artist lying around. If I were to look at that painting and think anything along the lines of "It looks like junk to me," then my search spell wouldn't register it as an object of value.

The results were entirely based on the caster's frame of mind. That incredibly vague style was both this spell's biggest strength and most critical weakness. Although in the painting example, it would probably react if I found out about the painting's worth after the fact.

At any rate, she did have a point. My frame of reference for treasure was mainly things like gemstones, golden crowns, decorative swords, or piles of old money. *In which case, the term I should home in on is...*

"[Search]: Historical Relics." *This way it should catch objects of historical value in its net.* Or so I thought until I remembered that I had no way of knowing that at a glance... *Hold on...* "...Huh, I found something."

"Eh?!" "What?!" "E-Excuse me?!" There it was, an object of historical significance. The ruins themselves were also included in the results, but there was something else nearby as well. I honed my senses in on it. Yup, there it was.

"Wh-Which way is it, the direction?!" Elze exclaimed.

"...It's over this way. I can feel it over there. What the heck is this? It's pretty big."

"It's big?!" they all screamed in unison. We groped around the inside of the ruins as we pressed forward. Everyone followed my lead until we eventually came out in front of a big pile of rubble. Hmm...?

"Below? It's coming from underneath this rubble?" Just as I was wondering what to do with the several tons of the building debris before us, Linze stepped forward and fired off a spell.

"Burst forth, Fire! Crimson Eruption: [Explosion]!"

The rubble was blown into tiny pieces with a tremendous kaboom. *Isn't that overdoing things a bit, Linze?!*

"...I've taken care of it." Not paying my stunned stature any mind, Linze set right about to examining the ground where the rubble had been. *Where'd all that sudden zeal come from?*

As I stood where the rubble used to be, I felt the signal grow stronger once again. It was... under here? Looking carefully, I noticed something half-buried in the dirt...

I called everyone over and we started digging away the dirt around it. When we finished unearthing it, it turned out to be a pair of large steel doors that were roughly two tatami in size and shape. Why was it hidden in a place like this...?

We combined our strength and pried the doors open. For some reason it opened smoothly, showing not so much as the slightest trace of having rusted. It was possible that it wasn't made of steel.

After we pried open the doors, what we found waiting for us was a stone staircase eerily beckoning us into the depths...

"Come forth, Light! Tiny Illumination: [Light Sphere]!" Linze created a small light that floated in the air. With cautious steps, we proceeded down the stone stairs.

The staircase was a spiral one and it looked like it was going to go on forever. As we proceeded, I was filled with anxiety. It was almost like we were headed into the bowels of the earth itself.

After some time, the stairs opened into a long, stone passageway. The path was straight onward, and so dark I couldn't make anything out. It was moist, foisty, and humid... The whole place had an atmosphere that gave me the creeps.

"Th-This place is freaking me out... Are there ghosts around here?"

"Wh-What are you saying, Elze-dono?! Gh-Ghosts won't come out here, they won't!" Yae responded to Elze's mutterings in a hyperbolic manner. *That aside... can you girls quit yanking on my coat? It's difficult to walk like this...*

Linze, on the other hand, was firmly walking along the hallway. *Strong-willed, that one.*

Linze's light was the only thing illuminating the area, so we followed behind her. As we carried on through the passage, the ceiling gradually got higher until it opened up into a large chamber.

"What's this...?" I saw what appeared to be some kind of lettering drawn on the wall ahead. It was four meters tall and ten meters across... lines drawn across it separated the writing into columns. Each column was around thirty centimeters across, and contained each individual piece of lettering.

Looking closer, they seemed to be more like pictograms than letters. Sort of reminded me of ancient languages, like that of the Mayans or Aztecs.

"Linze... can you read this at all?"

"I can't... I don't understand this lettering. It's not an ancient magic language, either..." Linze didn't look at me as she answered my question; she just kept her focus on the wall.

This place was clearly of historical importance. Even an untrained eye like mine could recognize that. Rather than treasure or loot, this was something very different. My [Search] spell must have reflected that feeling when I used it.

Oh, right. I should capture this moment in a picture. Smartphone in hand, I hit the capture button on my photo app, and a dazzling flash illuminated the room for a moment.

"Ah?! What was that?!" Yae and the others were startled by the sudden flash. I held up my smartphone to show that everything was fine, and they exhaled in relief. *Guess they've finally gotten used to my eccentricities. Wait, I shouldn't say things like that about myself.*

I took several pictures of different sections of the wall, making sure that I got at least one photo of every part. Really though... why was something this unusual in a place like this?

"Hey, guys! Come over here a sec!" Elze, who was searching around elsewhere, suddenly raised her voice. She was pointing at a part of the wall on the right side of the chamber.

"There's something buried here." About level with my eyesight, there was a muddy brown-yet-clear stone embedded in the wall. It was about two centimeters in diameter. A jewel...? A low-quality and filthy one, at that.

"That's... a spellstone. It's a spellstone with the Earth attribute! If it gets some magic flowing through it, something will probably happen."

"Something...? What if it's a trap?"

"I can't say for sure that it isn't a trap... but something like this wouldn't be considered conventional with regards to warding off intruders." Linze's explanation definitely made sense... But I still couldn't shake the anxiety. When there's a switch, naturally you'd want to push it, right? In that case, it could've really been a trap... *Well, maybe I'm just overthinking it.*

"Well, Touya. Get some juices flowing through it already!"

"Why me?!" I quickly turned to Elze in response to her casual remark. *Don't you care that it might be trapped, girl?!*

"It's an Earth magic spellstone, so it's not like anyone but you can do it anyway, right?"

Hrm... I guess she has a point. Linze had affinity for Light, Water, and Fire... Elze had Null affinity, and Yae didn't have any aptitude for magic at all. Me being me meant I *obviously* had an affinity for all the elements. *So I guess I've really got no choice, huh...*

"...Why'd you guys all back away just now?"

"Just in case..." "Y'never know!" "Better to be safe than sorry, it is." Everyone backed away from me, smirking softly as they narrowed their eyes in anticipation. With a sigh, I channeled magic through the old spellstone.

Bzzzzzzzz... The ground itself began to rumble and shake, then suddenly the wall in front of me crumbled away into sand, revealing a gaping hole. *Pretty flashy opening for a big door...*

"What the heck...?" We looked through the hole left by the crumbling wall, and saw something in the middle of another room. Something covered in dust and sand.

The best way to describe it was... I suppose the first thing that sprung to mind was an insect. A cricket, maybe? Yeah, it looked like a cricket. It had a round central body, kind of like a rugby ball or an almond, with six thin legs protruding from it. Some of them were broken, however.

It was around the size of a small car, as well. Imagine a dead cricket with all of its limbs torn off, kind of like that...?

But it also had a streamlined, simplistic form. More like it was designed as a machine than a living creature. It honestly looked a bit like some piece of abstract art.

"What is that thing? Some kinda statue?" Elze looked at the thing from a variety of different angles. Looking closely, there was a red orb around the size of a baseball visible inside the thing's... head? Torso? Well, it was inside what could've been either the head or the torso of the thing.

I couldn't tell because of the dust and sand covering the surface, but it seemed to be made out of a semi-transparent material... *Is it made out of glass?* I couldn't really see very well due to the darkness.

"Linze... how much longer will you be able to maintain that **[Light Sphere]?**"

"Eh? Well... Light magic isn't my forte... but I should be able to hold it for about two hours." Linze puffed up her cheeks, looking up at the sphere of light suspended in the air.

"Huh? Isn't the light growing a bit dimmer?"

"There's no growing about it. It did get dimmer... W-Wait..."

"Touya-dono!" Following Yae's shout, my gaze turned back to see the red orb begin to glow inside the cricket-thing's head. The cricket began to stir and shake a little bit.

"Touya! It's absorbing the magic from the **[Light Sphere]!**" *So that's why the light was growing dimmer!* The glowing of the orb inside the cricket-thing began to intensify and brighten, and before long the cricket itself began to stir even more violently. *No way... is this thing actually alive?!* Its broken legs were slowly regenerating themselves. Was it lying dormant, waiting for magical power to come by and power it back up?

Sssskkkkkrrrrreeeeeeee!   **Sssskkkkkrrrrreeeeeeee! Sssskkkkkrrrrreeeeeeee!**

"Gah...! What the...?!" A sudden high pitched noise reverberated across the chamber, directly assaulting my ears with a ringing pain. The noise ripped across the room, enough to make my body shudder as if I'd been electrocuted. The sound even began to damage the structures around us. *Oh crap! We're gonna get buried alive!*

"**[Gate]!**" The door of light appeared at my command. Everyone ran in one after the other in order to reach safety above ground. I was the last one to enter the [Gate], but not before I saw the cricket-thing get up and head straight for me at a monstrous speed. Like a launched spear, it hurtled toward me and closed the gap to just five meters in an instant.

I tumbled through my [Gate] and landed flat on the ground. I closed the [Gate] spell as soon as the above ground ruins came into sight. We just barely avoided being buried alive...

"What the heck was that?"

"I've never seen such a monster before, I haven't..." Elze and Yae looked over the entrance to the underground ruins, both brimming with tension and anxiety. A deep rumbling came from underground... almost like an earthquake was going on down there.

A roaring sound echoed out from the depths of the ruins, accompanied by a whoosh of debris and a cloud of dust. The underground chamber had probably caved in... At the very least, that darned monster cricket was definitely crushed to pieces down there.

There was nothing but silence all around us as everyone found their breath caught in their throats.

......**Rrrrreeeeee**......

That noise... No way...!

Kkkrrreeeeee...

It's getting closer.

Sssskkkkrrrrreeeeeeeeeeeeee!!! With the sudden crash of splitting earth, the creature burst through the ground and appeared before us.

An almond-shaped body with six elongated legs jutting out from its frame. A crystal body, beautifully shimmering and shining like water beneath the sun. This translucent being was alive, some kind of crystal creature.

The creature extended its legs and began a sideways crawl. The walls of the ruins crumbled as it moved, cut like a knife through tofu. *C'mon, that's stupidly sharp!*

"Come forth, Fire! Crimson Duet: [Fire Arrow]!"

Linze attacked the cricket thing with a repeated barrage of flaming arrows. But the creature didn't even try to dodge, choosing to just stoically shrug them off instead.

No wait... it's absorbing them. The flame arrows were being sucked into the cricket thing, one after another!

"It absorbs magic attacks?!"

"Darn... In that case...!" Yae darted forward, striking the cricket thing with lethal force. However, what was supposed to be a sure-kill shot was nothing more than a scratch on it.

"It's extremely hard, it is!"

"Take this...!" Elze followed Yae's attack up with a massive punch to the cricket's side. However, even though she staggered it a little, her punch had no real effect.

One of the creature's crystal legs seemed to aim at Elze. She dodged it. Good thing too, as it would've skewered her.

"How do we stop this thing?!" It absorbed magic... blades couldn't damage it. *What should I do...?! Wait... if head-on attack magic does nothing, then... maybe we can try an indirect approach.*

"[Slip]!" The moment I cast the spell, targeted beneath the cricket thing's feet, it stumbled and crashed to the ground. *Alright!*

"Linze! Don't cast spells at it; use indirect environmental effects to harm it!"

"I see... Understood, then! **Come forth, Ice! Grand Frozen Mass: [Ice Rock]!**" Linze decided to cast an ice spell. An enormous mass of ice appeared over the creature and... fell right down onto it. *Ouch. That's gotta hurt.* It could absorb attacks directly made out of magical energy, but it had no such luck absorbing objects formed from magic.

Skree! Screaming with a sound eerily similar to a rusty door hinge, the creature was clearly enraged. But it seemed like even magically created objects could only cause minor damage at best, the darn thing was built too solid!

Taking advantage of its brief incapacitation, Else jumped in with bullet speed.

"[Boost]…! Full Throttle." Using **[Boost]**, the Null magic spell that enhances physical ability, Elze delivered a devastating kick to one of the creature's legs.

The leg was demolished in a heartbeat, accompanied by the sound of shattered glass.

"Awesome!" Of course the thing could be damaged. *Even if it was just a little damage at a time, that meant we'd be able to win!*

Skkrrrr… Sssskkkrreeeeee! The cricket thing let out another piercing shriek, and the red orb inside its head began to softly glow. Almost as if reacting to the glow, the shattered leg effortlessly regenerated itself. *Hey… no way that just happened.*

"It regenerated…" Elze stood stunned for a moment, giving the newly regenerated leg an opportunity to strike. In an instant, it shot out and pierced her deep in the right shoulder. Her timing was off, so she'd failed to avoid it.

"Gwagh…!"

"Sis!" Elze leaped back to escape any more opportunistic attacks. Blood began to flow from the wound on her shoulder, staining her clothes a deep crimson. She was brought to her knees with sweat pooling on her brow.

"Yae! Linze! Stall that thing!" The two nodded and got to work. Yae distracted it with sheer speed while Linze conjured up more hunks of ice. While the two girls had the creature distracted, I made my way over to Elze and cast some Healing magic. A gentle light enveloped her shoulder and blood stopped flowing from the wound as it closed itself up.

"Thanks... I'm fine now, though." *Like hell are you fine.* Even if the wound had closed up, the damage was still done.

Regeneration... magic absorbing properties... an abnormally tough carapace... how could we beat it? Did it even have a weak spot?

"Even if we smash it, it can regenerate! It's futile!"

"...Wait a second... when we found the creature, it was broken in several places, so why is it fine now...?" I remembered that it absorbed Linze's spell and then regenerated... Wait, did it need magical energy in order to regenerate? The orb inside its head was glowing back then, too. Could it be that the orb was the nucleus, of sorts?

"Elze, c'mere." I told Elze the plan I'd thought up.

"Huh? Can you actually do that?!"

"Not sure... But it's worth a shot, right?"

"...You're right." I steadied my breath and looked toward the creature, focusing my mind on what it was I wanted. Because it had a transparent body, I could make out my target perfectly!

"[Apport]."

Suddenly, the small, soft red orb was in my hands. Alright, we did it!

"Elze, do your thing!"

"[Boost]." I lobbed the little orb high into the air, where it soon met Elze's fist. Finding itself sandwiched between Elze's fist and the ground, the little orb was finally shattered to pieces.

"How's that?!" Its nucleus plucked, the cricket stopped moving. Eventually, cracks spread and splintered across its entire body, and it collapsed with a crash. The crystal creature had finally fallen, its remains glimmering in the sunlight.

We waited a while to see if it would regenerate, but it simply never did.

"Hm…" There was a sudden lack of tension in the air due to our victory, so I sat down on the ground.

I was just glad the idea I suddenly had at the time worked out so well. If [**Apport**] had failed, who knows what I'd have done. I cast my spell faster than it could absorb it, and it seemingly worked just fine, given that I managed to pull out the nucleus.

I looked over to see that Yae and Elze were also sitting on the ground. Meanwhile, Linze seemed to be busy investigating the broken fragments of the monster.

"This… could actually be a material similar to spellstone."

"Spellstone, really?"

"The properties of spellstones include magic amplification, build-up of magical energies, and the discharge of said energies. The monster absorbed the magical energies of others, and used it to regenerate itself… or perhaps it was more of a defensive ability… Regardless, it used the magical energy to attack as well. Amplification, build-up, and discharge… The three properties of a spellstone."

Could it be that it had no ability to make magical energy of its own…? Was that why it was frozen in place in the ruins? But wait, magical energy flowed throughout the world. Did that blocked off room have some sort of anti-magic seal, then? The whole matter was an enigma wrapped up in an air of uncertainty.

"Shouldn't we report this kind of thing to the guild, we should?"

"No. Given that this involved the ancient ruins of the former capital, we should probably inform the government directly. We should take this to the duke, I think." Well, that made sense to me. It seemed a smart choice given the situation. With that, we were off to see the duke.

"[Gate]."

"I see. So there were such ruins at the old capital..." Duke Alfred folded his arms as though thinking, then leaned back in his chair. Sue and Duchess Ellen had gone out on a walk, so unfortunately I didn't get to see them. We were let on through to the parlor where we gave the duke the gist of what had happened.

"Alright then. This situation may concern the royal family. I'll arrange for a search party on behalf of the country to be sent out to investigate. Of course, we shall try and find out more about that monster, too."

"Oh, umm, the underground ruins collapsed, so it might be a bit difficult to investigate..."

"What? Oh dear... I was curious as to what may have been written on that mural you mentioned..." The duke drooped his shoulders disappointedly. *We did something bad back there...* No, wait, *we* didn't do anything! That monster wrecked the place, not us!

"Oh, the mural. Don't worry, we might still be able to do that. I took a photo of it."

"Pho-to...?" I opened up the picture in my smartphone's gallery app and showed it to him.

"Wh-What in the world is this?!"

"One of my Null spells. It allows me to record images of things that I've seen."

"I-I see... Always full of surprises, aren't you?" Duke Alfred was wonderfully fooled by my white lie. *I'm sorry,* I apologized internally. *It's a bit difficult to explain, you see.*

"If you give me some time, I can transcribe it for you."

"Please do. This could just be the key to solving the mystery of the capital's relocation a thousand years ago." Oh, it seemed the people of the country themselves didn't even know why the capital was moved.

I thought they would have left a record of such a huge event somewhere in some official archives. Then again, if he was right, then that record could even be exactly what we just found. It might even have had information about the crystal creature we encountered.

I'd grasped the creature's weakness. I was confident I could probably beat it if we ever had to fight another one.

But I still couldn't get something out of my mind. I had a feeling that the old capital being run down into that state had something to do with the crystal creature...

With a feeling of uncertainty over the whole ordeal weighing us down, we left the rest in Duke Alfred's hands and departed from his estate.

A few days later, I finished transcribing the mural onto paper.

What came in handy during that was a little Null magic spell called [Drawing] that I learned. It allowed me to take anything I saw and replicate that perfectly on paper. In short, I became a photocopier.

In fact, I didn't even touch pen to paper. The spell worked by conjuring up the symbols straight onto the paper, so I really *was* like an actual photocopier. I simply had to look at the image on my smartphone's screen in order to finish copying it down. The spell was less [Drawing] and more [Printing], not that I really cared too much about the name either way.

The important part was that with the spell, I had effectively acquired a printer. As a test, I took down several new recipes for sweets and gave those to Aer, and she almost exploded with joy. I was thankful that I was able to translate the words as part of the printing process, if I focused hard enough. The only downside was that I had to use [Search] to find the actual ingredient names one by one.

I'd learned to use one of the one hundred yen coins that I had been carrying to deal with anything concerning weight. *Notice these things sooner, idiot,* I told myself.

My next job was to deliver the mural transcript to the capital. I did ask the others if any of them wanted to tag along, but it seemed like the thought of meeting the duke again made them all too nervous, so they declined.

It was at those times that I really felt the difference in my perception of what a noble was, compared to how everyone else thought of them. I mean, there weren't exactly any nobles back in Japan. Though, strictly speaking, there may have *been* some in the past.

I took the bundle of transcribed papers in hand and cast my trusty [Gate] spell. Stepping through the light, I arrived directly in front of the gate to the duke's estate.

"What the—?!"

"Whoops, sorry about that..." The guard was startled by my sudden appearance. To tell the truth, I had been startling this poor guard like that every time I came to the duke's estate. I kind of wished he'd just get used to it already, but that was still going to take a while from the looks of things.

Wait a sec... The gate opened and a carriage came out. Were they going out somewhere? I figured I had timed my visit poorly.

"Touya, is that you?! Thank the heavens! Please, get in!"

"Huh? Wait... Wha?! What's going on?!" The carriage door swung open and the duke swept down like a bird of prey, grabbed me by the arm, and whisked me up into the carriage in one movement. *Seriously, what the heck?!*

"To think you would appear with such impeccable timing...! You're truly a godsend. I give Him my thanks." The duke started fervently praying.

I mean, technically God did *send me here, so...* At any rate, the duke's behavior was definitely not normal. I'd never seen him so frantic before. I wondered what in the world had happened.

"What happened, exactly?" At my sudden question, sweat appeared on the duke's forehead as he answered in a rather panicked tone.

"My brother has been poisoned."

...*Come again, sire?* Wasn't the duke's brother... the king? Was this a case of royal assassination?

"Fortunately, treatment was delivered swiftly, so he's still hanging on... For now." The duke's voice came out trembling as he sat face-down, gripping his hands together tightly. I mean, his brother was on the verge of death. Anyone would be worried in that situation.

"Do you have any idea who the culprit could have been?"

"...There's one prime suspect, but we have no proof. Surely you remember the incident where Sue was attacked, yes? I believe both of these crimes were orchestrated... by the same individual."

"But why would they want to kill the king? Oh, hang on, could it have been an assassin sent from outside of the country or..."

"If only it were that simple..." The duke let out a sigh and raised his head. He wore a terrible expression on his face.

"Our Kingdom of Belfast is surrounded by three other countries. To the west is the Refreese Imperium, to the east sandwiched in the Melicia mountain range is the Regulus Empire, and to the south by the Great Gau River is the Kingdom of Mismede. Of these, we have been on good terms with the Refreese Imperium for a great many years." *I see, I see.*

"As for the Regulus Empire, we signed a nonaggression pact after the war twenty years ago, but I cannot exactly say that we're on good terms. It wouldn't be strange if they launched another attack on us at any moment. Now, as for the Mismede Kingdom, this is where things get complicated."

"Complicated how, exactly?"

"Mismede is a new kingdom that was established during the war with Regulus twenty years ago. My brother has been trying to form an official alliance with this new kingdom, partly to stave off the threat of Regulus, and partly to open up more trade routes between our two kingdoms. However, there are some nobles who are very displeased with his decision."

"What's their problem?" If the Regulus Empire could attack again any day, then it would make more sense to gain as many allies as possible before that happened. Maybe it wasn't so simple, though.

"Mismede is a kingdom of demi-humans ruled by a beastman king. Some of the older nobles despise the idea of, well... forming an alliance with a kingdom like that."

"...Okay, but why?" These nobles would even go out of their way to obstruct things that would benefit the country just because they didn't like the idea of an alliance with demi-humans? I couldn't understand that reasoning at all. If they were simple beasts who couldn't be reasoned with, then that was one thing, but the beastmen were perfectly capable of holding a conversation. And that little beastgirl Arma was such a nice kid, too.

"In the past, demi-humans were seen as an inferior race and were the target of much discrimination. They were treated like a race of crude savages. However, this all changed during our father's generation. A law was created such that demi-humans no longer be treated as inferior or discriminated against. With that, the old ways died out, and demi-humans were able to walk around with their heads held high without worry. Even as we speak, there are plenty of them in the castle town itself. On the surface, discrimination against them is all but gone, but in reality there are still some nobles stuck in the past who refuse to treat them fairly."

"Discrimination, huh..."

"That's correct. Their opinions are that we should not have to join hands with a country of savages. Some even insist that we should simply destroy their kingdom and claim the land for our own. To the nobles of that disposition, my brother is a very big nuisance."

That made sense. So the culprits behind the assassination plot were probably those old nobles, but was it really necessary for them to go so far? I felt that it was all wrong. Could it really be so bad that they'd want to kill the king over it? Hell, if the king died, wouldn't those nobles be the ones to suffer the most?

"Were my brother to die, the throne would go to his lone daughter, Princess Yumina. The older nobles are probably seeking to have the princess marry one of their sons or relatives in order to claw their way into the royal bloodline. After that, they would be free to abuse their power to purge all of the demi-humans from the country... I'm beginning to think that the ones who tried to kidnap Sue were not trying to twist my arm, but my brother's instead."

A case of "Do as we say if you value your niece's life," then. They wanted to cut off relations with Mismede bad enough to take hostages. The princess probably had strong guards protecting her, so they would've aimed for a relative like the king's niece instead... And then they might've gotten carried away and demanded that the king marry his daughter off to one of their sons. Something about the whole thing just felt like the plot of a goofy evil mastermind from a cartoon or something. The culprit was probably a complete idiot.

If they were caught, they'd probably get the death sentence right away. I could almost picture them as the villain in some period drama. Like a greedy merchant or a corrupt magistrate, something like that.

"So, uh, what do you need *me* to do?"

"I need you to expel the poison from my brother's body, by way of the same spell you cured Ellen with." The spell that heals any status ailments, [**Recovery**]. That made sense. With that spell, not only the poison itself, but all of the effects it had on the body would be reverted to normal. That explained why the duke whisked me up into the carriage. And in such a rush, too.

While we were discussing all of this, the duke's carriage pulled through the castle gates, across the drawbridge, and into the castle grounds. The duke then rushed me into the castle in a flurry, and we were greeted by a massive hall covered in bright red carpets. It was my first time in a castle. Everything there was massive.

From where we were in the center of the hall, I could see a pair of staircases to the left and right, curved around and leading up to the next floor. On the ceiling there was a brilliant chandelier, sparkling like stars in the night sky. It didn't appear to have any candles, though. Was it infused with Light magic? The duke and I made a dash up the red-carpeted stairs and got up to a small landing where we crossed paths with a certain man.

"Well well, if it isn't Your Highness the Duke. It is good to see you again."

"Tsk...! Count Balsa..." The duke met the man in front of him with an intense gaze. He was a plump, thin-haired little man in a showy outfit. His appearance called to mind the image of a toad. The toad gazed at us with a large, slimy grin.

"You can rest easy. We've captured the one who tried to assassinate His Majesty."

"What did you say?!"

"That's right, it was the ambassador from Mismede. His Highness collapsed after drinking a glass of wine, and we later discovered that it was the very wine the ambassador had offered as a gift."

"That's absurd..." The duke's expression changed. He clearly doubted what he just heard. If that story were true, then it wouldn't just open a rift between the two kingdoms, it could easily lead to all-out war.

I really doubt that's what happened. Doesn't make sense for the other kingdom to do something like that.

"The ambassador is currently being confined in another room. We should have that filthy animal executed immediately. Chop off her head and send it back to Mismede, I say..."

"We shall do no such thing! These decisions are for my brother to make! You will keep the ambassador alive in that room until my brother comes to a decision!"

"Very well... You really do show far too much sympathy to the likes of a beastman... At any rate, I will see that she is kept restrained for the time being. However, if the worst should come to pass, I will not be able to keep the other nobles in check. They will likely all respond exactly as I wished to." Count Balsa stood there with a repulsive smile on his face. *I see... So he's one of the old nobles who're opposed to the king's decree on the treatment of demi-human species. No, he could even be the very mastermind behind the poisoning...*

From the way the duke was glaring at the toad, it seemed my guess was dead on the mark. Yup. This guy? Guilty. Case closed.

"Well then, allow me to be on my way. It seems things are about to get quite exciting around here." With those words, the toad began to descend the stairs with a lumbering gait. Things were going to get exciting? Why, because the king was going to die? The duke's hands were trembling with rage as he saw off Count Baldy. *Alright, let's give this toad a little taste of justice.*

"**[Slip]**."

"Urrbuoah?!" The toad slipped magnificently and rocketed down the stairs with unparalleled grace. Nothing could stop him as he went tumbling down, rolling down the stairs until eventually his momentum catapulted him out onto the carpet of the bottom floor.

"Oof!" Upon reaching the bottom floor, the toad tried to put on a mask of composure as he tottered to his feet. The surrounding maids and the knights on guard duty were all trembling trying to suppress their laughter. *Damn... He made it out mostly fine...*

The blank-faced duke turned to me when he heard me clicking my tongue, and inquired of me.

"Was that your doing?" No words were necessary. I threw him a thumbs up with a smile as clear as the day blue sky. The duke was absolutely astonished with me at first, but eventually his face softened into a smile as well.

"Now, we can't keep dawdling around here all day. We must make haste!" We resumed our journey up the stairs and proceeded down a long corridor. At the end of the corridor was a door guarded by the king's strongest personal guards. The guards noticed the duke approaching and respectfully bowed their heads as they opened the large door behind them.

"Brother!" What I saw as I walked into the room with the duke was a gorgeous bed with a large canopy, bathing in the sun's rays and surrounded by a number of people. All of the people in the room were gazing at the figure on the bed, most likely the king himself, with sorrowful expressions.

Gripping the king's hand as she sat by his side was a young girl. Next to her was a woman sitting in a chair, crying. The others present were an old man in gray robes with a grave expression, a jade-haired woman with downcast eyes holding a golden khakkhara, and a splendidly mustachioed man in a military uniform whose shoulders seemed to be shaking with rage.

The duke strode up briskly to the side of the bed and began talking to the old man in gray robes.

"What's my brother's condition?!"

"We've done all we can, but we've never seen these symptoms from any kind of known poison... At this rate, I fear the worst..." The old man closed his eyes and lightly shook his head. Just then, the king began talking in a very hoarse voice.

"Al..."

"I'm here, brother."

"...I leave my wife and daughter... in your hands... The alliance with Mismede... you must..."

"Touya, please help!" I snapped out of observation mode and rushed to the king's side. The military man made moves to stop me, but the duke held him back.

The king rested there, gazing at me with clouded-over eyes like a dying fish, and mouthed "Who is that?" in a wordless voice. Between his pale complexion, his dried out lips, and his incredibly faint breathing, he was the very picture of death itself. I had no time to waste. Focusing my magic, I extended the palm of my hand out to him.

"**[Recovery]**." A gentle light flowed out from my hand and into the king. Eventually the light petered out, and the king began breathing easily again. His complexion grew more and more healthy before our very eyes. After blinking a few times, the light returned to his eyes. Suddenly, he shot bolt upright in bed as if he'd been sleeping on a springboard.

"Father!"

"Sweetheart!" The king opened and closed his hand while looking at the woman and young girl clinging to him.

"...I feel quite grand. All that suffering, now gone without a trace..."

"Your Majesty!" The old man in gray robes rushed over to the king. He took the king's hand, measured his pulse, and examined his eyes, among various other tests. So that person was the royal physician. That made sense.

"...You are the very picture of health. How could this be...?" Ignoring the dumbfounded doctor, the king turned to face me.

"Al... Alfred... Who is this boy?"

"This is the same young Mochizuki Touya who cured my wife's eyesight. By sheer coincidence, he had come to visit my estate. I brought him along with me, knowing that he would be able to cure you."

"...Aha... yyyyeah. My name's Mochizuki Touya." With absolutely no idea how to introduce myself to a king, I responded suitably. Like a simpleton. Only after the fact did I worry that I'd gotten something horribly wrong.

"I see. So this is the boy who cured Lady Ellen...! You have saved my life, and for that you have my sincerest gratitude!" I had no idea how to act after being thanked by a king, and before I knew it the mustachioed man came up and started patting me on the back with vigor uncalled for. *Hey, whoa, that hurts, you know!*

"You've done a great service in saving the king's life, boy! Sir Touya then, is it?! I like the look about you!" So said the mustachioed geezer as he relentlessly continued in his efforts to break every bone in my back. *Seriously, that really hurts!*

"General, that's enough of that now. Still, to think I'd be able to see the non-elemental spell [**Recovery**] nowadays... How curious..." The lady with the golden khakkhara smiled as she put an end to the general's ruthless onslaught. *You've saved my spine, ma'am.*

"Now brother, we must talk at once about the ambassador from Mismede...!"

"What of the ambassador?"

"She is currently being held captive by Count Balsa as the suspected ringleader of this assassination attempt. What do you think about that, brother?"

"How utterly absurd! What could Mismede possibly hope to gain from my death?! This is without a doubt the work of those who see me as an obstacle!" In that case, that old toad was the most suspicious after all.

"Unfortunately... the fact of the matter is that Your Majesty collapsed upon drinking the wine brought forth by the ambassador. There were several witnesses present at the time. Unless we can clear up those suspicions..."

"Hrmph..." The king fell deep into thought at General Whiskers' words. Well, it was only natural that they couldn't release a suspect without first proving their innocence.

"We don't even know what type of poison was employed. It could even have been a special type of beastman poison. We'd need to investigate that in order to find out..." The elderly physician mumbled in a troubled voice.

Apparently they'd already used every known method of detecting and identifying poison, but the wine had shown no reaction whatsoever. Without knowing the type of poison, there was no way to know what kind of antidote was necessary. As a result, the king had been teetering on the brink of death for close to an hour.

Ordinary Healing magic couldn't cure physical status ailments like paralysis or poison. If I hadn't arrived, the king would have been in heaven at that very moment. Just as the culprit had planned.

"For the time being, I would like to meet with the ambassador. General Leon, escort her to me."

"Yes, Your Majesty!" The mustachioed geezer left the room as fast as his feet could carry him.

It was almost certain that the ambassador had been framed. Erase the bothersome king and conveniently pin the crime on the ambassador. This would create a fissure between the two kingdoms, and Belfast would be free to wage war under the pretense of a just cause… Yeah, that was probably the plan. By that point it was almost clear as day, really.

"Uhm…" While I was deep in thought, a girl called out to me. I raised my face to see that it was the princess — Princess Yumina as I seemed to recall — who had been standing and staring at me.

She looked to be about two or three years older than Sue. Maybe around twelve or thirteen? She wore a fluffy white dress, and in her hair sparkled a silver hairband. She had the same gorgeous blonde hair as Sue, and her large eyes were very captivating. Looking closely, I noticed that her left and right eyes were actually different colors. Her right eye was a vibrant blue, while her left eye was a light green. I'd heard about situations like that before; it was called heterochromia.

"Thank you very much for saving my father's life." The princess thanked me and quickly bowed in my direction. She sure was well-mannered. I was worried she might be some high-handed spoiled brat of a princess.

"Please, don't worry about it. I'm just glad he's feeling better." The way everyone kept thanking me made me feel embarrassed, so I tried to just smile my way out of it. But the princess merely kept staring at me veeery closely. What, was there something on my face?

Staaare…

Staaaare…

Staaaaare…

Staaaaaare…

"Err… can I help you?" I couldn't withstand being engulfed in her burning gaze any longer, so I shifted my gaze as I asked that question. The princess blushed slightly and spoke almost in a whisper.

"…Do you dislike younger women?"

"…Come again?" Unable to comprehend the meaning behind her question, I tilted my head in confusion. Just then the door opened, and in came General Whiskers with a beastgirl who looked to be around twenty. *Hmm? Haven't I seen you before?*

"I, Olga Strand, have arrived as per your summons." The beastgirl genuflected before the king, who was still sitting in bed. Atop her head were a pair of animal ears standing upright, and from her lower back protruded a tail. The tail of a fox.

"Let us get right to the heart of the matter. Did you come to this country with the intention of killing me?"

"I swear on my life, I would consider no such thing. I would never think to poison Your Majesty!"

"I had thought as much. You do not strike me as the type of foolish person to do such a thing. As such, I trust you." The king spoke with a smile, and the Mismede ambassador's expression turned to one of relief.

"Still, the fact remains that it was your wine from which the poison came. How would you explain this turn of events?"

"Th-That is…" Unable to respond to the words of the woman with the golden khakkhara, the foxgirl simply let her head hang listlessly. Of course she had no way to prove her innocence. It didn't seem like the khakkhara lady was accusing her because of that, though. It felt more like she was asking "What can we do to help figure this out?" or something. *Hmm...*

"Er, excuse me a moment?"

"Wait, is that Touya?" the foxgirl questioned.

"So it was you...!" The foxgirl turned to face me when I called out, and was surprised when she saw my face. Oh, looked like it really was the same lady from back then. She was the older sister of that young foxgirl, Arma, who I'd found wandering lost in the capital on my first visit. So the older sister's name was Olga, huh?

"Are you acquainted with the ambassador?"

"I made friends with her younger sister, but we only met in passing, really. Anyway, putting that aside for a moment..." I made a gesture of picking up a box and moving it to the side as I brushed off the duke's question. Nobody seemed to get it. Ouch. Moving on, I asked General Whiskers about something that had been bothering me.

"Where in the castle did the king collapse?"

"That would be the main dining hall... What of it?"

"Has the crime scene been left untouched?"

"Huh? Well, yes, it's exactly as it was at the time of the incident... No, wait, we removed the wine in order to test it for poison. The tests are still ongoing..." Which meant that they still hadn't found any trace of the poison whatsoever.

I was pretty sure I had figured it all out, then. It was a common trick. Heck, it didn't even really count as a trick. The moment anyone realized that there was no poison in the wine whatsoever, the truth would be blatantly obvious. This plan had so many holes that it would've made a good fishing net. I wanted to check one last thing though, just to be sure and all.

"Could you guide me to that room? I might be able to prove the ambassador's innocence." Everyone in the room exchanged glances, but the king gave his permission, so General Leon led me to the room.

The room itself was a large hall. It had a big white-brick fireplace and a single massive window, which was adorned with blue curtains and looked out over the gardens. The walls were lined with several expensive-looking paintings, and on the ceiling was a magnificent sparkling chandelier. The long table was covered in a white tablecloth, atop which rested silver candlesticks plus plates and cutlery with the food still on them.

Upon my request, the general brought me the wine in question. "Is this wine rare at all?"

"I'm not too sure myself, but apparently so. According to the ambassador's story, it's only produced in a certain village in Mismede. It's supposedly very valuable due to that fact."

"Alrighty then." *Okay, it's about time to test out my theory.*

"[Search]: Poison." I activated my search-fu. I looked over the wine, continued on through the rest of the room, and passed my gaze across the whole of the tabletop. Yup, just as I'd thought. I was pretty sure it would've been found out eventually, but I was the only one who could use search magic to quickly confirm it for sure.

The fact that I could find it with the [Search] spell must have meant that if I ever consumed any, I would know immediately that I had been poisoned. The thought made me never, ever want to try that.

Now, what was to be done? At the rate things were going, the chance that the truth would remain unknown was relatively high. The crime was probably plotted out with that thought in mind. Even if it failed, the worst the real culprit would get off with was being suspected, and little more. I could prove the ambassador's innocence with what I had, but we wouldn't be able to catch the real culprit that way... *Okay, think I got it.*

"I think I get the gist of it. General, could you get the king to summon everyone to the dining hall? Oh, that's including Count Balsa, by the way. Also, I have a small favor to ask..."

"A favor?" The general tilted his head quizzically, but he heard out my request. If there was no solid evidence, then all we had to do was get the culprit to fess up themselves.

Alrighty then, time to put on a little act...

"Y-Your Majesty! You're already back up on your feet?!"

"That is correct, Count Balsa. As you can see, I am the very picture of good health. Though I seem to have caused a lot of worry for everyone." The toad burst into the great dining hall, and His Majesty the King answered his inquiry most casually. He even beat his fist against his chest as if to prove it.

"I... see... Hahaha, well now, this is quite something. I'm very glad to see that..." The count was already covered in cold sweat as his smile twitched and he nervously rubbed his hands together. The king looked him over with completely sober eyes. Oh, seemed like the king had noticed it, too. This guy was undoubtedly the true culprit.

"I thought I had met my end for a moment there, but then young Touya arrived and cleared up the poison in my body in the blink of an eye! I must say, I was tremendously lucky today. That truly was a close call." At the king's words, Count Baldy looked at me as though he loathed my very existence. *Oh, come on, he's practically giving it away! Now I can't even picture anyone besides him as the culprit.*

"Alright, Touya. Everyone is gathered. What next?" Holding her golden khakkhara, the jade-haired court magician, Miss Charlotte, asked me.

The people gathered in the dining hall were: His Majesty the King, Princess Yumina, Queen Yuel, Duke Ortlinde, General Leon, Charlotte, Doctor Raul, Olga, and Count Balsa. I had them all stand before me, then began talking.

"As we all know, the king was poisoned just a few hours ago. The crime took place in this very room, the dining hall. The room has been left exactly as it was at the time of the crime. Well, maybe 'exactly' isn't the right word, since the food's gone cold and all, but that's not the issue at hand. The real issue is the identity of the criminal behind the Case of the Failed Royal Assassination. And..." I let my words hang in the air as I savored the moment, and then spoke the words.

"The culprit is right here among us."

I've always wanted a chance to say that line! The room's atmosphere changed in an instant, and Olga went pale. Her ears jolted upright, and she looked around with pleading eyes as if trying to say "You're wrong, it wasn't me!" *Don't worry, we already know that.*

When he saw Olga's pale face, Count Balsa's lips curled up into a smile.

Come on, dude, it's almost like you want to be caught. He hadn't seemed to notice it himself since he was staring at Olga, but everyone else in the room had already turned their eyes on Count Baldy as if they unanimously agreed he was the culprit. Having everyone besides Olga already know the culprit's identity kind of sucked some of the fun out of it, honestly…

"To start off with, we have the poisoned wine." The general handed me a wine bottle, and I held it up for all to see.

"Now, Olga. This is, without a doubt, the wine that you brought with you, yes?"

"Th-That's right, that is the wine I brought with me, but I didn't do anything like poisoning it…!"

"Silence, you wretched beast! Do you still intend to act innocent? Have you no shame?! Everyone agrees, right…?!" Watching the toad verbally abuse Olga with a sidelong glance, I took a large swig straight from the wine bottle and gulped it right down.

I'm a minor, but that's no big deal! After all, I'm in another world!

"Ah, it's delicious!" I slammed the bottle down onto the table. To be totally honest, I didn't actually know how delicious the wine was, because I had no others to compare it with. I just told you I'm a minor! Looking around, I saw that everyone's mouths were agape as they locked their eyes onto me.

"S-Sir Touya, a-are you alright?!"

"I'm fine, General. I mean, after all, there was never any poison in the wine to begin with!"

"What?!" Everyone looked around amongst themselves, trying to figure out what in the world I was talking about. Everyone except the count, that is, who was now visibly sweating bullets. *Good, I have him all scared.*

"Now, I have with me here a bottle of wine from the Far East. It's a very rare type of wine born from a secret formula, and it's the finest wine that I can think of." I took in my hand a bottle with a label that read "Bowjolly Noovoe." The label had in fact been made by me and simply pasted onto the side of a bottle of some cheap wine. As if to show that my wine was more precious, I took a glass from the vacant table and poured some wine into it.

"This wine will expose the culprit." I held the wine glass aloft toward the chandelier, which caused a dazzling array of lights to reflect off the glass and bounce around the room. I made my way over to the others and offered the glass to the general.

"Could I ask you to drink this?" The general gave me a doubtful look, but he downed the glass anyway.

"How's the taste?"

"Ohoh! This is wonderful! It is better than any wine I've ever tasted! Delicious! Count, would you like some?" Oh god, his voice was completely monotonous. It was completely monotonous, but the general did *exactly as I had asked earlier* and offered some wine to the count.

"Eh? Err, well then, alright…" After the Count nodded, I made my way over to the table and picked up *the glass that had been at the king's seat* and poured some wine into it. The moment I did so, the count's face changed immediately.

"I'm *extremely* interested to hear your impressions of my finest wine."

"Ah, no, actually I think I'm fine!"

"Come now, just one drink!" I grabbed the count as he started to back away and forced the wine glass into his hand.

"Drink it with spirit, my friend!" I beamed a smile as bright as the sun straight into the Count's eyes as I spoke. But he simply stood there flooded in cold sweat, making no move to drink from the glass.

"What is the matter, Count? Won't you have a drink?"

"Er, well, you see… it's just…" The count began lightly rocking the glass with shifty eyes as the king spoke. Whoops, wouldn't want that falling to the ground now.

"…Can you not drink it? In that case, this may be rather forward of me, but I'll simply have to help you along."

"Wha?! Mgh! Argh?!" I forced the glass to the count's lips and poured the wine down his throat. Choking all the while, the count reflexively swallowed some of the wine that was trying to make its way down his gullet. Realizing what had just happened, he stood terrified.

"Ugh! Uwah! Uwaaah! H-Help me! The poison! It's coursing through my veeeiiins! I'm dying! I'm dyiiing!" The toad writhed around, gripping at his throat all the while. Anguish coated his face as he continued to squirm. How embarrassing. *I wonder what it is about us humans and our powers of imagination that can drive us to act in such overblown ways.*

"Urrrgggh! I-It hurts to breathe! The poison! The poooiiisooon! S-Somebody, help me…!"

"Alright, you can calm down now. That glass you just drank from? It was a fresh new one."

"I'm dyiiinggg, I'm… pardon?" The puzzled count stopped writhing and rose to his feet, lightly patting at his throat.

"…I feel just fine."

"Of course you do. It was just a glass of cheap wine. I'm sorry for forcing it down your throat, but…" I left a deliberate gap before asking the deciding question.

"What made you think it was poisoned?"

"Uh…" The count's face froze over. *Checkmate.* This man had outed himself with that little display. Fearful of a nonexistent poison that he believed he had been forced to drink, he writhed around on the floor for no apparent reason. Anyone who didn't know the trick behind it would never have reacted like that. I had forced him to show his own hand.

"...What does this mean, then?" The duke spoke up all of a sudden.

"The poison wasn't in the wine that Olga brought, it was coated on the inside of the glass itself."

"On the glass...? I see. No wonder we couldn't find any traces of poison in the wine."

"I have a spell that lets me detect poison, so I found out the trick to it straight away. The perpetrator was most likely one of the chefs or waiters, I would imagine. They probably intended to dispose of the glass after the incident itself, but our good general here was quicker in securing the crime scene, meaning they couldn't get to the glass without raising suspicion. All that was left for me to do was find a way to corner the mastermind... which ended up being way easier than I thought." Then again, looking at the guy again, I really couldn't picture anyone else as the mastermind. I'd thought to myself that all I had to do was create a situation that he couldn't bluff his way out of, but having it resolved so easily was a bit of a letdown, really. After all, the trick, if you could even call it that, was so unbelievably simple.

Heck, even if I hadn't done a thing, someone would have eventually discovered the truth once they realized that the wine itself contained no poison. At the end of the day, I just really wanted to play the role of the detective at least once in my life, even if the culprit did happen to be a bumbling buffoon, you know?

"...Gah!" The toad set his sights on the door and dashed for it. He really didn't know when to give up. Really, all that meant was that he was an incompetent third-rate scoundrel of a man who never considered the consequences because he had deluded himself into believing he was better than everyone else. Nevertheless, that idiotic plan almost claimed the king's life. The price for that crime would be a heavy one.

"**[Slip].**"

"Uohwhah?!" The count slipped with incredible vigor and bashed the back of his head against the floor.

"You little…!" Almost as if she were channeling all of her resentment for the man into her own strength, Olga slammed into the count with a fearsomely powerful kick straight to the gut. He lost consciousness instantly. *Oof, that's gotta hurt.*

Olga's actions were rather unbecoming of an ambassador, but not a soul in the room felt like voicing any complaints.

"According to the general, there were two accomplices: the waiter and the poison tester. They also found poison of the same type that had been coated on the glass in Count Balsa's residence. And finally, Count Balsa himself confessed to attempting to kidnap Sue. Looks like this case is closed." The duke spoke happily as he sat on a chair in one of the rooms of the royal castle.

We were accompanied in the room by His Majesty the King, Princess Yumina, Queen Yuel, and Charlotte, who all sat around the same table leisurely drinking tea.

"What'll happen to the count?"

"A plotted assassination of the king is no less than high treason. The man himself will be executed, his residence and assets confiscated, and the grounds sealed off." Well, that was only natural, really. Feelings of guilt… didn't even cross my mind, for some reason.

Probably because the guy got what was coming to him. It was hard to show sympathy for a man like him.

"What about his family?"

"Treating them as accomplices and executing them all... would be rather excessive. At the very least, they will lose their status as nobles and be banished from the country. That said, the man had no wife or children, and his other relatives were all actively opposed to letting demi-humans integrate into our society. With them gone now, things should be somewhat easier on my brother." The duke kept up his cheerful tone as he spoke.

I see. This incident can be used to set an example for any other nobles who are against the alliance with the beastmen, and keep them in check.

"Honestly, my boy, I am truly in your debt. I should very much like to bestow a gift upon the man to whom I owe my life. Is there anything you desire?" The king almost seemed to be pleading, but honestly, I wasn't exactly wanting for anything at the moment.

"Please, don't worry about it. I just happened to be passing by on my way to see the duke while all of this was going on. It was just a stroke of luck for Your Majesty. Simply chalk it up as a coincidence." I really didn't do much with my own power, that much at least was true. The only reason I could even use the [**Recovery**] spell was thanks to God. If I tried to take advantage of an unfair skill like that, karma surely would've found its way back to me...

Hmm? Hang on, I thought, *weren't things like that God's area of expertise? Just spare me another lightning bolt incident. Seriously. Please never do that again.*

"A man lacking in avarice as always, eh, young Touya?" The duke said, while returning his teacup to the saucer on the table.

"Isn't it only natural to help a friend in need? It's not like I did any of this because I wanted a reward. I wanted to do it. No more and no less." That was genuinely how I felt about it all. If, on the other hand, Count Balsa had come to me asking for help, I wasn't sure I would've done anything for him. In the duke's case, I knew the type of person he was, and seeing him in trouble made me want to help him to the best of my ability. That was all there was to it.

"You truly are one curious person. The ability to use two Null spells, both [**Recovery**] and [**Slip**]… That's quite the rare gift indeed." Charlotte spoke to me with a bright smile. Being praised for my magic by the court magician herself made me turn a beet red.

"Two? Heavens no, young Touya can use far more than just two unique spells. Even as he came to visit me, he did so by way of the [**Gate**] spell. Then he used yet another to detect the poison, and I seem to recall him telling me that the shogi sets he brought as gifts were crafted through non-elemental spells as well."

"Wh-What?" Charlotte grew visibly tenser the more the duke spoke. *Hmm… Guess the best course of action here would be to just be honest about it,* I concluded.

"Er, well, about that… See, it seems like I can use every non-elemental spell there is. Though there's always the chance that some won't work, I'm not sure on the details." At the very least, I had never failed to learn any of the spells that I'd tried to acquire so far. Well, excluding that one time where I failed to cast [**Apport**] properly. Even then, I did eventually manage to add the spell to my repertoire, though.

"All of them…?! If that's really true, then this could be a momentous occasion…! P-Please, excuse me for just a bit!" Charlotte burst her way out of the room, clearly in a frenzy… *I hope I didn't say something I shouldn't have just now…*

"So, you were the one who crafted that shogi set, Touya my boy? Al brought it over and praised it greatly, and upon taking to the board, I was absolutely enthralled with it! It truly is an interesting game. So then, what's this about it being constructed by way of magic?"

Yup, just what I'd been worrying about. The king got hooked on it too. These brothers really are cut from the same cloth.

To demonstrate, I took a glass from the table and cast [**Modeling**] on it. The glass gradually changed shape, and within thirty seconds I had completed my glass figure rendition of the king himself. It was a ten centimeter tall glass sculpture, which, if I said so myself, really captured his majestic aura.

"And, well, that's pretty much how it works." I handed the figure over to the king. Since the model for the piece had been sitting right in front of me, I was able to capture even the tiniest of detail. The only real problem was that, being made of glass, it would still shatter if dropped.

"Th-This is incredible… I seem to recall there being someone from Refreese who could use similar magic, but to see such affection poured into one's creation to the smallest level of detail…" Refreese… The Refreese Imperium, was it? If memory served, they were one of the neighboring countries. Non-elemental, Null magic was primarily comprised of unique, personalized spells. It was entirely possible for several people to share similar, yet subtly different forms of their personal non-elemental spells.

The king held his little figure up in the sunlight and marveled at how it sparkled. Seeing that, I felt that I should really complete the set since just the king alone would be somewhat lonely, so I took two more glasses in hand and set to work.

Before long, I had completed two more glass figures: One of the queen, and one of the princess. I gave them to their respective owners. They accepted the figures with beaming smiles, then chatted joyously as they compared each other's figures before lining up all three on the table. *Yup, I knew it was a good idea to trust my instincts. The completed set really paints a lovely picture with the whole family together in one place.*

"This is truly a wonderful gift."

"Nah, the glasses I used to make them were yours to begin with. If anything, I'm sorry for using them as crafting materials without asking first." I lowered my head to the king to show my small apology. When I raised my head back up, the duke's pleading little face caught my attention immediately. He really was the type who made no effort to hide his emotions.

"…I'll make some figures of the duke's family too, the next time I'm around for a visit. Promise."

"You truly would not mind?! You have my gratitude!" If I was going to make more figures anyway, it'd be much easier with the models themselves in front of me as I crafted them.

I gave a wry smile at the duke's calculated assault on my generosity, when all of a sudden a loud crashing sound resounded through the room and the door flew open as Charlotte charged in, carrying a large number of things in her arms. She approached me with the appearance of some terrifying apparition and held out a parchment with something written on it.

"Child… c-can you read this?!" Charlotte loomed closer and closer. *What? What is this, what's going on? Why do I always end up in these scary situations?!* Giving in to Charlotte's sudden compulsive behavior, I ran my eyes over the parchment. Whatever was written on it was in a language I'd never seen before. I couldn't make out a single word.

"…Can't make heads or tails of it. What is this, exactly?"

"So you can't read it, right? Alright, how about this non-elemental spell? Do you think you can use it?" This time she took out a bulky tome and turned to a specific page. I could read this one. Let's see... Null magic spell... **[Reading]**? According to the book, it was a spell that allowed one to read a number of different languages. The one stipulation was that the caster had to at the very least know the name of the language he was trying to use the spell on. Oh, that made sense. It was possible I'd be able to decipher the parchment with that spell.

...Wait a minute. If I'd had this spell earlier, then I wouldn't have had to rely on Linze to teach me how to read and write...

"I think I can probably use it now, but... do you know what language that parchment is written in?"

"It's written in Ancient Spirit Script. There's almost nobody in the world who can read it." Hmm... Well, it was worth a shot.

"[Reading]: Ancient Spirit Script." I activated the spell... My eyes darted back toward the parchment. *Uh... Mm...*

"This is..."

"Y-You can read it?!" Charlotte locked her gaze on me as I noticed stars in her eyes. In comparison, I probably had something more like a cloudy night sky in mine.

"Sorry... I can make out the characters now, but I have no idea what's actually written here."

"You can read it... but you don't know what it says?! Wh-What do you mean?!"

"Well, let's see... 'By taking a Degment, which lacks any meaningful arts to access the Origin Magic, and introducing that to the nature of the Soma-arts' method of blasting magic in order to cause a change in the Edos...' And well, it's all stuff like that. I can't really make heads or tails of it." I really didn't understand a

177

single word. In the first place, reading something and understanding it were two different things. Whatever that parchment had written on it, it was far too difficult a subject for me to ever hope to grasp.

"So you really *can* read it! Touya, that's amazing! With this, our research will begin making progress by leaps and bounds…! Sorry, could I get you to read this one, too?"

"Wait, wait, just hang on a second!" I broke Charlotte's barrage of demands off even as she made her way toward me once more with yet more documents. Evidently, she was so excited that I could almost see steam coming out of her nose! *Geez, lady! Calm down a little!* "Charlotte, would you calm down for a moment?"

"Y-Yes, of course! I-I-I'm very sorry about all of this! I appear to have gotten caught up in the moment…!" Having regained her senses, Charlotte hung her head as a huge blush spread across her face.

"I'm well aware that you've been passionately studying the field of Ancient Spirit Magic for the longest time, so it's not as though I don't understand your feelings on the matter."

"That's exactly right! Until now, we've been struggling to piece it all together one word at a time, sometimes taking many months or even years, our research riddled with problems such as the occasional mistranslation or whatnot… But Touya, he read it in an instant! Touya, I beg of you, please assist us in translating these scripts for the sake of our research!" *Huh? She wants me to keep on reading this stuff…? Without end, for all of the foreseeable future?*

"About that… Roughly how much is there that needs translating?"

"Let's see… Well, there are countless documents which still need to be translated… If we were to start with the documents pertaining to the ancient civilization of Partheno, then…"

"That's enough! Thanks, but no thanks!" From the moment she uttered the word countless, I had already mentally thrown in the towel. I didn't mind helping out every now and then, but I had *zero* intention of making a career out of it! I had no plans to work as a translator anytime soon.

At my rejection, Charlotte made a face that could easily have convinced anyone that the end of the world was nigh. I couldn't live with myself if I left her like that...

Oh, there was an idea...

"Excuse me, Your Majesty. Could I borrow one more glass?"

"I do not mind, but what are you planning to craft with it this time?" That took care of the glass part, which only left the metal... I supposed some silver coins would suffice.

Taking my silver coins and placing them next to the glass, I cast my [Modeling] spell and began reshaping the materials. I crafted the frame out of silver coins, then inserted two glass discs into the openings on the front. With that, my creation was complete.

Humbly designed though they were, I had, indeed, just invented glasses. Well, the lenses were made from regular glass, so they were just mock-glasses. For now...

Charlotte was the only one who was truly amazed by what I'd just done, but I was still just getting started.

For the next step, I cast [Enchant] on the glasses in order to imbue them with a special effect.

"[Enchant]. Imbue with [Reading]: Ancient Spirit Script." The glasses glowed faintly for a moment before the light gradually dissipated. I took the completed glasses and wore them on my face before taking another look at the parchment from before. Yup, a resounding success. I could read it again. Having confirmed that fact, I took the glasses off and gave them to Charlotte.

"Please try wearing them just like I did."

"Hm? Well, alright…" Charlotte put on my special mock-glasses as I'd instructed her. *Oooh, this is beyond my expectations! They suit her perfectly! On this day, this world bears witness to the birth of the bespectacled beauty!*

Finally, I handed the parchment back to Charlotte.

"Now, please read exactly what you see written here."

"Eh…? Umm… 'By taking a Degment, which lacks any meaningful arts to access the Origin Magic, and introducing that to the nature of the Soma-arts' method of…' I-I can read it! I can really *read* it!" A job well done, then. And so, on that day translation-vision glasses were brought unto the world.

Seeing Charlotte grow happier and happier as she quickly glanced over several more of the documents made her look so adorable that it was hard to believe she was an adult woman.

"The effect should at the very least be semi-permanent, I think, but if it does wear off, then please don't hesitate to bring them back and I'll enchant them for you again."

"I will! I-I mean, wait, does that mean you're giving these to me?!"

"Of course. They're all yours now."

"Thank you so much! Really, thank you!" Good grief. Well, at least I'd managed to escape the wicked fate of having to go through a class change to Translator of all things.

Charlotte was in such high spirits that she blurted out something like "I'd like to put these to work on my research immediately!" and left the room like a brisk summer gale.

"My apologies for that. Once something catches that girl's interest, she tends to tune out everything else around her… She *is* the most talented magic researcher we have, as well as the pride of our research team, but even so…"

"Oh my, I would rather say that that is precisely what makes her so appealing, do you not think so?"

"...Well, I'm just glad she was pleased with my little gift." The king and queen made an amusing image at that moment, him shaking his head as if to say "What am I to do with that girl?" and her giggling at his side due to the whole exchange. The sight made me relax in my chair once more, which in turn made me bring the chilled tea to my lips for a drink. Even lukewarm, it tasted quite delicious. I supposed that was probably part of what made it first-class.

Staaare...

Staaaare...

Staaaaare...

Staaaaaare...

...Now, who does that burning, intense gaze that's been honing in on me this entire time belong to? Why, the princess, of course.

She had completely wrapped me in her sights with those mismatched blue and green eyes of hers, and showed no signs of relenting. It was like she had locked onto me as some sort of target. Had I done anything to rub her the wrong way...? Actually, it seemed like her face was a bit red...

Her visual assault came to an end all of a sudden. I cast a glance in her direction, and she had risen from her seat. She was now standing facing her parents, the king and queen.

"What's the matter, Yumina?"

"Father. Mother. I have made my decision," Princess Yumina declared.

I wonder what this decision she's talking about is, I thought to myself as I took another mouthful of my cold tea, watching the conversation with a sidelong glance.

The princess' face turned bright red as she spoke once more.

"I-I would like to… I would like to take Mochizuki Touya as my husband!"

Pfffffft!!! The princess dropped a bomb that detonated in the form of cold tea soaring through the air. Ah, what a graceful display.

What'd she just say? Husband? Hundred? Huntsman? Oh, it must've been hostage. "I would like to take Mochizuki Touya as my hostage." Yup. That makes absolutely zero sense.

"…Sorry. Yumina, could you say that one more time?"

"As I said, Father. I would like to take Mochizuki Touya as my husband."

"Oh my, oh my," the queen muttered, clearly amused. Yumina repeated herself for the benefit of her father, His Majesty the King. Queen Yuel, still sitting next to the king, opened her eyes wide and took a good look at her own daughter.

Watching all this from the side, the duke was utterly gobsmacked as his gaze drifted between his brother and niece repeatedly.

"Your reasons?"

"Well, him saving your life, Father, does indeed factor into it… But more than that, my Touya has a strange charisma that brings smiles to all those around him. Even just from his interactions with Uncle Alfred or Charlotte, he has done nothing but bring them joy. I find his kindness appealing beyond words, and for the first time in my life, I thought that… I would be happy to live out the rest of my days by a person's side."

"…I see… If that is your decision, then far be it from me to stop you. I wish the two of you nothing but happiness!"

"Thank you, Father!"

"Hooold it right there!" I raised my hand to interject for a moment. If I didn't cut them off, things would've surely spiraled completely out of control. Actually, it was already well beyond any kind of control.

"Excuse me, but I would *really* love to have a say in all of this!"

"Ahh, my apologies, son. I'll trust you to take good care of my daughter."

"No, no, no, no, *hell* no. This is all messed up! Your Majesty, you've gone mad!" I understood fully well that I'd just said some outrageous things to the king, but I didn't exactly have the time to care about manners. My entire future was on the line!

"You barely even know anything about me! Are you really fine with just marrying your daughter, a princess at that, off to some complete stranger?! I could be the baddest brigand in all the lands, for all you know!"

"No, there is no chance of that. Yumina has approved of you, so at the very least it is certain that you are not a bad person. My daughter has an ability which lets her see the true nature of a person in that way." Huh? She could grasp a person's nature? What did that even mean?

"You see, Yumina was born with Mystic Eyes. They allow her to see the true nature or personality of anyone she lays her eyes on. I would say it's somewhat similar to intuition, but in Yumina's case, she's never been wrong." The duke explained the situation to me along those lines. So put simply, she could instinctively tell whether someone was a good person or a bad person? I had no idea her odd eyes held such a power. Well, in Count Balsa's case, even *I* could tell that he was a rascal at a glance, but if that power of hers was genuine, then Yumina would never be taken in by any shady fellows.

Being recognized as a good person by a girl like that didn't feel half bad at all, but that was completely irrelevant to the situation at hand.

"...Plus, I mean, just how old *is* Princess Yumina?"

"She turned twelve years of age not long ago."

"Don't you think it's a little bit early for her to be thinking about marriage...?!"

"Not at all, it is quite a common thing for the royal family to find their life partners by age fifteen. I recall that I was fourteen when I got married to my wife." Gah... This was the problem with other worlds... As I made a face like I'd just swallowed a bug, I felt a hand tugging at the sleeve of my coat.

"Touya, do you dislike me...?" Princess Yumina clung to my sleeve and gave me the sad puppy eyes routine. *Hold up, stop right there! Foul! Red card! Offside! Anyway, that's just unfair!*

"Well... I don't really... *dislike* you or anything, it's just..." *This isn't even a question of like or dislike! I just don't even know you very well.*

"In that case, it shouldn't be a problem!" Yumina's face immediately returned to a blissful smile... *Man, she sure is cute... No! Pull it together, dumbass!*

What should I do? True enough, I didn't have any real reason to dislike her as of yet, and it wasn't like I had anyone I was in love with, either. Her parents had approved of it, and I'd never struggle for living expenses ever again. Wait, what? Hang on. Thinking about it, I had absolutely no reason to decline at all!

No! Marriage is where your future goes to die! My older cousin said so! He accidentally got a lady pregnant, so he got married to her, only to be slapped with divorce papers just three years later! He had no idea why! And then, after having taken out a huge loan under her impossible demands for a house, he was driven out of it without a say in the matter. As a final nail in the coffin, he ended up having to pay child support for a kid he wasn't even allowed to visit. As if *that* wasn't bad enough, it turned out that his ex-wife had mainly been using the child support payments for her own sake instead of the child's. It was so bad that whenever the relatives got together at New Years, everyone would try to cheer him up as he comforted himself with alcohol.

I couldn't ever shake the image of my cousin's withered face from my mind…

Okay, I've decided! I'm going to live like royalty as a bachelor for the rest of my life! I'll never become a member of royalty, mind you! "…Where I come from, men can't get married until they turn eighteen, and women can't get married until they're sixteen. Besides, I don't really know the first thing about the princess, and certainly not enough to make any decisions about marriage!"

"How old are you right now, Touya?"

"I'm fifteen. Soon to be sixteen, I guess." I answered Queen Yuel's question. If I remembered right, my birthday should have been in around two months' time. Of course, that was all assuming that the dates in this world matched those of my old world. I didn't know enough about the world yet to say for sure.

"Which means the wedding ceremony will take place in two years' time. Until then, you can just remain betrothed to give you time to think. Those two years should give you ample time to get to know my daughter Yumina better." *Hey, I see you trying to trick me, you know?! Even after two years, Yumina'll still only be fourteen! Man, this queen is off her rocker too!*

"Touya, boy."

"Whahyyes?!" I almost jumped out of my skin and ended up letting out a weird voice when the king called out to me. *I can't help it, alright?! Just look at this situation! Even I can tell that I'm working myself up into a panic over it!*

"Why not take the two years to get to know my Yumina a little better? If, after those two years, you still cannot consider marriage, then we will give up on the idea. How does that sound for the time being?"

"Er, well... I guess that sounds like a more reasonable idea..." It was many times better than considering something like marriage right off the bat. I was sure that, after enough time passed, Yumina might calm down or possibly even find someone she really did love... And besides, maybe if she looked at reality a little bit she'd realize how ridiculous the idea of marriage at her age was. It didn't seem like I could bargain with them any further... And so, I decided to resign myself to these plans for the time being.

"Good for you, Yumina. Now, you've got two years. Give it your best shot and steal that boy's heart, you hear? If you fail to snatch his heart even after two years, then prepare to live out the rest of your days as a nun!"

"Of course, Mother!"

"Wait, what?!" I knew that accepting that proposal was a bad idea! I was too hasty! Heavy! The burden of it all was *way* too heavy for my poor soul! *Now I see! They're trying to cut off all my escape routes one at a time!* Why would me turning her down equal her becoming a nun? Surely she could just search for someone better!

"I'll be in your care from now on, my Touya..." The Princess flashed a smile worth more than a bag of priceless jewels. The best I could conjure up in response was a hollow smile of my own.

Aaahh, I can hear my cousin calling out to me. He's saying "Don't you ever end up like me."

"Geez... what in the world have you gotten yourself into *this* time?"

"You know, I've been asking myself that same question all day..." Upon returning to the Silver Moon Inn, I relayed the tale of my exploits to the rest of my party. Elze sounded exasperated right away.

"So Touya-dono is going to be getting married, is he..."

"It's a real shock, isn't it...?" Both Yae and Linze aimed their dumbfounded gazes at the girl who seemed to be affixed to my left arm.

Yes. This is exactly what it looks like. I brought her along with me. I brought the gosh-darned princess of this country back with me.

Yup. Princess Yumina Urnea Belfast, the one and only. Great.

"A pleasure to meet you all. My name is Yumina Urnea Belfast." Minding her manners, Princess Yumina bowed before everyone as she introduced herself. Her beaming smile was a deadly weapon that made my chest feel heavy.

"So, Princess, whatever are you doing here right now, pray tell?"

"Yes, well. My father has decreed that I live together with my Touya as a part of bridal preparation. I'm sure that my ignorance of the outside world may cause problems every now and then, but I would really like to get to know all of you better." And that was the situation. The princess had basically been handed right over to me. What in the world was that loopy king thinking?

I seemed to recall that he went on about how being close to someone was the quickest way to get to know them better or some nonsense. He could have at least assigned a guard or two! Wasn't he worried about his daughter's safety in the slightest? No, wait. What if she *did* have a guard assigned to her, and it was some ninja hiding up above the ceiling this whole time? Right as that thought crossed my mind, I heard something clatter above me. It was probably just a rat... right?

"Live together? You mean, like, here? I mean, you're a princess and all. Are you gonna be... Will you be okay in a place such as this?" Elze was the only one speaking any sense here. I agreed with her wholeheartedly. I simply couldn't picture a princess, who'd been surrounded by servants that met her every need, suddenly adapting to a life where she had to do everything on her own.

To be completely honest, a little part of me had been hoping that the difficulties of single life would hit her hard enough to convince her to scurry along home...

"Please, you needn't be so stiff when you're talking to me, Elze. For the time being, I'll try to do my best at what I *can* do, and if I ever require assistance, I'm sure I can rely on my Touya to help me out. I'll do my best to ensure that I do not weigh everyone down!" The princess made two small fists and held them up to her chest, striking a pose that showed she was brimming with motivation... *Gosh, she's such a darling little thing... QUIT THAT! Snap out of it!*

"...Uhm, did you have something in mind?" Linze raised her hand and asked a simple question.

"Why yes. I was thinking I could get registered with the guild for a start, and try to reach the point where I can be of assistance during any requests we take on."

"WHAT!" "Uhm..." "Huh?!" "Pardon...?!" Our surprised reactions were growing more harmonious by the day. For the princess to say that she wanted to get registered with the guild... Was she planning on living the life of an adventurer?!

"Excuse me, Princess? You do realize what it means to get registered with the guild, right?! There are any number of dangerous situations we could wind up in, and…"

"I'm well aware of that. And please, don't call me Princess all the time. I'd like it very much if you would call me Yumina, my darling."

"Well, I'd like it very much if you'd cut out the 'my Touya' and 'my darling' stuff!"

"Then please call me Yumina from now on." The princess… No, Yumina, declared so with a sugary sweet smile. Hrmmm… The girl could be unexpectedly stubborn about things. I realized that I couldn't afford to underestimate her just because she was younger than me.

Anyway, I got her to stop calling me "my Touya," and of course "my darling" was right out of the question. We settled on just Touya and Yumina for each other, respectively.

"I've learned the basics of magic from Madame Charlotte, and I'm also well trained with a bow. I'll have you know that I'm actually rather strong, despite my appearance."

"Bows and magic… Indeed, more long-range offensive power would be a wondrous asset to our current party, it would! What might be your magical alignments, then?"

"Wind, Earth, and Dark. I can only summon three types of contract beasts, however." Wind, Earth, and Dark. That certainly would fill in the gaps perfectly, since those were all elements that Linze had no affinity with. Although we still didn't know just how capable with magic Yumina really was…

"Hmmm… So, what's the call?" Elze crossed her arms as she spoke to Linze and Yae. What she was really asking was "Do we let this girl into the party or not?" and checking with the others about that.

"…For now, why don't we accept a request… and see how things go…?" Linze slowly muttered.

"I see. A trial by fire then, is it to be?"

"Guess so, yeah… Well, if it gets dangerous, then I'm sure Touya will just leap to her rescue. So that settles it, then." There were so many things wrong with the situation, but I felt like trying to argue back would be like poking at a hornet's nest, so I obediently decided to abide by the party's decision. Though, hell, something in the atmosphere told me that I had no right to voice my opinion to begin with.

The girls decided on their plan of action, and so we would be heading to the guild office the next day to get Yumina registered.

With that out of the way, we went to talk to Micah to see about getting Yumina her own room. She insisted that she would be happy to share a room with me, but I very much had to draw the line there for a whole variety of reasons, so she was booked into her own separate room. After that, we all had dinner and went to bed in order to prepare ourselves for the next quest.

I returned to my room, alone at last, and collapsed right into bed. The day's events had left me utterly exhausted… So very, very exhausted…

Just as I felt that I was being dragged into the murky depths of sleep, I heard my smartphone's ringtone for the first time in a while. It was set as Suppe's *Leichte Kavallerie*. An upbeat little tune, which, at present, served only to irritate me somewhat.

I removed my smartphone from my pocket and saw the words on the phone's screen: Caller ID: God.

"…Hello?"

"Aaah, it certainly has been a while. Congratulations on your engagement, Touya my boy."

"...Why do you even know about that...? Oh, but I guess it wouldn't be all that strange for God to know about these things, huh...?"

"Ha ha ha. It was a mere coincidence, I promise you. I had thought to check in on you, only to find you in quite the amusing state of affairs." I could picture the jolly old man's face even as he spoke.

"There's nothing amusing about it... I just can't bring myself to think about marriage at this age."

"She seems like a good girl. What more could you possibly want for?"

"It's not like that. Yeah, Yumina's really cute, and I'm sure she'll grow up to be a really beautiful woman. Her honest, straightforward personality also makes her my type, too. But that's got nothing to do with all of this marriage stuff."

"How stubborn you are. You know, in that world polygamy is perfectly normal and widely accepted. That being the case, you should take any girl who strikes your fancy and make wives out of them!" Huh, I didn't know that... The duke and the king each only had one wife, so I thought for sure... No, no, that wasn't the real problem. I had absolutely no intentions of turning my life into a harem story.

"At any rate, everyone is looking forward to how things go for you from here. Do your best out there, yes?"

"That's easy for you to say... Wait a sec... What do you mean, everyone?"

"Why, all the gods of the Divine Realm, of course. When I showed you to them, they all took an interest in you, you know? Although I am sure most of them are only checking in on you every now and then for a bit of amusement." Wait, huh? What did that mean? There was more than one God?

"You said gods, right? Does that mean there are others besides you?"

"But of course. Though I would like to say that I am the world god, the highest of all. Besides me, there are the lower gods such as the god of hunting, the god of love, the god of swords, the god of agriculture, and many, many more. Oh, and the god of love, in particular, has taken quite the interest in you." *Don't go sticking your neck into people's love lives, God of Love.*

"We were talking about how we would all turn up for your wedding ceremony as your relatives. It was quite the fun discussion, I must say. Oh, and I would be turning up as your grandfather, of course."

"Now you listen here..." Those gods must have had a lot of free time on their hands. What in the world would that even be like? A wedding hall filled with nothing but gods of all kinds. I mean, yeah, it wasn't like I had any relatives in this world or anything, but still.

"I seem to recall you saying something about being unable to interfere once I was down here, or am I misremembering things?"

"I believe I said that I would be unable to do much for you *directly*. There are no problems with me descending to that world myself in human form if I so choose to." I was sure there was a mountain of problems with a plan like that... But it felt like commenting on the matter any further was only going to make me seem the fool. When I thought about it, the gods of mythology back in my old world supposedly visited the human world on occasion too.

"Anyhow, I am right here watching over you, my lad. Do take your time to think things over such that you will live a life that you may look back on fondly in your later years. I am wishing you all the best and hope that you find your own path to happiness. With that, I suppose I really must be going. I will check back in on you again. Goodbye."

"Yeah…" I cut off the call after giving a vague response. Live a life that I can look back on fondly one day, huh…?

What did it even mean to be engaged to a twelve year old…? Thinking of it in terms of a high school freshman and a girl in her sixth year of elementary school, the age difference seemed overwhelming. On the other hand, looking at it as a mere four year difference in our ages, it wasn't really that big of a deal, was it…? Even my parents had a six year difference in their ages. I also seemed to remember hearing something about some entertainers whose wives were as much as thirty years younger than them.

Back to the situation at hand, I hadn't gone out with a girl even once in my life. There was no way I could be expected to understand the concept of marriage.

Hell, I just don't get what's even going on anymore. I should just sleep on it all for now. Yeah, I think I'll do just that.

The next day, we all headed off toward the guild together.

Yumina's clothes were too showy for her to be wearing around in public, so she had borrowed some clothes from Elze and Linze.

She wore a white blouse with a blue ribbon, and a black top over that. She also wore a dark blue culotte skirt and black knee socks. They suited her quite well considering they were borrowed clothes, though they still seemed a little big for her.

She had also bunched her long blonde hair into one large braid so that her movements were less restricted.

Personally, I had been worried that her heterochromia would be the thing to give her away, but apparently heterochromia wasn't a sign of having Mystic Eyes.

And so, we'd succeeded in making her look like a normal girl. Well, her looks were still champion-class, which made it hard to classify her as a normal girl, so it was difficult to judge her based on such standards.

"I've been wondering for a while now, but if Touya and Yumina got married, wouldn't that make Touya next in line for the throne?" Elze pondered.

"Yes, that's right. I'd be happy if that ever came to pass. But in order to make that a reality, we'd need to have the nobles and the citizens approve of him first. On the other hand, if my parents were to give me a little brother, he would be the next to inherit the throne instead." On the way to the guild, I happened to overhear Elze and Yumina's conversation. I prayed from the bottom of my heart for Yumina to get a kid brother.

I'm beggin' ya, King, you've gotta get this girl a younger brother, stat! I'll even look up the recipe for stamina drinks on my smartphone for you... No, damn it, not this pattern again! Making plans like that is the same as admitting defeat in this marriage tug-of-war!

"Just so you know, I really have no intention of becoming the king of anywhere."

"I'm aware of that. The same would hold true if my uncle had a son, or even if, um, i-if our child was a boy, th-then he would be the one to succeed the throne!"

Really, you're pulling out "if our child was a boy"?! Also, don't go blushing when you're the one who said it! Now you're making me feel embarrassed!

Before dropping by the guild, we took a detour to the weapon shop, Eight Bears, so we could get Yumina set up with the appropriate equipment. When I asked if she had any money on her, Yumina took out a jangling bag of coins and said that her father had given it to her as a parting gift. I had a really bad feeling about that, and sure enough, when I opened the bag to check, it was filled with fifty platinum coins. Back in my world that would've been about fifty million yen... Bit much for a parting gift, wouldn't you say...?

Once in the store, I asked Barral to show us his selection of bows. His selection wasn't as varied as those stores in the capital, but the store still stocked some high-quality weapons. Yumina picked up a few bows and tested the bowstrings intently. In the end, she went with a light, M-shaped composite bow.

Rather than prioritize firing distance, she went with a bow that was easy to handle and quick to shoot with. Made sense, really. She probably couldn't handle a huge longbow properly at her height and build.

She also bought a quiver, which came with a set of one hundred arrows. Finally, she bought a white leather breastplate and matching white boots.

Alrighty then, looks like we're just about ready to roll out.

We took Yumina into the guild office, which was bustling with life like always.

Another thing that was just like always was the number of intimidating gazes locking onto me. In fact, some of the male adventurers shot me some particularly nasty glances.

At first I'd had no idea why that kept happening to me every time I went there, but by that point I understood all too well.

You didn't have to look very hard to tell that Elze, Linze — and Yae, too — were all beautiful girls. And I was the "lucky fella" who was in the same party as all those cute girls. This was why I, in particular, was the object of their resentment. Their gazes stung like daggers from all directions.

To tell the truth, there had already been a few incidents where other adventurers had come up to me and said and done things like "People like you really piss me off" or "Come lend me your face for a second." Guess they were trying to knock me down a peg or whatever it was those types of people do in this world. Naturally, I politely declined by making them pass out, but the real solution to it all was to just not even give people like that the time of day.

I guided Yumina over to the receptionist's desk and helped her through the registration process. Meanwhile, Elze and the others went to go look over the details of some of the currently available requests.

When Yumina's registration was complete, she and I made our way back to the rest of the group to find Elze holding a Green-level request paper.

"Did you manage to find a reasonable one?"

"Hmm... I guess I just thought this one might make for a decent starting point." She handed me the paper. It was a monster hunting mission. Let's see here...

"Defeat five King Apes... What kind of monster were they again?"

"They're basically just large apes. They tend to move in groups and attack using pack tactics. They're fairly unintelligent monsters, so traps are highly effective against them. The only thing to watch out for is their sheer brute force attacks. Based on our experiences so far, I believe we can defeat them without a problem." So they were a type of monster that relied on brute force. Still, for monsters with "King" in their name to form groups struck me as really weird. Such thoughts drifted through my mind as I listened to Linze's explanation, and I passed the request paper over to Yumina.

"Well? Thoughts?"

"Not a problem. Let's accept this one." Our guild card was the Adventurer's Green, whereas Yumina's was the Beginner's Black. There was no real need to bring her along on one of our higher level requests, but Yumina insisted, so we simply gave in to her demands.

I recalled that the ranks went in ascending order of Black, Purple, Green, Blue, Red, Silver, and Gold. Basically:

Black - Beginner.

Purple - Adventurer-in-training.

Green - Adventurer.

Blue - Veteran Adventurer.

Red - First-rate Adventurer.

Silver - Elite Adventurer.

Gold - Hero.

And that was what the ranks were like. Naturally, every time you went up a rank, the time it took to ascend to the next one got longer and longer. Incidentally, there were no Gold Rank adventurers in the whole country, apparently. Seemed that Heroes weren't exactly all that easy to come across.

For the time being, we took the King Ape extermination request to the receptionist and officially accepted it. The location was somewhere to the south, across the Alain River.

Unfortunately, we had never been that far south before, so we couldn't just use my [Gate] spell to drop us off right where we needed to be like we usually did. Instead, we settled for renting a wagon.

Elze and Linze sat up front in the driver's seat, while Yae, Yumina, and I sat in the back. By the way, it turned out Yumina was good with horses, too. Even though she was a princess. No, maybe *because* she was a princess? Was she used to traveling long-distance? It might've just been that those who couldn't handle horses were the minority in this world…

"Hrmm… We're renting wagons a lot these days. Maybe it's about time we just went and bought one?"

"There are all kinds of wagons, but even the cheapest would cost a fair bit, they would. Not to mention the need to look after the horses, yes. And we certainly could not leave a wagon parked up at the Silver Moon all the time, not at all." Yae had a point. There were both merits and demerits to owning a wagon. Hell, I didn't know how to look after a horse. Someone like that definitely shouldn't be allowed to keep a horse of his own.

Three hours passed as we chatted idly in the back of the wagon, before we finally crossed the Alain River and arrived at the southern woods.

Now, where were those King Apes? It would've been nice if my [Search] magic located them, but if they were within range of that spell, then we'd have noticed them already even without having to cast it. I also had [Long Sense] at my disposal, but that spell worked sort of like creating a double of one's self which took the shape of heightened senses, meaning I'd be the only one searching through the forest. There was certainly less danger that way, though.

Looking at my smartphone's map, it was a surprisingly large forest, too. It'd be fairly difficult to find one type of monster in particular in a place that large. Wasn't exactly like I could use the search function on my phone's map to find animals or monsters, either…

We had no choice but to search the forest on foot. But just as we were about to do so, Yumina stopped us.

"Sorry, do you think I could use my Summoning magic before we head into the forest?"

"Summoning magic? You're gonna call on a contracted beast?"

"Yes, that's right. I think I have just the thing to help track down those King Apes." Yumina made some space between us and began her incantation.

"Come forth, Dark! I seek the proud beasts wrapped in silver: [Silver Wolf]!" When she finished the incantation, a number of Silver Wolves rose out from the shadows at Yumina's feet. Five in total. Each was about one meter from head to tail. They wagged their tails happily as they raced in circles around their summoner. Out of them all, one of the wolves in particular was slightly larger than the rest, and it had a cross-shaped mark on its forehead.

"I'll have these boys look for the monsters. We're mentally linked so that even if we're apart I'll be able to tell immediately once they've found the enemy."

I see... Dogs... no, uh, wolves had a good sense of smell. They'd probably be able to find the monsters we were looking for quite quickly.

"Alright boys, I'm counting on you!" They barked in affirmation at Yumina's order and dashed off into the forest. So this was Summoning magic. I had wondered back during the Lizardman incident, but could I summon creatures like that, too? I decided to ask Yumina while we made our way through the forest.

"It all comes down to whether or not you can form a contract with the creature you've summoned. If you can form a contract, then you'll be able to summon and control that monster at will. The condition for contracting with those wolves was fairly simple, so I had no problems with them at all. Some of the conditions for contracting a monster include fighting it to show off your own strength or even just answering a question correctly. They can vary quite wildly. But as a rule of thumb, the stronger the monster, the harder it is to keep them under your control." Right then. So the stronger the summoned beast you wanted, the harsher the conditions for contracting with them were. Though I guess that was just stating the obvious.

I was searching the surroundings as such thoughts rolled through my head when Yumina came to a sudden halt.

"…Looks like one of them found the enemy. Hmm, there are more of them than the request stipulated… Seven in total."

"Seven, huh…? How do you wanna do it, then? We only really need to beat up five for the request." Elze beat her gauntlets together with a loud clang.

"We should probably take care of all of them, just to be safe. If even a single one gets away, there's a chance it could return with backup." I agreed with Linze's opinion. There was always the chance that there were more than just seven in the area. We should charge in and take care of them as swiftly as possible.

"Yumina, any chance you'd be able to lure those King Apes over this way somehow?"

"I can, but… do you have a plan?"

"Let's set up some traps. We can make some pitfalls using Earth magic." After Yumina and I used our Earth magic to set up a few pitfalls, I hid in the shadow of a tree. Before long we all heard a loud roar, and Yumina's wolves came rushing past with several large apes charging after them.

They were slightly larger than gorillas and had larger teeth, with pointed ears and red eyes. They chased after the wolves looking utterly ferocious.

The wolves leaped over the hidden pitfalls and perfectly avoided the traps. Not questioning their behavior in the least, the King Apes charged forward with reckless abandon and fell straight into the traps.

"Goh-gruagh?!"

"Now!" Spotting our chance, Yae, Elze and I leaped out from behind the trees. There were three apes caught in the traps. They were buried in up to their chests and struggling to climb their way out.

One of those apes was immediately hit with an arrow to the eye. Must've been Yumina. Approaching from the monster's now-blind spot, Yae sliced open an artery in its neck.

"Come forth, Fire! Whirling Spiral: [Fire Storm]!" The remaining two in the traps were devoured by the firestorm that Linze had called forth. Burned completely black but still alive, Elze and I finished them off.

The other four King Apes came charging at us before we even had time to catch our breath. They came at us while wildly swinging their huge, bulky arms, roaring all the while and causing small tremors in the earth.

"[Slip]."

"Grruaaah?!" The King Ape that I'd aimed for tumbled to the ground with all of its momentum as soon as my spell hit it. Before it could get back up, a storm of arrows pierced its large frame. As a final blow, Yae put all of her body weight behind one thrust aimed at the beast's chest, piercing straight through its heart.

"**[Boost]!**" Elze activated her magic nearby and charged straight at one of the other King Apes, before delivering a series of tremendously heavy blows to its abdomen. Unable to withstand her brutal onslaught, the ape collapsed to the ground and Yumina's wolves came rushing out to finish the job. Two left.

"**Come forth, Lightning! Pure Sparking Javelin: [Thunder Spear]!**"

"**Come forth, Fire! Crimson Javelin of Flames: [Fire Spear]!**" Yumina and Linze's magic shot forth. Two magical spears glided through the air — one Wind-type, and one Fire-type — and hit the bullseye smack bang in the center of the apes' chests. Both of the apes dropped to the ground, writhing and spitting out their death rattles as they collapsed.

Whoa, that's incredible. Looked like Yumina's magic was at least as powerful as Linze's. With the two of them together, they were even better than me with the main six magic elements. Apparently my problem was that I didn't have very good control of my magical output, and as a direct result I had yet to acquire even a single high-tier spell. Offensive magic was particularly difficult for me. Well, at least I was fairly proficient with Light-type magic.

We had wiped out all seven of the King Apes. Our battle was over for the time being. We'd taken care of that more easily than I'd expected.

The five summoned wolves leaped back into Yumina's shadow and disappeared.

"Umm, how did I do?" What Yumina was trying to ask was, had she held us back in any way during that skirmish. Honestly, it was the complete opposite. She had proven herself a great asset to the party. I had no idea that covering fire could be so effective.

"No problems skill-wise, that's for sure," Elze barked out enthusiastically.

"Your magic was also, erm, quite impressive…"

"As I suspected, long-ranged support is incredibly helpful, it is." All of them approved of her abilities in succession. They all made valid points, but… I still didn't feel good about exposing a twelve year old girl to such a dangerous environment… Hrmmm.

The girl in question intruded on my deep thoughts by staring at me at length with an anxious expression. *Now see here, those puppy-dog eyes are against the rules! …She couldn't be doing this on purpose, could she?*

"…I'll be counting on your support from now on, Yumina."

"Of course! Leave it to me, Touya!" Yumina wrapped herself around me with the biggest smile on her face. *Whoa, hey, time out! Could you at least not do that while everyone's watching?!* Once I finally managed to pry Yumina off of me, we set about collecting the King Apes' ears as proof that we'd fulfilled the request.

"But now that Yumina has joined the party, that makes four girls with me as the only boy here…" I let out a little sigh.

"Umm, is that a problem at all?" Linze tilted her head. The fact that she didn't get what I meant was a problem in itself.

"It doesn't look like you three have noticed at all, but we really stand out at the guild… and the harsh looks I get from the other adventurers really sting."

"Hm? Why would that be happening, Touya-dono?"

"Well, I mean, if a guy's surrounded by cute girls all the time, then there's any number of people who'd get jealous. And come on, Elze and Linze, and Yae too, you're all exceptionally good looking, you know?"

"What?!" "E-Excuse me?" "Whatever do you...?" Everyone froze up. *What? Was it something I said? It's true, though. If I were one of those guys at the guild and I saw some guy coming and going, always with some cute girls in tow, even I'd get pretty jealous.*

"Wh-What are you even saying, Touya? I still don't get your sense of humor. It's mean to tease and call me cute like that..." Elze muttered, clearly flustered by my words.

"Huh? I was serious."

"..." "..." "..." *Why's everyone turning bright red? Are they coming down with fevers or something?* "A-Anyway, we should r-really be getting back now, d-d-don't you think?!"

"W-We s-sure should, Sis!"

"L-Let us be on our way, i-indeed!" The three of them marched off, backtracking through the forest. *...What just happened?*

I felt a gentle tugging on the sleeve of my coat.

"Touya, what about me? Am I cute?"

"Huh? Well, I mean, yeah. Of course you are."

"Ehehe..." Yumina blushed, grinned, and wrapped her arms around me. *Please stop doing that, this is bad for my heart!* Eventually we made it back to the wagon. I cast **[Gate],** and we were back in Reflet in the blink of an eye.

So, how about that Summoning magic, eh...? My first exposure to it had been that man summoning swarms of Lizardmen, which gave me a fairly bad impression of Dark-type spells. For that reason, I hadn't tried dabbling in it at all. But since I learned that there were animals like Yumina's wolves among the creatures that could be contracted, I decided that it might not be a bad idea to try contracting myself with a single monster just to test the waters a little. *I should have Yumina teach me more about it later.*

"The first thing to do when handling the Summoning spells unique to Dark-type magic is to draw a magic circle and then summon a creature. The creature you summon is completely random, though some say that it's influenced by the caster's magic or that it reflects the caster themselves. That's all just speculation though, so we don't really know for sure why people end up with the contracted beasts that they do." Out in the back garden of the Silver Moon, Yumina drew a large magic circle while explaining how Dark-type magic worked. She held a book in one hand and a piece of chalk in the other as she carved out a magic circle that was filled with complex patterns. The chalk supposedly had fragments of spellstone put into it during the manufacturing process.

"The hard part is forming the contract itself. In order to successfully contract with the creature you've summoned, you need to pass a sort of test first. These tests come in all forms, from the incredibly simple to the nigh-impossible depending on the strength of the creature itself. The test I had to pass to contract with my Silver Wolves was to feed them until their stomachs were full." Yumina finished drawing the magic circle, then went over and patted the head of the Silver Wolf she had summoned a little while ago. It was the wolf with the cross mark on its head that I'd seen before out in the forest. Apparently this was the first of the wolves she had formed a contract with. The other wolves she had summoned were its subordinates. Incidentally, his name was Silva. *Please, someone in this world, put more thought into naming things,* I pleaded internally.

If you contracted with a powerful creature, apparently you could summon a number of others to work as the primary beast's subordinates. That Lizardman summoner who attacked Sue had probably similarly contracted with a strong Lizardman that acted as the head of that group of them he kept bringing forth.

"If you fail to meet the conditions of the contract, then the creature you summoned will vanish. After that, it'll never appear before you again. You only get one chance to meet the conditions of their contract." Right then. So I had to make the most of our encounter and try my best to fulfill the conditions... Hang on a second.

"This isn't dangerous or anything, right? Like, the thing I summon won't suddenly attack me or anything, will it?"

"Without a contract to bind them to this world, the summoned beasts cannot exist outside of the bounds of the magic circle. Long range attacks will also be absorbed by the magic circle's barrier, so it's perfectly safe. The one exception is if the summoner themselves steps foot within the magic circle. The conditions for some creatures can sometimes be along the lines of fight and prove your strength, after all."

Yeeeah, that sounded a bit violent for my tastes. Well, if I ended up summoning a creature like that and judged that I had no chance of winning against it, I supposed I could always just politely decline and let it return back to whence it came. It may have seemed like a waste, but that was my decision.

"The summoned beast I end up with won't be decided solely on my magical prowess or anything, yeah?"

"That's right. There are many stories of complete beginners summoning incredibly powerful creatures on their first attempt." Which meant there was a chance for me, too. Although in the end it was still essentially a raffle...

"Alright, guess I'll give it my best shot, then." I stood in front of the magic circle and clapped my hands together to get myself fired up a bit. Then, I focused all of my Darkness together and directed the flow of my magic into the center of the magic circle. A black fog slowly built up within the bounds of the magic circle until it completely filled the space, when suddenly an absolutely explosive burst of magical energy emerged from within.

"...Art thou the one who summoned me?" The dark fog dispersed before my eyes to reveal a single large, white tiger. Was that tiger the source of that voice? Its eyes were sharp and discerning, giving off an incredibly intimidating aura. It also seemed to have exceptionally sharp fangs and claws. Great. I'd gone and done it again. I'd summoned something utterly ridiculous with my God-cursed magic... I could feel the tiger's magical energy emanating like waves coursing through the very air itself. This wasn't your zoo-variety tiger, that much was for sure.

"This aura, that white visage... It can't be... the White Monarch...?!"

"Hoh. You know of me?" Behind me, Yumina was cowering on the ground, hugging her wolf for comfort as the tiger stared her down. The wolf, Silva, had also assumed a completely submissive position, lowering his ears and curling up his tail out of fear. Well, being glared at so intently by a tiger would've made anyone cower in fear. Hey, hold up a second. There was a Japanese saying that went like this! "A tiger in front and a wolf at the rear." This was the very picture of that situation! Well, not really, since the meaning behind that saying was closer to "Stuck between a rock and a hard place." The more you know.

"Please try not to look at them so intensely. You're frightening them."

"…You are awfully calm given the circumstances. To think you're still standing after taking the brunt of my magic-laden gaze… How very intriguing."

"Well, I mean, I *was* a little surprised at first. I'm used to that kind of thing by this point, I guess, so it doesn't really affect me much anymore. Anyhow, Yumina. What's this White Monarch thing you mentioned?" Yumina looked in my direction and tried to answer, but her voice kept shaking… She couldn't even speak properly! It probably had to do with the immense aura of fear that the white tiger was continuously exuding.

"Look, could you stop with that for a second? I can't even get a proper conversation out of the poor girl. I can't say that intimidating people weaker than you is a particularly praiseworthy thing, you know?"

"…Very well." I voiced protest to the white tiger, and the oppressive air melted away in an instant. *Well, would you look at that. Looks like it's a pretty reasonable tiger after all.*

"Alright, then. Yumina, what exactly is this White Monarch thing all about?"

"Of all the monsters… that can be summoned through Dark magic… it's one of the four strongest, most sacred of beasts… It's the Guardian of the West and the Main Streets of the cities, the Ruler of all beasts… Really, it's not even a monster at all; it's a Heavenly Beast…" Still shaking in her boots, Yumina awkwardly tried to answer my question. *A Heavenly Beast, huh? It'd be pretty interesting if it were one of God's pets or something.*

"Alright, so how might I go about getting contracted with you?"

"…You wish to form a contract with me? Are you even aware of how nonsensical your words must seem to your comrades at this moment?"

"Well, I figure it's at least worth a shot. If I can't fulfill your request, then I'll obediently give up on the idea."

"Hmm…" The tiger stared at me intently, twitched its nose a little, and inclined its head.

"How curious… I feel a rather strange power about you. The protection of the spirits…? No, something far greater than that… What is this curious power?" *The protection of the spirits? Sorry, bud, but I don't really have any ghosts that I'm on particularly good terms with.*

"…Very well. I'd like to see a display of the quality and quantity of your magical energy. You claim to want to contract yourself with a Heavenly Beast, after all. If your magic is half-hearted, then this whole negotiation will fall through without a moment's consideration."

"You want to gauge my magic?"

"That is correct. Place your hand upon me and pour as much of your magic into me as you possibly can. Keep going until you can barely force another ounce of it out of you. If you have even the minimum amount required to satisfy me, then I will consider forming a contract with you." I could almost see the tiger laughing to itself. It'd consider it? Meaning this wasn't even the main test itself, just a warm-up?

Still, the tiger had come up with a dangerous warm-up exercise. It wanted me to channel all of my magic? So in video game terms, it wanted me to reduce myself to 0 MP? I wouldn't be able to use any magic at all for a while after that. No, wait, it said until I could barely force another ounce, meaning I could keep 1 MP in reserve just in case.

No, hang on a second. Was magic even a thing that decreased as you made use of it…? I'd never felt anything like that in all my time casting spells. I recalled Linze saying that I had an abnormally large amount of magical energy. Was that why I had never felt it before?

Putting that aside, I walked into the bounds of the magic circle and placed my hand on the tiger's head. *Oooh, who's a fuzzy-wuzzy widdle kitty-cat?*

"So you just want me to flow as much of my magic as possible straight into you, yeah?"

"Correct. Just channel all of your magic directly into me. I'll be the judge of it. And I will say this in advance: If you run out of magic and collapse during the examination, the contract will be off the table." Hmm... I wasn't exactly desperate to form a contract with it or anything. If I started to feel ill during the whole exam, I decided I'd just give up on it. I didn't exactly feel like pushing myself to the brink of collapse over something like this.

"Alright, I'm going for it. Brace yourself." I directed all of my magical reserves toward the palm of my hand and began gradually channeling it into the tiger. *Good, I'm not feeling any negative effects from it so far.*

"Hrm... This is... What?! What is with the ridiculous clarity of this magical energy...?!" The tiger seemed to be commenting on my magic. Come to think of it, Linze had said something similar once before. Well, whatever. Things seemed to be going well, so I decided it was fine to go a bit further. I opened the floodgates of my mind and sent a massive burst of magic straight into the tiger.

"Hrnnn!!! Wh-What is this?!" Hmm... didn't feel like my magic had decreased much at all. Did I need to pile on some more before I started to feel any negative effects? I fired up my mental garden hose and set it to full blast.

"Hrg… th-this is… W-Wait a moment—!" Yeah, still nothing. I resorted to the Broken Faucet method.

"P-Please… wai… A-Any more and… aahhh…!" Time for my last resort. I removed my limiter and blasted as much magical energy as I could muster straight into the tiger… *Oh, I think I'm starting to feel it a bit. I'm getting a little bit worn out now. So this is a taste of what it feels like to be running low on magic.*

"… P-Please, I beg of… stop…!"

"Touya!" I snapped to my senses when I heard Yumina's voice and took a look at the tiger in front of me. Its body was convulsing and foam was coming from its mouth. Its eyes were rolled back and it seemed that the only reason it was still standing was because it was being forcefully held up due to being unable to remove its head from my palm.

I panicked and immediately cut off the flow of magic I had been pouring out. The moment I removed my hand, the tiger's body shook violently as it collapsed down onto the ground.

"…Huh?" Had I done something wrong? *Should I try using Healing magic on it?* The big cat was twitching on the ground… its tongue was hanging out and everything.

"Come forth, Light! Soothing Comfort: [Cure Heal]!" I instinctively cast a Healing spell on it. When I did that, the tiger's eyes reverted to normal and it rose unsteadily back to its feet before approaching me.

"…I would just like to ask one thing. That magical energy you were channeling into me… you still had a little room to spare at the end, didn't you?"

"Huh? No, I was doing fine. Honestly, it hardly feels like my magical reserves have depleted at all… No, wait. Kind of feels like it's already filled itself back up."

"Wha…?!" The tiger was speechless. *I see. So that's it! The reason I've never felt my magic being consumed by my spells until now is because it was passively recovering itself at absurd speeds! That's one mystery solved.*

"So yeah, about the conditions for the contract…"

"…Might you grace me with your name?"

"Hmm? Mochizuki Touya. Oh right, Touya's my given name." I threw a curious glance at the tiger, who'd suddenly become so humble, and it bowed down before me.

"Master Mochizuki Touya. By my judgment, there are none I have ever crossed paths with more suitable for the role of my master than you. I would be honored if you were to form a Master-Servant pact with me." Aww yeah, White Tiger joined the party!

"So, uh, what are the conditions for the contract?"

"Please, bestow a name upon me. That shall be the proof that seals the contract. It will also serve as a bond that allows me to exist freely in this realm."

"A name, huh…? Hmmm…" *A tiger. A white tiger… Let's see here…*

"Kohaku. What do you think of Kohaku as a name?"

"Kohaku?"

"It's a name from my homeland. It means Amber, and it's written like this…" I drew the characters for Kohaku on the ground in Japanese, as 琥珀.

"The character on the left is taken from the word for tiger, and the one on the right is taken from white. The little characters stuck to the left side of each of them both mean king. Put it all together and, in my language, it reads as Kohaku. What do you think?"

"The White Tiger who stands by the king's side. Truly, there could be no other name more suitable for me. My gratitude to you.

213

Henceforth, please do call me by the name Kohaku." The contract was sealed. Kohaku stepped slowly out of the bounds of the magic circle and into our realm.

"...Touya, that was incredible...! You actually managed to form a contract with the White Monarch...!"

"Young lady, I am the White Monarch no longer. Please, call me Kohaku."

"Umm, of course... Kohaku." The White Monarch — now named Kohaku — corrected the stunned Yumina. Behind Yumina, Silva the Silver Wolf still cowered in fear at Kohaku's gaze. Panicking, it retreated into Yumina's shadow and disappeared.

"Master, I do have but one humble request."

"What's up?"

"I would like to request that I remain in this realm permanently."

"Hmm? How would that work?"

"Under normal circumstances, a summoned being can only remain in this realm for as long as the summoner's magic will permit. We consume our master's magic simply by materializing in this realm. Once our master's magical energy runs out, we fade back into the other side. This is the normal way of things. However, ever since our contract was formed and I set foot in this world, I've felt that your magical energy has hardly depleted in the slightest. That being the case, I should like to humbly request your permission to remain in this realm indefinitely."

Yeah, I think I know why that is. In short, my magical energy is recharging so fast that it's even counteracting the normally massive amount of magic required to keep a Heavenly Beast in this realm. Well, I see no problem keeping Kohaku materialized as long as it doesn't cause any problems, but...

"I don't mind letting you stay materialized if that's what you want, but, uh, I don't really know how I'd feel about walking through the streets with a huge white tiger in tow... you know?"

"I see... In that case, I shall change my form."

"Change your what now?" Before I had even finished my sentence, Kohaku had morphed into the form of a white tiger cub. I had no idea it could do tricks like that.

What was once a large tiger had turned into roughly the size of a small dog. With those stubby little legs and that stubby little tail, its aura of intimidation had decreased by 100%, and its aura of adorability had leaped up by 100%.

Kohaku was so adorable, in fact, that I couldn't resist picking the little cub up and cradling it in my arms. *Oh gosh, oh gosh, so fluffy-wuffy! I'm so glad I summoned Kohaku,* I thought, feelings welling up from the bottom of my heart.

"I believe I should not attract any undue attention in this form." *Oh my gosh, it talked! So cuuute!*

"I think you'll be attracting attention in a totally different way in this form, but that's A-OK in my book!"

"Very well then. Thank you very much for allowing me to— Gufhu?!"

"Kyaaaa! So *cuuuuute*!!!" The one who snatched Kohaku from my arms for the purpose of much hugging was none other than the Phantom Thief Yumina. She rubbed her face against Kohaku's fur and hugged it tightly even as Kohaku struggled to break free from the Fort Knox-level hugging techniques that Yumina had been practicing on me.

"Wait, stop! Cease this insolence immediately! Who are you that you would dare commit such acts?!"

"Oh right, I hadn't introduced myself yet. My name is Yumina. I'm Touya's wife."

"Master's wife?!" Even Kohaku's stunned face looked like a national treasure to my eyes. *Hang on just one minute, Yumina! You can't just go around introducing yourself as my wife like that!*

Kohaku dejectedly endured being petted by Yumina for a while.

It seemed that Kohaku had qualms about putting up any real resistance to her master's self-proclaimed wife, so it soon stopped struggling and let Yumina play to her heart's content.

Her dose of fluffy-wuffy satisfied, Yumina released the captive Kohaku... only for Elze and the others to appear and, as if a switch had been flipped in each of their brains, they all became exactly what Yumina had been just moments before. Only this time the onslaught of cuddles was triple what it was moments ago.

"M-Master! Please, assist meee!"

"Grin and bear it. They'll calm down once they've had their fill."

"Maaaasteeer!" And so, our party gained a new member that day. Well, maybe "gained a mascot" was a more fitting way to put it.

Once everyone had gotten their fill of fluffy-wuffy time, I decided to partake of it myself.

I looked up to the sky as Kohaku's pleasant screams filled my ears. *Such lovely weather we're having.*

God's in His Heaven, all's right with the world!

I took the day to go and visit the guild's reading room, so that I could read through the Monster Encyclopedia they had. With Linze's help, my literacy had improved substantially.

In my world, a Monster Encyclopedia would be like one big book full of mythological creatures and plots for kaiju movies. It was a really fun read.

There were entries for all different kinds of monsters, magic beasts, spirits, and even Heavenly Beasts, each with their own detailed illustrations. However, there were some that lacked illustrations, which I assumed meant they were as-yet unidentified.

Out of all the monsters in the world, the ones I could find the least information on were Dragons.

Dragons were monsters, yet not monsters. That alone already made them a different kind of lifeform. It was written that the optimal means of dealing with a Dragon was to run away. It seemed like they were considered the strongest things around even in this world... Not that my old one actually *had* any real Dragons.

The guild didn't allow anyone to check any books out of the building. If you really wanted to refer back to anything you'd read, then you just had to note it down. I, however, had the ultimate ally in the form of my smartphone.

I used my smartphone's camera to photograph all of the pages containing info on any local monsters. It was so that I could refer back to it later to look up any of their behavioral traits, valuable body parts, and general points of notice. *Don't try doing this at home, folks.* I'd have been fine simply copying the pages with my [**Drawing**] spell, but the room was protected by a barrier preventing any spells from being cast. These sorts of books were apparently pretty valuable, so it was entirely plausible that some people had tried to use magic to steal them in the past. I didn't really mind just photographing the pages instead, since it took up less room that way anyway in addition to being far easier to sort through.

I also found books with details on demi-humans. It surprised me to find out that this world even had demonkin in it, which were a separate thing from actual demons.

One major difference was that these demonkin weren't inherently evil. Instead, they seemed somewhat similar to demi-humans.

Really, the term demonkin in this context referred to things such as vampires, werewolves, alraunes, lamias, and ogres. These races weren't immediately hostile to humans in the way that monsters were, but they didn't exactly seem to be on good terms, either. Most of these so-called demonkin apparently kept to themselves in a place known as Xenoahs, the Demon Kingdom, far to the north. They rarely ever approached countries inhabited by humans.

I couldn't be sure whether they were being isolated or whether they were deliberately staying out of the way of humans... But, well, even beastmen were discriminated against. Demons seemed like they'd have it even worse than that.

One thing I found interesting was the difference between werewolves and wolf beastmen. Basically, a wolf beastman was like a human, except they had wolf ears and a tail. A werewolf was a human-sized wolf standing on its hind legs, with five-fingered hands and five-toed feet. In other words, werewolves still had the faces of wolves.

Also, werewolves didn't transform under moonlight or anything. They wore clothes and could still talk just like any other demi-human.

Still, between a human with wolf ears and a man with the face of a wolf, I could see the former being accepted among a human community far more easily. Though if we shared languages and could still communicate with them, then physical appearances didn't seem like such a big deal to me.

Other types of demi-humans included winged races, fairies, aquatic races, horned races, dragonfolk, elves, and dwarves.

Even beastmen could be further divided into sub-types like dog or fox, so it felt pretty difficult to grasp just how many different kinds of demi-humans there were.

Looking at a world map taught me that while the world was fairly big, its climate was a complete patchwork mess. Countries didn't get colder in the north or hotter in the south, or follow any kind of consistent logic like that.

This climate was said to be caused by the spirits dwelling in the lands, but the details were unknown. Hell, I couldn't even be sure that the world was even spherical like Earth. It wasn't secretly being held up from beneath by elephants or turtles or anything like that, right? I was surprised yet again to find out that there were completely accurate world maps. Then again, even without blimps or planes, there were still winged demi-humans and probably even magic allowing for human flight, so it wasn't actually *that* strange.

Oh, time's up... The guild charged extension fees if you used their services for too long, so I closed up the book and decided it was time to leave.

There were a bunch of adventurers talking in front of the request board when I returned to the first floor. More than there would normally be at this time of day. Was it because it was the weekend? I made my own way over to the request board to see if there were any exceptionally good jobs available or anything, though I had no real intention of accepting any.

We had decided to take the day off since Elze was feeling "under the weather." It must've been tough dealing with... girl problems like that. Even my [Recovery] spell had no effect. Probably because it wasn't classified as an abnormal status condition, or so I figured. If anything, that kind of pain was proof that her body was functioning properly.

I had been looking over the request board when I heard angry yelling coming from outside.

Guild offices typically stood next to bars, most of which also stayed open throughout the day. They mainly sold light meals during the day, but they still served alcohol regardless of the time.

There was also a larger inn than the Silver Moon fairly nearby, and its guests would frequent the bar due to the convenient location.

All of those things combined meant that there were drunkards out and about at all times of day. It should go without saying, but most people who did just want a light meal wouldn't usually go to a bar for one. That much was obvious.

I'd only ever been in the place a handful of times at most. I didn't drink alcohol, and I hated having to deal with drunkards.

The high number of drunkards also meant that loud arguments were a common thing. People inside the guild building had gotten used to it, with it maybe arousing a few complaints at most. Under normal circumstances, at least. It was a different story when you could hear the sounds of clashing steel.

I ended up leaving the guild office to join the crowd of onlookers. Out in front of the bar, two adventurers were glaring at each other red with anger. One was a bald-headed bearded man, and the other had a mohawk and a long face. Both of them already had their swords out.

"What's going on? A duel?" They had their swords drawn in the middle of the road, so it wasn't just your average scuffle. Worst case scenario, someone could end up dead.

Honestly, it wasn't my first time witnessing a duel. Typically a duel went the way of stating your name and the reason for the duel, and then you get the consent of the other party. After that had been established, outsiders would refrain from butting in. But this wasn't anything as sophisticated as a duel. Just a pair of drunkards at each other's throats. Neither of them had any acting witnesses, so it was clearly no formal altercation.

The townsfolk were treating them like a pair of pests, too. If it wasn't a duel, then a patrolling knight would probably be around to stop it before long.

"…How stupid. They should at least take their fight somewhere out of everyone's way."

"Alright, where's the smartass who said that?!" The bearded baldy turned in my direction, looking like he was about to blow a gasket. Seemed he'd overheard me.

The other onlookers moved out of the way like a sea being parted. Every last one of them fled as if explicitly telling me not to get them wrapped up in it. *Dang, that's cold.*

"Were you the one that called us stupid?!"

"He called us what?!"

"No, I said that what you were *doing* was stupid. I didn't mean to personally offend either of you by it…" I made a small attempt to explain myself. It was true that I thought they were a pair of idiots, though.

"Hold on… You're that brat who joined the guild recently, the one that's always bein' followed around by a buncha girls! You've been pissin' me off for a while now, y'know that?! You tryin' to show off how popular you are? You makin' fun of the rest of us?! Well, are ya?!"

"Yeah, Mr. Bigshot! Unlike you, there're some *real* adventurers out here putting our lives on the line! The guild ain't your playground, so go screw around somewhere else!"

"…I see. So being an adult means getting drunk and hacking away at each other with your swords in the middle of town? It really does make *me* look like the childish one when you put it that way, doesn't it?" I ended up spitting out some sarcasm after what those guys said annoyed me a little.

Don't lecture people for being childish when you're going around picking fights with literal children. That's about as immature as you can get.

The two men who had been fighting mere moments ago united in their hostility toward me instead. Apparently they saw me as a common threat.

"Bastard… You've got real guts, you know that? Feel like finding out what color they are, do ya?!" The bearded baldy moved toward me. There were veins bulging on his forehead. He was over two meters tall, so I ended up having to crane my neck to meet his gaze.

The man before me had muscles like a pro wrestler. Plus, his behavior gave the impression that he was a real nasty guy. But in all honesty, I wasn't intimidated in the slightest. I had memories of being yelled at by my late grandfather that were far scarier than the guy in front of me. When I realized that, I accidentally let a laugh slip out.

"You son of a…!" As I thought, the guy hesitated to draw his sword on me. Instead, he swung his massive left fist straight toward my face.

Yup, I can read his every move. I tilted my head to the right a little and cleanly avoided his punch.

Using my opponent's momentum against him, I grabbed hold of his arm and pulled in order to break his balance before sweeping his legs out from under him. The bearded baldy who'd come charging at me dived straight to the ground in a single breath. *Alright, I managed to pull it off. Glad I got Yae to teach me how to do that.*

"C'mere, brat!" This time the mohawk rushed at me with his sword. *You shouldn't point sharp things at other people.*

"[Slip]."

"Ghwah?!" I knocked down the crazy mohawk guy using my trip-up spell, making the sword go flying out of his hand in the process. I picked the sword up and, very carefully so as not to get noticed, cast [**Modeling**] to bend its shape with my hands as though it were made of rubber. This spell made me able to change the shape of any material in front of me into something else. Any complex new shapes or sculptures took a lot of time, but something simple was a piece of cake.

I threw the bent sword back down in front of the mohawk guy.

"What?! Eep!!!" Mohawk guy let out a squeal of terror as he crawled away. Seemed like he was so scared that he couldn't even stand. He probably thought that I had superhuman strength after a display like that.

"You goddamned...!" This time the bearded baldy came charging at me from behind, swinging his sword down on me without a shred of mercy. *Does nobody around here have any manners?* I sidestepped to avoid the bearded baldy's attack and moved behind him, sweeping at his legs from the back this time.

"Ngwuh?!" He let out a grunt after falling backward and hitting the back of his head against the ground. He probably had a minor concussion. He was already drunk, but was now unable to even keep his head straight as it bobbed from side to side.

I picked up the bearded baldy's sword and worked my spell on it, same as with the mohawk guy's. The man went pale as he watched his sword being bent out of shape before his very eyes.

"D-Dammit! I'll get you for this!" With the parting words of a two-bit thug, both of the idiots ran away.

Don't go around being an angry drunkard in the middle of the day, for heaven's sake. You're making trouble for everyone around.

"Hey, you gonna be alright, man?"

"Yeah, I'm fine. Not like they managed to actually hit me." One of the onlookers showed what appeared to be concern for my well-being, so I waved my hand to show him I was just fine.

"No, not like that... I mean, those guys were with the Steel Fangs and Poison Snakes, right? They'll probably bring a whole bunch of scary guys to get back at you." *Steel Fangs? Poison Snakes? I don't get it.* As it turned out, they were a pair of adventuring parties that happened to be somewhat well-known in the area. Not that I'd ever heard of them. We never really interacted with other parties outside of our own. And we didn't have any reason to hang out around the bars, either. I guess we were short on local knowledge thanks to little things like that. From what I'd heard, the Steel Fangs and Poison Snakes were both parties mainly composed of Blue-rank adventurers.

We were a party of Green-rank adventurers, so technically both of them outranked us.

Your guild rank rose based on the points you'd earned from completing requests, and it went up starting from Black-rank, going up through Purple, Green, Blue, Red, Silver, and Gold, in that order. This didn't mean that higher ranking people were more amazing by default, but naturally, ascending through the ranks got harder and harder the more you rose through them.

It got so difficult to attain the highest ranks that almost nobody ever made it to Silver, let alone Gold. Hell, there was only a single person in the whole world who currently held the status of Gold adventurer. It took an absurd amount of points even just to rise from Red to Silver.

That's why Red-rank adventurers were generally considered to be some of the best around. The ones below them in Blue-rank were generally considered Veterans for the most part.

…Neither of those guys just now had seemed very *veteran* to me, though. They were both stupidly weak. Then again, them being a higher rank was a separate issue from how strong they actually were.

I honestly didn't believe that either of those parties had so much free time that they'd bother coming back for revenge or anything of the sort. Quarrels between adventurers were practically an everyday occurrence, and it wasn't like I'd seriously injured either of them.

At that time, I had no way of knowing just how wrong I was…

"Care to explain what you've gone and done, would you kindly, Touya-dono?"

"Well, I don't really recall doing anything that would get us in *this* kind of situation…" The next day, following right after Elze, Linze started having her own "girl problems," so I went with Yumina and Yae to the eastern forest on a hunting quest.

Our target was a monster called a Wind Fox — a fox that attacked with blades of wind like a kamaitachi youkai. *I thought that myth was about a weasel spirit? Why the hell is it a* fox *in this world?*

We had defeated the monster without any trouble whatsoever and cut off its tail for proof when we were suddenly surrounded by a group of mean-looking adventurers.

"Hey there, brat. We've come to pay you back for yesterday." Among the group of adventurers, there was one that I recognized. It was the bearded baldy who had been causing a bunch of trouble on the street in front of the bar the other day.

Huh? Is this what I think it is? Did all of these guys seriously come here for a petty reason like that?

"…Hmm… So basically, you were so embarrassed yesterday that you brought all your friends along thinking to teach me a lesson, is that about right? Picking on a kid I can brush off as immature, but this is just pathetic."

"Shut the hell up! If I just left things as they were, it'd be like smearing mud all over our reputation! I'm gonna show you what it means to pick a fight with the Steel Fangs!" The adventurers around the bearded baldy all smirked as they readied their weapons. There were quite a few of them. One, two, three, four… Nine in total. Seemed like the Steel Fangs were a fairly large group after all.

"Bringing a whole group of people to settle a score with someone makes you a pathetic excuse for a man — no, a pitiful outline of human-shaped scum. Touya, what's the plan here?" *Geez, Yumina, even trash has feelings. I mean, look at poor old bearded baldy. Being lambasted by a twelve-year-old girl is making him red in the face. Look at the steam rising from him, I could probably cook an egg on his head!* I was surprised by the backbone on Yumina. Quite honestly, I thought she'd be a bit more scared in these types of situations. I guess she wasn't just a princess for show.

"Well, in this case it's justified self-defense, so I think we can afford to go a little overboard just so long as we don't actually kill anyone."

"Indeed. Fellows of this sort are utterly abhorrent, they are." Yae drew her sword and turned the blade around to face the blunt side at the enemy. Upon seeing her motion, the Steel Fangs made their move.

Before they could even reach us, one of Yumina's arrows pierced one man's right shoulder.

"Urgh!" The moment the man dropped his weapon, I got right up close and pressed my fingertip against him.

"**[Paralyze]**."

"Hrngh?!" With my magical paralysis sapping all the strength from his body, the man collapsed on the spot.

"C'mere you little...!" A man wielding hatchets in both hands came charging at me, swinging his weapons around wildly, but there was absolutely no edge to any of his movements. Maybe it was because I had started training with Yae recently, but it looked like he was moving in slow motion.

Finding the first suitable opening between his attacks, I rushed in and punched him in the stomach while activating **[Paralyze]** yet again. Just like the first guy, this one dropped to the ground with a thud.

[Paralyze] was a great spell for rendering an opponent harmless, but it had a large weakness in that it required me to make physical contact with the target. In addition, if the enemy had a magic-defense talisman of any kind on them, then regardless of how weak that talisman was, [**Paralyze**] would have no effect.

Though talismans, even the weakest ones available, sold for quite a high price, so there weren't many who were likely to just casually have one on them.

"Strike forth, Earth! The Fool's Abyss: [Pitfall]!"

"Arrghhhhh…!!!"

"Noooooo…!" I glanced behind me to see Yumina casting an Earth-type pitfall spell. Given that the men's voices were literally echoing as they fell, it had to be a pretty deep one… Would they be okay after a fall like that? "Hrgh!"

"Gwah…?!" To the side, Yae had already knocked two men down with the blunt side of her sword and was busy dealing with a third. By that point, the Steel Fangs had already lost their numerical advantage, leaving us with just the bearded baldy and two other men.

"Th-This is ridiculous…! We're Blue-rank adventurers! Why are we struggling so much against a bunch of brats like this…?!" *Again with the rank stuff, huh?* I didn't know how long they'd been running around doing guild quests, but given enough time wouldn't just about any semi-capable person reach Blue-rank without any real trouble? With a large number of party members and accepting nothing but simple requests, you could slowly but steadily earn points and rise through the ranks that way. On the other hand, that method would only take you so far. If you really wanted to aim for Red-rank or higher, it would take forever.

In the end, all it meant was that there was no real correlation between one's guild rank and one's actual abilities. At least for those below Red-rank, anyway. Getting to Red-rank or higher seemed like it required actual skill and ability, or else you'd likely never make it that far.

"Mrgh?!"

"Ugaaah!!!" Yae took out another two men, leaving just the bearded baldy facing off against the three of us.

"What a pain. You guys are still adventurers, even if in name only, right? Aren't you ashamed of yourselves for picking a serious fight against a group of kids?"

"Shut the hell up, you snot-nosed brat! You're dead for th—!"

"Oh, shush already. [Paralyze]."

"Gfhuuh?!" I didn't feel like going through the same conversation all over again, so I knocked the guy down with a swift application of magic. There was no point trying to reason with thugs like him. Even if you fended them off once or twice, they would probably just keep coming back for more.

In which case, the only way to truly drive them off was to utterly crush their spirits. *Heheheh...*

"I do believe this is rather overdoing it, do you not think...?" Yae muttered a bit to herself as she averted her gaze, her cheeks flushed red.

"Really? They go around as a group ganging up on people, so surely they were prepared for something like this to happen to them one day, don't you think?" I had erected nine posts by the side of the highway leading toward Reflet, and dangling by the ankles from each post was a stripped-naked member of the Steel Fangs.

To complete the display, I had put up a sign that said "We're the adventuring party called the Steel Fangs! Currently recruiting new members."

"Say cheese!" I took a photo of them with my smartphone, then cast [Drawing] to transfer the image onto paper. When I showed that image to the Steel Fang losers, they started crying and whimpering through their mouth gags.

"If you keep bothering us, I'll spread this image all through the streets of Reflet... No, I think I'll post it up all around the capital for everyone to see. If you're fine with that, feel free to come pick more fights with us. I've still got plenty of punishments in mind, you know?" I let out a deliberately evil "Heheheh..." as I called out to the men. With that threat still lingering in the air, I smiled as innocently as possible and delivered the finishing blow.

"...Next time you try anything like this, I'll slice the tip right off with a razor blade." The thought alone was too much to bear, so one man wet himself. As he was hanging upside down, he ended up soiling his own whole body.

Yumina and Yae naturally found the whole thing a bit too much, and stood with their backs to the scene the whole time. Even so, they clearly understood what was going on.

"You're really merciless today. Did you need to go that far?"

"Don't you get it? The next thing guys like this tend to do is go after anything they might see as my weakness. That could mean them trying to kidnap one of you or hold you hostage. I definitely don't want to see that happen, so I'm crushing their spirits so badly that they won't even consider the idea." This fight was my problem and mine alone. I didn't want to get Yumina or the others involved any further. Anyone who would dare lay a finger on my precious companions didn't deserve any mercy, even as a second thought. "When you crush someone, make sure they're crushed utterly and thoroughly." That was something my grandpa taught me.

...Wait a second. That other guy from yesterday's fight belonged to a different party, didn't he? The Poison Snakes, I think it was. Wait... don't tell me...

"[Gate]!!!" I had a bad feeling about things, so I opened up a [Gate] straight to the Silver Moon and took Yumina and Yae back with me immediately.

We stepped out of the [Gate] and stood outside the Silver Moon.

What we found was a group of seven unconscious men in the middle of the street.

I recognized one of the guys on the ground. It was that stupid mohawk guy. Wait, did that mean these guys were Poison Snakes?

What in the world...?

"Oh, welcome back. That sure was fast."

"Howdy there, Touya." Welcoming us back were the master of the Silver Moon Inn, Dolan, and the owner of the Weapon Shop, Barral. The two of them were sitting on a bench out front of the Silver Moon, playing a quiet little game of shogi with a pile of unconscious men right next to them.

"What happened here?"

"Well see, these guys came marching up while we were playing shogi and demanded I bring Elze and Linze out immediately. I told them the girls weren't feeling well and to go away, but they went and barged right on into the place. I flipped on 'em and it ended up like this."

"We sparred with them a little an' they just up and collapsed on us. Didn't even put up much of a fight. Y'sure these guys're even adventurers?" Barral muttered. I looked down at the Poison Snake guys, completely dumbfounded. I found myself pretty surprised by how strong Dolan and Barral were. *Geez...*

That said, both of them were built pretty well, and they worked at an inn and a weapon shop respectively, so they were probably used to dealing with tough-guy types. If they couldn't fit the job, then they could easily go out of business.

"So what's the deal with them, anyhow?"

"Er... Well, I think they came to settle a score with me. Probably planned to hold the girls hostage or something..."

"What, so they were a gaggle of human garbage, then? In that case, we should've roughed them up a little more." Dolan clicked his tongue as he said that. Micah came out front shortly afterward. She had an annoyed expression on her face. Well, that was understandable. There was a bunch of trash outside her inn, after all.

"Oh darn it, this is nothing but a nuisance. Touya, it's your fault these guys are here, right? Could you do something about this?"

"Oh, uh, sure. Just a second." I knew instinctively not to try arguing given the situation. I used [**Power Rise**] to pick up all the unconscious men, then I tossed them through a [**Gate**].

Back out on the highway, I strung the Poison Snakes up the same way as the Steel Fangs — bare naked and by the ankles. They came to their senses and noticed their pitiful state immediately.

When they then noticed the Steel Fangs hanging up opposite them, they went completely pale.

I did the whole routine a second time, putting up a signboard, taking a photo, and scaring the living daylights out of them.

They tried to scream about something, but I didn't give a damn. They could stay there all week repenting for all I cared.

From what I heard later, it seemed that Dolan and Barral were both former adventurers. Both of them reached Blue-rank, but never made it to Red. Though since they were both solo adventurers, that was still mighty impressive.

I couldn't get over the fact that those losers were the same rank that Dolan and Barral used to be. Adventurers really did come in all shapes and sizes.

You couldn't judge a book by its cover... except Dolan and Barral were both exactly as strong as they looked? One was a red-haired giant of a man and the other was built like a bear, after all...

I ignored the hanging dimwits and returned to the Silver Moon through my [Gate].

"Hmm, sounds like you've been keeping yourself busy." Back in full health, Elze was getting a story about the other day's events from Yae and Yumina.

Linze wasn't quite back to her usual self yet, but it didn't seem so bad anymore, so she joined us at the dinner table.

"Still, that was a sight I shall not be forgetting anytime soon, I won't. You should have seen the look on Touya-dono's face the moment he thought that Elze-dono and Linze-dono were in trouble."

"He looked dead serious, didn't he? It was almost frightening." *Oh c'mon, haven't you talked enough about that already?* Finding myself getting all fidgety, I downed the rest of my fruit juice in one gulp.

"Hmmmm? Did you get all worried about us when you thought we were in trouble, didja?" Elze closed in on me, no doubt to tease me about the whole thing even more. *Now see here, you…*

"Of course I was worried. Felt like my heart was going to burst when I thought that something might have happened to you. Dolan and Barral saved the day this time, but if they hadn't been here and something had happened to you two, I'm pretty sure I'd have done something unspeakable to those thugs."

"H-Huh? Oh, i-is that so…"

"Ah…" Elze and Linze both turned their faces downward, red as tomatoes. *Huh? Was it something I said?*

"Touya, what if it had been me or Yae in danger? Would you have reacted the same way for us?"

"Well yeah, of course I would. Both you and Yae are my precious companions. I'd go to any lengths to save you if you were ever in trouble."

"I-Is that so, is it…?"

"That's my Touya!" This time Yae turned her bright red face downward, while Yumina shot a beaming bright smile at me. *What the hell's up with this mood…? Ah, whatever.*

"C-Come to think of it, those two parties seem to have broken up after what you did, Touya-dono. All of their members also skipped town as if fleeing from some horrible monster, they did." Well yeah, that was a pretty natural reaction. I had pretty much expected that to happen when I went and did those horrible things to them. Though it did make me somewhat infamous in the process. That didn't really bother me so much, since it meant that fewer people were likely to target us.

Those parties weren't particularly liked among the guild members either, so nobody filed any complaints against me or anything of the sort. As a general rule, the guild didn't involve itself in conflicts between adventurers.

"I never thought you were capable of such nasty things."

"You reduced two groups of men to tears, you did… It was quite the off-putting sight, it most certainly was."

"I understand that villains of that sort need to be thoroughly taught a lesson lest they try something even more foolish, but even so…"

"I still think… that sounds like a bit much…" Linze gave me a fairly rigid little smile.

No, see, it's not like that, right? I felt like someone needed to teach them a lesson… No, phrasing it that way still makes me sound like a villain… Hrm… I did it so that they'd never try something stupid like that ever again…? Right, it was to protect me and my friends! I psychologically tortured them into submission for the sake of protecting my friends! I derived no sadistic pleasure from it whatsoever!

…I'm not lying, okay?

"The reason why I chose Touya…?"

"Yup, yup. I mean, you *are* a princess and all, and he's just an adventurer. You wouldn't normally picture a couple like that getting married, right? What was the one thing that made you want to marry him? *Was* there even any one thing in particular, or was it really just love at first sight?" In the dining room of the Silver Moon sat Yumina, tilting her head quizzically at Elze's interrogation.

She was able to explain, of course, but she wasn't entirely sure she could get other people to fully understand. Sitting next to Elze were Linze and Yae, both also looking at Yumina in anticipation of her reply.

"Let's see… Well, you know about my Mystic Eyes, correct?"

"I do recall hearing from Touya-dono that you could use your eyes to judge a person's nature, as it were." There was a theory that the Mystic Eyes were another form of Null magic. It was supposedly one's own personalized magic permanently fused with one of their body parts — in this case, the eyes.

For example, were the Fire spell [**Ignis Fire**] to dwell in a person's eyes, it would give them the Mystic Eyes of Conflagration, and if the Null spell [**Paralysis**] were to dwell in one's eyes, they would become the Mystic Eyes of Petrification. Yumina agreed with this hypothesis and thought of her own Mystic Eyes in the same way.

"My own eyes are known as the Mystic Eyes of Intuition. They allow me to visually perceive the corruption of a person's soul."

"So, put simply… it's basically a heightened sense of intuition? Like when we might look at someone and think 'this person seems nice,' or 'this person seems suspicious to me…' taken to the extreme?"

"Yes. That's the best way I can explain it." Yumina nodded to Linze's words. In truth, it wasn't quite as simple as that, but Yumina decided that it would be confusing to try and explain it any further.

"I can grasp now that you would look at Touya-dono and see that he is not a bad person. However, what we're curious about is how that would immediately lead to a decision of marriage, you see." This time the twins nodded in agreement.

"Then I'll continue. You see, it was when my father was on the verge of death that Touya appeared and saved his life as though it were the most natural thing in the world. Naturally thinking that he may be plotting something, I used my Mystic Eyes to try and sense for any ulterior motives, but I felt not a single corrupt thought in his mind."

"Yeah, I mean, normally in that situation you'd have the thought at least *somewhere* in the back of your mind that you'd be able to claim some kind of reward for saving the king's life or something, right?"

"I believe so too, yes. Even were it not one's actual motive, the idea would normally at least briefly cross one's mind, I would think." That, in itself, wasn't necessarily a bad thing. All people in the world tended to have at least some small sense of risk and reward, some selfish desire calculating things to work out in their best interests.

Yumina had seen many types of people from her time in the castle. Sometimes it was necessary to make use of talented people in order to keep the country going, even if said people were working under utterly corrupt motives. Even if Yumina used her Mystic Eyes and judged that someone were a complete villain and scoundrel, there was no way she could use that alone as an excuse to drive someone out of the castle. Were it so simple, people like Count Balsa would have been dismissed a very long time ago.

Yumina learned from a young age that it was necessary for the king of a country — and by extension, for the royal family, too — to be open-minded enough to associate themselves with people from all walks of life.

And in the middle of all of this appeared a mysterious boy in whom Yumina's eyes reflected no such complex things as purity or corruption. He was the kind of person the likes of which Yumina had never seen before in her life. The fact that his gentle face was just her type was simply a nice bonus on top of that.

"To stray from the topic for a moment, I should mention that our kingdom's royal family currently has no male heirs to the throne. If things continue as they are, I will eventually be crowned Queen Regnant, and have to take a husband as Prince Consort… and then our firstborn son would succeed the throne. That is how it would normally go, but I don't want to have to marry someone I don't even have feelings for." This was a comparatively peculiar trait of the Belfast royal family, but there were many among them — the men, in particular — who were monogamous in their relationships.

In this world, polygamy was considered the norm. Although naturally, one had to be able to sustain their household financially for as many partners as they had.

In spite of that freedom, both King Belfast and even his younger brother, Duke Ortlinde, each took only a single wife.

The duke aside, it made far more sense for a king to have multiple concubines to increase the chances of birthing a worthy successor, but King Belfast firmly rejected the idea.

Going back through the family tree, the father of the two monogamous brothers — the previous king, Yumina's grandfather — also took but a single wife and had only two sons of his own.

Even his predecessor, and the predecessor before that, going back for generations, the royal family tree was like a long, narrow tightrope walk. It was almost a miracle that their bloodline had lasted so long, but now that there was currently no male successor to the throne, the royal family was beginning to feel the weight of that responsibility.

"So, because you didn't want to marry someone you don't have feelings for, you decided to make use of Touya?" Linze knit her eyebrows slightly.

"No, that's not it, either. My father would never have given his blessing had that been the case. But he would have had trouble handling any cases of potential suitors should I reject them simply because I did not truly love them. It would be… somewhat difficult to get society to believe that it was simply a case of us not being right for each other."

"Hm…? Ahh, I see. Due to your Mystic Eyes, is that it?"

"Yes, that's right. Because my Mystic Eyes are public knowledge, society would potentially see anyone I rejected as being unfit to succeed the throne. They might easily be suspected of having foul motives or a twisted personality, even were that not truly the case. This could potentially cause trouble not only for the man himself, but even for his friends and relatives." Were the suitor an aristocrat of the same country, then things might have still worked out, but were he the prince of another country, then all manner of hell could break loose. The truth was that Yumina herself wanted to find a romantic partner before she reached the age where problems like that might begin to arise.

"The first time I laid eyes on Touya, I thought to myself, 'He is the one.' I cannot say for sure whether that was a byproduct of my Mystic Eyes, whether it was love at first sight, or whether it was a calculated decision for my own selfish sake. The fact of the matter is, though, that I've truly and utterly fallen in love with him."

"Love at first sight is one thing, but marriage at first sight is a bit extreme, don't you think?"

"Had I not made such an extreme decision, then my relationship with Touya would have ended then and there. As you said earlier, Elze, I am a princess and Touya is a mere adventurer. I had to be the one to take action, or else our relationship would have remained one of Princess and Adventurer; no more, and no less. The problem of our difference in social status does remain even now, but that is becoming less and less of a problem as the days go by." Touya was genius-levels of proficient in every type of elemental magic, and even had the White Monarch bound to him as a familiar. Those facts alone placed him in an entirely different league from your run-of-the-mill adventurer. It was plain as day to anyone with working eyes that he would go on to do magnificent things. Only the man himself was oblivious to it all.

"It sounds as though you had to take a great many factors into consideration when you proposed to Touya-dono, it does."

"True, but I have no regrets. I've already decided that I will do everything that I must in order to make Touya fall in love with me."

"What if… just, hypothetically, what if Touya were to fall in love with someone else instead?" Linze spoke up, her words tinged with nervousness. Yumina, on the other hand, replied with a smile on her face and not a shred of hesitation.

"I wouldn't mind at all. I would just have to put in the extra effort to make him love me the same as that girl. I'm not particularly dead-set on keeping Touya all to myself, given the circumstances. I wouldn't mind at all if he had a mistress or two or three." The three girls sitting across the table were rendered utterly speechless by the young princess' declaration.

"Why do you ask, did anyone in particular come to mind?"

"N-No, not at all! I just meant, well, you know, purely hypothetically…" Linze hastily gave as evasive an answer as possible. Yumina smiled slightly as she watched Linze's face turn bright red.

"Out of curiosity, what sort of impression does Touya leave on you, as a person?"

"Hmm… well, he has a lot of really weird knowledge in that head of his. Just the other day he went and gave some weird little tool to Aer."

"An Ex-Ricer, was it not called?" What Yae had meant to refer to was an egg slicer. A kitchen utensil for slicing hard-boiled eggs quickly and evenly.

"Also, just recently, he was helping Micah manage the Silver Moon's account book. Just because he was bored, he said. He was very fast with his mathematical calculations. He seems to be extremely well-educated in such areas."

"I'm sure Touya said he came from Eashen… Do you suppose he's the son of some prominent Eashen nobility?" Were that the case, then the difference in social status between them would practically be rendered a moot point. Alas, Yae, who actually *was* from Eashen, shook her head.

"Nay, he claimed not to be from Eashen itself when I asked about it, he did. Even if he were, there is no prominent Mochizuki Clan to my knowledge, there is not. I believe it is more likely that he is of Eashen blood, but born and raised in a different land, I might guess." Whenever Touya himself was asked about his homeland, he brushed the question off with a vague answer. Everyone simply assumed that he had his reasons, and decided not to stick their noses in any further.

"And while he has all of that weird knowledge knocking around inside his head, there are a whole bunch of things he's just completely clueless about."

"Did you know that, at first, he didn't even know the most basic of basic facts about magic?"

"He cannot even properly handle a horse, in fact. Do you suppose, then, that he has simply led a very sheltered life, possibly?"

"No, I've definitely led the more sheltered life, I think…" Yumina drooped her shoulders in some sense of defeat, so Elze hurriedly tried to follow up on what Yae had said.

"Nah, see, you're a princess, Yumina, so that's only natural for you. Touya, though, well… You think he's secretly the prince of some country or other, and he's just not letting us in on that fact?" For all his princely aspects, Touya practically exuded the aura of a commoner most of the time. All of those mismatched traits came together to form a patchwork picture of the person known simply as Mochizuki Touya.

"In short, he's just a weirdo."

"He is a weird person, I think…"

"He holds a queer character about him, indeed he does."

"He may be weird, but he's my prince charming." The three girls watched as Yumina smiled and blushed, and were by that point convinced that it was simply love at first sight for her. At the same time, all three of them also felt a tad embarrassed by the fact that they sort of understood how she felt.

"Achoo!"

"Got a cold?"

I don't think so... Just felt this sudden chill down my spine. Is someone talking about me somewhere...? I answered Dolan, the Silver Moon's owner, by telling him that I was fine.

I was in the capital for the day.

I had been specifically nominated for a special guild quest in helping the local shop owners stock up on goods from the capital. Dolan and Barral were naturally present, but plenty of other shopkeepers had come along, too. The reason they specifically requested me was because of my ability to use the [**Gate**] spell.

"You really don't get the chance to go to the capital all that often, y'know?"

"And to go there and back in a single day is like a dream come true." Barral of Eight Bears and Simon the item shop owner were chatting happily in the front seats.

We were riding in a fairly large wagon, supposedly the biggest one in all of Reflet. It made sense when you considered that we were on our way to pick up a bunch of weapons and food supplies and stuff.

I looked around and noticed that everyone around me was acting like a bunch of restless kids. What in the world had them so excited? It wasn't like it was their first time visiting the capital or anything.

The wagon pulled up in front of a large inn just a little ways off the main road. Apparently they would look after your wagon for a short while if you paid for it.

Huh? We aren't going to just take the wagon around all of the shops? Every last one of the shopkeeps was practically glowing with excitement as they stepped out of the wagon.

"Alrighty then, let's all meet up back here in about, oh, five hours or so. Sound good?"

"Huh? We're not going around the shops as a group? I mean, with all the luggage we'll have to carry, wouldn't it be more efficient to move as a unit...?" Simon the item shop owner saw my startled reaction and spoke to me in a hushed voice.

"Y'don't get it, do you, Touya? We haven't been to the capital in ages. We wanna mess around for a bit, you know what I mean? Dolan's a widower and all. You get what that means, right? Ah, and keep this a secret from Micah, yeah?"

Mess around? Widower...? Wait, that couldn't possibly mean...?!

"You feel like visiting one too, Touya? If you want, I can take you to this great place I know. They're even open during daylight hours." I found myself unconsciously gulping at the anticipation of what came next.

"Visiting... *what*, exactly?"

"A brothel." *I knew it! So that's why everyone's been all fidgety until now?!* While my mouth was flapping open and closed like a fish out of water, Barral interjected for a moment.

"Right then, now that it's all out in the open, I'd just like to remind you to keep this a secret from the women! I think you'll find that part, in print, specified on the quest paper, too." *That's playing dirty! Now I know why you didn't want me to bring Elze or any of the girls along! I knew it was suspicious of you to specify that!*

"Okay then, see you all in five hours!" The geezers strolled off merrily down the lane and out onto the main street. *Does this situation really warrant literally skipping? Seriously?* Simon had invited me to go along with them, but I politely declined. I mean, I *was* technically engaged to this country's princess. I couldn't afford to do anything rash like visiting a brothel. You never knew where the king's subordinates could be watching from the shadows.

At least, that was the excuse I gave. In truth, I just didn't have the guts. Yes, I was a chicken.

"Well, guess I've got five hours to kill..." I wished I could've at least taken Kohaku along. Kohaku was probably resting, or more like recovering, on my bed, in my room, with the door locked up all tight and safe.

Given that the girls had been fawning over that tiger non-stop for the past several days, I felt that a day of rest was more than deserved to give even a moment's peace from that hellscape.

I decided to take a walk around the capital. Unlike the small town of Reflet, the large capital was full of all different races of people. There were beastmen that I'd seen before, but apart from them I could also pick out people with horns growing out of their foreheads, and people with long, pointed ears. The latter... were probably elves. I'd only ever seen them in video games before, but I could spot all sorts of people like that walking around.

That upstart Kingdom of Mismede... it was supposedly composed mostly of demi-humans, with a beastman majority. Given that Belfast was trying to form friendly relations with them, it only made sense that the capital would see more demi-humans visiting as a direct result.

There were still many countries that discriminated against them quite fiercely, so Belfast was a far more welcoming place for them in light of that fact.

"Hrmm... Should I just go pick up a simple quest from the local guild? I'll just tire myself out walking around for five hours, anyway..." Aside from the typical monster hunting and herb gathering quests, there were plenty of other unusual quests that found their way to the guild. From helping someone move, to advertising for a store; some of the weirder ones involved things like looking for lost cats. Naturally the rewards for quests like those were fairly cheap, but they were generally aimed at beginners anyway. They were less quests and more part-time jobs.

My [**Search**] *spell could help find lost cats immediately. No, wait, that doesn't seem like such a good idea after all. I nearly forgot that* [**Search**] *only scans a very small area around me.*

I'd been to the guild in the capital once before. The quest we accepted that time was the Dullahan extermination one, which subsequently got out of hand.

I walked down the main street and eventually the guild office came into sight. It was way bigger than the one in Reflet…

Attached to the building was a bar, owned and managed by the guild. Apparently you could get discounts on food and drink in there simply by displaying your guild card. Not that I'd ever used that function.

At the end of the day, there are a lot of hooligans amongst the adventurers. I didn't want to take the risk of getting caught up in any drunken brawls again, and I wasn't too keen on the idea of getting drunk myself, either. And if I wanted food, then I'd just go to a regular restaurant.

The entrance to the capital's guild was a pair of wooden swing doors like something out of an old fashioned Western movie. I swaggered through them like a cowboy and into the guild itself.

There were fewer people around than I'd expected to see. When I considered that the time was somewhere around 10 AM, though, it made sense. People accepting any day-long quests would have been long on their way by now, and it was still far too early for anybody to be returning from just having completed anything.

For the time being, I went over to examine the quest board. I was currently Green-rank, meaning that I could still only accept Black, Purple, or Green level quests.

Most of the Green quests were for monster hunts, and those that weren't still required me to leave the capital anyway, so I gave up on those ones. Between Purple and Black quests, there were plenty that seemed doable in a fairly short period of time.

"Don't feel like becoming a babysitter, so that one's out…" *Roof repair? I can probably manage something with my* [**Modeling**] *spell, but… Oh?* The one that caught my eye was a house demolition quest. For manual labor, my [**Boost**] spell definitely seemed like it was up to the task.

Then again, [**Boost**] only stayed active for short bursts of time, so it might not have been up to the task… Well, even if it wasn't, I always had the muscle-enhancing spell [**Power Rise**] to cover for that, so I was sure it would work itself out. I took down the quest scroll from the board and carried it on over to the reception desk.

The job location was right next to the rich-folks' western district. It was a fairly old-looking building, and several men had already gotten to work on tearing it down. When I reported in to the site foreman and told him I'd come from the guild, he instructed me to go and take all of the junk out from the storehouse located over in the corner of the estate.

Apparently the foundations of the main building itself had rotted over the years, so it had to be torn down for safety reasons, but the shed that had been used as a storehouse was still plenty usable if they fixed it up a little.

It seemed the owner of the place had passed away, and everything in the shed was to be disposed of anyway, so I didn't have to handle any of it with care since it was effectively junk. If I just quickly got my job done… I'd have had time left over, so I decided to go about it at a slightly more leisurely pace.

"Man, it stinks of mold in here." I used a handkerchief as a makeshift dust mask and set about removing all the junk from the building, starting with the things closest to the door.

An old chest of drawers, a broken table, a wall clock with no hands, a saucepan with a huge hole in it, a bed with broken legs, a doll with no arms, a chipped teacup… it really was all just a bunch of useless junk.

Except for that sword over there! …Or so I thought, until I removed it from its scabbard only to find that the blade was broken. I don't know what I expected.

I found a shield, too, but there was a huge crack in it. There were suits of plate armor as well, but they were bent out of shape in several places and couldn't be worn anymore. There was a battle-axe still in comparatively good condition, but it was so rusty that it probably wasn't worth much anymore.

The whole shed really had just been used as a storehouse for a bunch of old junk. An abnormal amount of it seemed to be weapons and armor, however. I briefly wondered if the former owner of the estate had been a knight or something along those lines. Then again, would a single knight really need so many different types of weapons and armor? It might've made sense if he were some kind of collector, but then why would they be in the junk shed…?

Clang.

"Hm?" *Did I hear something just now…?* I could still hear the demolition work going on outside, but I could've sworn I'd heard a noise coming from inside the shed. I looked around and listened carefully…

…*Nothing. Must've been my imagination.* I got back to work. I turned around and removed a cloth from a full-length mirror, and the reflection clearly showed the sight of a battle-axe aiming straight for my back, held aloft by a figure in full plate armor.

"Ah...?!" I managed to dodge the axe as it came thundering down with such tremendous force that it shattered the wooden floor at the figure's feet into splinters. *Holy shit...! That was too close.* I could see a sort of black mist leaking of from between the gaps in the armor. This wasn't the same inanimate suit of armor it was until a second ago.

With a sharp, grinding *creeeaaak*, the armor turned to face me. *Uh-oh, I felt like our gazes met just now...*

"Whoa-hoh?!" Twisting my body to avoid a second attack from the axe, I threw myself out of the shed in a panic.

The armor came chasing after me with a noisy *clank, clank, clank*, swinging its axe around as though in the throes of a frenzied rage.

"Wh-What the hell is that?!"

"A m-monster?!"

"Are you kidding? Is that seriously... a Living Armor?!" The demolition crew saw the armor chasing me and let out terrified screams.

Living Armor?! Aren't those monsters born from those who died and left behind heavy regrets?! I recalled what I'd read about them in the guild's reference materials and clicked my tongue. Well, at least now I knew that it was an Undead-type monster like the Dullahan. Strictly speaking, the Living Armor was basically a lower class of monster than the Dullahan, though I still wasn't confident that I could defeat one on my own... Well, either way, I had to try!

I recalled that Undead-type monsters were weak to Light-type magic.

"Strike true, Light! Sparkling Holy Lance: [Shining Javelin]!"
I pointed my index finger and middle finger together in the Living Armor's direction and shot out spears of light.

The spears violently tore the Living Armor apart at the waist, sending its upper and lower halves flying in opposite directions. The spears then continued on their trajectory and crashed magnificently into the side of the shed, dealing tremendous damage. *Whoops...*

Black mist leaked out from the upper and lower halves of the Living Armor, dissipating into the air. *Did I get it?*

"Hey, kid! The hell did you just do?!"

"I didn't do anything! That thing just pounced on me out of the blue! What the heck's a Living Armor doing in a place like this, anyway?! It's not like this is a graveyard or a battlefield or anything!" It was said that Living Armors were born from the restless souls of the regretful dead. Because of that, they would only appear in places where such regrets were likely to accumulate. Places like old battlefields or run-down graveyards.

"No, it couldn't be..."

"Sounds like you have some idea of where this thing came from." The foreman shifted his gaze to the shattered armor, and it seemed like he had just remembered something.

"The former owner of this estate was a kind-hearted viscount. One day, that viscount was tricked by a corrupt count, and ended up having this estate stolen from him along with his entire fortune. The viscount fell into despair after that, and he and his entire family committed suicide... If his hatred of the count remains even now, then maybe..."

There's no "maybes" or "couldn't bes" about it, that's clearly the only place a Living Armor could have come from! Which means what; the viscount's hatred of the evil count was intense enough to spawn a *Living Armor?!* Living Armors were born from people's negative emotions like regret or hatred, but they were completely separate beings from the dead that had produced those emotions in the first place. Such thoughts merely lingered in the world after death like the corpse of one's past. It wasn't fair for *us* to get attacked because of something some dumbass count had done a long time ago, but try explaining that to a corpse.

My thoughts came to an immediate halt as the foreman's words sank in. *Family suicide.* If the whole family died full of regrets, then the number of Living Armors that would be born from that was...

Expecting nothing but bad news, my vision returned to the shed only to see another Living Armor already slowly shambling toward us. *I knew it!*

"Why does this always happen to me...? Hey, what if we offered up that corrupt count to the Living Armors, do you think they'd let us go...?"

"Afraid that's not gonna be happening, kid. That same count was executed just recently... For high treason of all things." *Count Balsa, you goddamn slippery toad, I'd kill you again if I could!* Now that I knew who'd caused this mess, I couldn't help but sympathize with the poor viscount. Still, I had to clean this mess up one way or another.

Yet more Living Armors came tottering out of the shed. What was I supposed to do...? *If I cast* [**Shining Javelin**] *again, it might just end up causing more damage to the surroundings...*

I thought hard about what I could do in this situation... and then I remembered. I could use my [**Enchant**] spell to imbue my sword with some Light magic. I decided to try Healing magic, since that wouldn't damage the surroundings at all.

"**[Enchant]. Imbue with Light: [Cure Heal].**" I enchanted my blade with Healing magic, then dodged an oncoming attack from a rusty lance and brought my sword down with enough force to sever the monster's arm.

My sword cut through the Living Armor like a hot knife through butter, and its arm came flying off. *Yes! It's working! Wait, doesn't that mean I can just cast* **[Cure Heal]** *on them without having to enchant my weapon?* I thought about that for a second, but ultimately decided against it. Since **[Cure Heal]** needed an incantation to activate and only worked at close range anyway, it was quicker and easier to just imbue my sword with it and hack away.

Well, whatever. Right now I have to take care of this mess somehow. I took a battle stance as the remaining Living Armors came shambling toward me...

"What's got you all worn out? Ho ho, lemme guess. You regretted turning down my offer and found a place yourself, right? So, how was it? Feeling refreshed? Because I know *I* am! Gahahaha." There I was, collapsed in the wagon, without the energy left to even correct Simon's mistaken assumptions.

I somehow managed to defeat all of the Living Armors, but I got chewed out later for smashing up the shed's wall with my first attack. Since I protected everyone from the Living Armors, I wasn't penalized at all, but I should've been able to calmly handle the situation more carefully than that. If nothing else, the whole ordeal had at least taught me how flexible enchanting really was. It could potentially be used to make all sorts of things.

[Enchant] could be used to either temporarily or permanently apply the effects of a different spell to an object of my choice. For example, I could pick up a random stick and enchant it with the

[**Light Sphere**] spell to create a lightbulb…! Or so I thought until I noticed the fatal flaw in that plan. It would be extremely annoying to have a lightbulb that you could never turn off. Besides, activating an enchanted item required a small amount of magic, too.

I'd enchanted my blade with [**Cure Heal**], so all I had to do in the future was direct a little bit of my magic into it and it should become a powerful Anti-Undead weapon. At the very least, it didn't seem like a bad idea to have a few such Enchanted items close at hand.

…One such item that sprung to mind was my smartphone. Would [**Enchant**] work on it…?

"Alright, here we are! Dolan, Touya, this is your stop, the Silver Moon." My musings were cut short as Barral called out my name. I got down sluggishly from the back of the wagon and helped unload the supplies Dolan had bought for the Silver Moon. It was mostly food supplies and daily necessities, but there were some barrels of alcohol mixed in there as well.

"Welcome back. Did you manage to spot any good deals?"

"M'back… Nah, about that, I couldn't really find many good deals. Still, think I got enough to last us a while."

"That so? I wonder if the capital's seeing a recession, too, then." Micah came to meet us as we unloaded the supplies. She waved goodbye to Barral and the others before helping us carry the goods inside.

Dang, I'm beat. I just wanna go to bed…

"You sure took your time getting back for what little you bought. I thought teleportation magic let you move between here and there instantly?"

"Huh? Oh, oh yeah, right, right, there was some stuff that we had trouble finding, y'see…"

"Hmm…" Micah pointed her sharp gaze at Dolan, who was not helping the situation by acting so clearly suspicious.

Apparently unable to bear it any longer, Dolan picked up a couple of drink barrels and carried them off to the storehouse out back. Didn't he realize that only made him look even *more* suspicious…?

"So, Touya. Tell me about the girl *you* were out fooling around with today."

"I wasn't fooling around with anybody! I mean yeah, I was invited to go along, but I…" *Ohcrapohcrapohcrap.* I tried to plug up my big mouth as fast as I could, but the incriminating words had already been uttered. Micah flashed an evil-looking grin at me. *I've been had!*

"I knew it. I had a feeling that was what was going on. I mean, I do understand that my dad's been lonely ever since my mother died, so I'm not going to chew him out for that or anything." *Wow… Mister Dolan, you're a lucky man to have such an understanding daughter.*

"…Now what I *am* about to chew him out for is going off spending the money for our inn's important supplies and then trying to lie to me about it. Doesn't he have any idea how much I'm trying to cut back on unnecessary expenses here? I feel like he needs a niiice long talking to, so I'll see you later." Micah wore the smile of an angel as she walked off after Dolan… with a large wooden pestle in hand, for whatever reason.

It wasn't long before I heard a very loud, indescribably pathetic voice begging for forgiveness. There was nothing I could do for the man. He was reaping what he'd sown, and getting what was coming to him. I felt bad for poor old Dolan, but I was clocking in ahead of him.

Just as I was about to make my way up to my room, I noticed something poking out of Dolan's bag on the countertop. It looked like some kind of leaflet. When I pulled it out to have a look, it turned out to be an advertising leaflet for one of the brothels in the capital. It listed each of the girls working there along with such details as their measurements and personalities. The naked illustrations of each girl were impressively realistic and fantastically arousing.

What're you even thinking bringing this back here, old man...? You'd have been found out sooner or later even if I hadn't said a thing if you were silly enough to bring the incriminating evidence home with you.

"Oh, Touya, you're back."

"Hmm? Oh, hey, Yumina. Hey everyone. Yeah I just got back a... minute... ago..." *I have to hide this leaflet at all costs.* Only after I reflexively threw my hand behind my back did I realize how unbelievably suspicious I had just made myself look. Too late to stop myself, I had to play it off somehow. I wanted to yell at myself for even thinking to hide it in the first place. It wasn't even mine! But if I tried to explain that, there was no way anyone would believe me!

"...What's with the pose, Touya?"

"NO, IT IS NOTHING AT ALL."

"You're drenched in sweat, you are."

"I AM JUST EXHAUSTED. YES."

"Why are you speaking... stiffly, like that?"

"THAT MUST BE YOUR IMAGINATION. HA HA HA." Elze, Yae, and Linze took turns interrogating me as I walked backward toward the stairs. All four of the girls stared at me, trying to work out what I was doing, but I couldn't afford to let myself be caught here. I continued my backward march up the stairs.

"...For what conceivable reason are you walking up the stairs *backward,* pray tell?"

"I-It's just easier for me this way! Yeah! WELL — ahem — well then, I'm off to bed! Goodnight!"

"Eh? Wait, Touya?!" I dashed up the stairs at full speed. Backward. What did I think I was, some kind of shellfish?!

"...Definitely a weirdo."

"...Yes, a weird person."

"He holds a queer character about him, indeed."

"He may be weird, but he's my prince charming." I could hear the girls talking about something at the base of the stairs, but I couldn't make out what they were saying exactly. Not caring in the slightest, I unlocked my room and made my way inside. Kohaku was curled up sleeping soundly on my bed.

I collapsed onto the bed next to the little tiger. Kohaku almost got up when I jolted the bed, but calmed down as soon as I started patting that fluffy little head.

Man, all I'd done was succeed in tiring myself out even more...

I didn't even have the strength left to regret my actions. I was swallowed headfirst by the void of sleep, as I didn't even bother to put up any resistance.

I slept in the next morning, so the girls all came to wake me up. They discovered the leaflet on the bedroom floor. In the end, I got interrogated for almost an hour over it anyway. I decided in my heart of hearts that I would never, ever go with those geezers on a guys-only trip to the capital ever again.

Hello there, this is Patora Fuyuhara.

I'm not really used to appearing in the public(?) eye like this, so forgive me if I seem a touch nervouth. Whoops, bit my tongue there...

Er, well then, this work is an improved and revised version of a story I started working on back in 2013 for the "Shosetsuka ni Narou" website.

I originally began writing this story completely as a hobby, but I was able to get it physically published like this thanks to all of my readers. Really, thank you all for your support.

As I write this, I'm actually still worrying that the book will never actually make it to print, but, well, if you're reading this, then that must mean my worries were misplaced... I hope they were.

In Another World With My Smartphone, or Smartphone for short, is a story set in a world like a large hotpot, into which the ingredient known as Touya is suddenly thrown one day. From there I added a little bit of seasoning, skimmed a bit off the top, had some people do some taste-testing to see if it was any good or not, got informed on things that I'd done wrong, and then like some blindfolded bring-your-own-ingredients food party this work... became increasingly difficult to compare to a hotpot.

Anyway, Hobby Japan really has guts to bring a blindfold-hotpot to the dinner table like this... But that's just how I feel about it. I've already gone and made it now, though. All that's left is to hope that this first volume was to the liking of anyone who read it. Did you enjoy it at all? I plan to continue adding more and more ingredients to this blindfold-hotpot from now on, too. Something like a spy maid and a goth-loli girl, for starters. If you enjoyed this volume, then please continue to support Smartphone from now on! Thank you so much, really.

Now that the story is being physically published, I've decided to go back adding and removing little bits to keep the lore a bit more consistent throughout the series. With that said, I haven't made any major changes to the story, I'm not about to replace new characters, and I won't be erasing any existing characters or anything extreme like that, so fans of the original web novel can rest easy knowing I haven't mutated the work in any major way.

Come to think of it, I'd just like to mention that, in keeping with the title of this series, I've written the whole story so far on my smartphone without relying on my PC at all, except for making backup copies, of course. I guess you could call my story "Patora Fuyuhara, In The Real World With My Smartphone."

Personally I find I'm able to type much quicker on my phone than a keyboard, so this way is simply more convenient for me. Though sometimes I end up typing too fast and leaving a lot of typos behind, so checking for mistakes like that can eat a few hours away.

I do sometimes worry about accidentally dropping my phone or spilling water all over it, but thankfully I've managed to avoid any problems like that so far. Lately I've been thinking that I'd really like to get a newer model. I'm always using it for long periods of time, so the battery's constantly on the verge of death...

My wrist and hand actually start to hurt a bit if I've been typing on my smartphone for too long, so sometimes I'll even end up switching to typing left-handed. That's what I'm doing right now, actually. Could you tell?

Another thing is that, when I'm writing stories on my smartphone, from an outside perspective it just looks like I'm constantly playing games on my phone all day, which is unfortunate.

I get the feeling I'd look a lot cooler sitting at a desk, typing up my stories while sipping coffee. I already know that wouldn't really suit me, though.

I'm aware that Touya didn't really make much use of his own smartphone in this volume, but don't worry, it'll start gradually powering up from now on!

Finally, some words of thanks. Thank you, Eiji Usatsuka, for all of the wonderful illustrations. I look forward to working with you from now on.

Thank you, K, for reaching out to me and agreeing to be my editor. Thank you, everyone else at the Hobby Japan editorial department. A great big thank you to everyone involved in the publishing of this work.

And last, but certainly not least, a great big thank you to all of my readers, both those of you who might have read the web novel version of this work on "Shosetsuka ni Narou," and those of you reading this story for the first time with this officially published version. Thank you so very much!

- Patora Fuyuhara

Patora Fuyuhara
illustration: Eiji Usatsuka
VOLUME 2
AVAILABLE NOW!
In Another World With My Smartphone

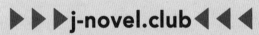

VOLUMES 1-2
ON SALE
FEBRUARY 2019!

How NOT to Summon a Demon Lord

J-Novel Club Lineup

Ebook Releases Series List

Amagi Brilliant Park
An Archdemon's Dilemma: How to Love Your Elf Bride
Ao Oni
Arifureta Zero
Arifureta: From Commonplace to World's Strongest
Bluesteel Blasphemer
Brave Chronicle: The Ruinmaker
Clockwork Planet
Demon King Daimaou
Der Werwolf: The Annals of Veight
ECHO
From Truant to Anime Screenwriter: My Path to "Anohana" and "The Anthem of the Heart"
Gear Drive
Grimgar of Fantasy and Ash
How a Realist Hero Rebuilt the Kingdom
How NOT to Summon a Demon Lord
I Saved Too Many Girls and Caused the Apocalypse
If It's for My Daughter, I'd Even Defeat a Demon Lord
In Another World With My Smartphone
Infinite Dendrogram
Infinite Stratos
Invaders of the Rokujouma!?
JK Haru is a Sex Worker in Another World
Kokoro Connect
Last and First Idol
Lazy Dungeon Master
Me, a Genius? I Was Reborn into Another World and I Think They've Got the Wrong Idea!
Mixed Bathing in Another Dimension
My Big Sister Lives in a Fantasy World
My Little Sister Can Read Kanji
My Next Life as a Villainess: All Routes Lead to Doom!
Occultic;Nine
Outbreak Company
Paying to Win in a VRMMO
Seirei Gensouki: Spirit Chronicles
Sorcerous Stabber Orphen: The Wayward Journey
The Faraway Paladin
The Magic in this Other World is Too Far Behind!
The Master of Ragnarok & Blesser of Einherjar
The Unwanted Undead Adventurer
Walking My Second Path in Life
Yume Nikki: I Am Not in Your Dream